LOCKDOWN CORNER

LOCKDOWN CORNER

WALKER UNIVERSITY STALLIONS
BOOK 5

AVA SUTTON

Visit my website at avasuttonbooks.com
Cover Designer: Enchanting Romance Designs
Developmental Editor: Jeannine Colette, www.jeanninecolette.com
Editor: Jovana Shirley, Unforeseen Editing, www.unforeseenediting.com
Proofreader: Tina Otero
Photographer: Michelle Lancaster
Model: Kally Grimmond
Text message photo: Shutterstock

This book is a work of fiction. Names, characters, places, and incidents either are products of the author's imagination or are used fictitiously. Any resemblance to actual persons, living or dead, events, or locales is entirely coincidental.
ISBN-13: 979-8-9946341-0-3

*For the brave hearts who said yes
to the risk, to the feelings,
and to the kind of love that changes everything.*

PROLOGUE

BROOKE

A SHIVER RUNS THROUGH ME, and it's not from the cold. Something is wrong. We should be celebrating Beck's win, but as we get closer to him, I see his brows pulled together and furrowed. His girlfriend, Charlie, is standing beside him, worry etched across her face. Beck is yelling at someone standing in front of him. It's a woman, but I can't see who she is since her back is to me. She's petite, with shoulder-length sandy-colored hair.

The look on my brother's face is one I haven't seen in a long time—not since a time we don't talk about. My heart starts racing, and when my dad takes my hand in his and squeezes it, I know for sure there is a problem.

We finally reach them and stand next to Charlie. She's aged, yet the lines on her face make her appear even older than she probably is. They're hard and deep. Like she's lived a rough life.

A life away from me.

I feel like I'm moving in slow motion as I watch my dad's gaze move from Beck's to the woman in pure recognition.

"Beck! What's going on? Stevie? What the hell? You're not supposed to be here," my dad whispers angrily.

I look up at my mother.

My heart races in my chest, and my lungs feel like they're packed with cotton as I stare at her.

Tears are running down her face, her hands covering her mouth. She's looking directly at me. "Brookie? Oh my God, you're so beautiful."

At the sound of her voice—and, *God*, the nickname—my spine straightens, and I freeze. I don't feel my dad release my hand, nor do I feel my brother protectively wrapping his arm around me.

Faint memories rush through me. They're flashes really. Tiny pieces that are buried deep in my mind.

Brookie.

She would always call me that when she apologized. That I remember. Clearly. My mother is an alcoholic, or she was anyway. She's supposed to be in prison for burning my brother's hand and arm. I have some memory of that day. Mostly of Beck's screams and me holding on to my mother's legs, begging her to stop hurting him. And the smell. Burning, smoke.

My dad's voice pulls me out of the memory.

I do what I do best. *Five, four, three, two, one.*

Five things I see. The Jumbotron blazing overhead. A hand-painted poster board bobbing in the crowd. A news camera angled too close. The orange Gatorade cooler by the bench. A man dancing like the world isn't watching.

Four things I can touch. The rough denim of my jeans. Turf biting through the soles of my sneakers. The soft cotton of Charlie's sleeve beneath my fingers. My own skin as my hand curls into a fist.

Three things I hear. A baby crying somewhere behind us. A woman cheering. My own breath—too loud, too fast.

Two things I smell. Sweat. Firework smoke.

One thing I taste. I dig into my pocket, find the mint I always keep there, and pop it into my mouth. Cool. Clean. Something solid to hold on to as I pretend like nothing bad is happening.

"Let's go, Stevie. Don't ruin this celebration by embarrassing him like this right now." My dad turns to us. "I got this, Beck. Go celebrate with your team. Brooke, you stay with Charlie, and we'll meet you in the waiting area." Then he turns back to my mother. "Start walking."

She tries to get to Beck and me, but he grabs her arm, stopping her from getting any closer to us. "Ryan, I just wanted to see him for just a minute. I haven't been able to see him or Brooke in two years! Just give me five minutes. If they don't want to speak with me, I'll go."

I glance at my dad's face, and it's starting to turn red. He's barely controlling his anger. "Nope. Not happening. You will not lay a single finger on my kids again."

"Ry …" she starts.

He bends down and gets in her face. His voice is quiet, trying not to bring attention to us, but I can hear him. "NO! I said no. If you don't start walking, I'm going to call your parole officer. You aren't supposed to be within ten feet of the kids. Ever."

He starts to pull her away from us, tilting his head and leaning it to the side. He leads her in the opposite direction from the locker room.

Charlie comes to stand beside us, reaching for my brother. Casey, her twin, is behind her. "Beck—"

"Not now, Charlie. Not here. I'll speak with you later." He turns to me and wraps his other arm around me, whispering into my ear, "You're okay. Just take some deep breaths. Stay close to Charlie and her parents. Don't talk to anyone. I'll see you at the hotel, okay?"

I haven't found my voice, so I just nod.

He kisses the side of my head, then turns to walk off the field toward the locker room.

"Char, let's give him a minute, okay? I don't know a lot about this situation, but I do know it's not good. I'll make sure he's okay. You take Brooke back toward the waiting area, and we'll meet you there." Casey wraps an arm around Charlie and reaches out a hand to me, but I still can't move.

She shakes off Casey's arm and reaches for me. "I'm so sorry, Brooke. I have no idea what's happening, but I'm so, so sorry."

I just look at her and nod again. That's all I feel like I can do.

"Let's go wait for your dad with my parents." She reaches for my hand.

The mint in my mouth has dissolved and so have my emotions as I focus on what's important. Beck.

I look around, watching everyone celebrating. "Right, yeah. Okay, let's do that. Um … where do we go?"

She leads me toward an exit off the field. "Let's go this way. It'll take us to the family waiting area."

When we reach the hallway, we turn the corner, and I can see my dad standing with Charlie and Casey's parents. The Kings have been like family to us since we moved in across the street from them years ago.

My dad has his back to us, but his arms are spread out to his sides, and he's shaking his head. I can see the Kings, looking rattled. I mean, what can they say? They know everything that's happened.

"I'll talk to him and tell him he needs to explain all of this to Charlie. I'm sorry about this. I had no idea she was coming," he says as we reach them.

Carol, Charlie's mom, reaches for her. "Charlie, are you okay?"

She then reaches out to me while holding Charlie. "Brooke, honey, are you okay?"

I swallow and try to seem calm, but when I speak, it's barely a whisper. "Oh, yeah, I'm okay. I think I'm just a little in shock, seeing her. It's been so long."

My dad puts his arm around my shoulders. "Why don't you go back to the hotel with the Kings? I'm going to wait for Beck to make sure he's okay."

I nod, but then shake my head, clearing my voice. "How will you get back to the hotel if we have the rental car?"

He looks over at Charlie's dad. "Tim will take the rental, and I'll catch an Uber when he gets on the bus to go back to the hotel."

"Tim, let's head out now," Carol says.

He places a hand on my dad's shoulder. "Yep, let's go, girls. Ryan, we'll see you back at the hotel in a bit. Let me know if you need anything in the meantime."

The ride back is quiet. We're all clearly worried about Beck. And based on Charlie's shaking leg, she is even more anxious to see him.

I'm not really sure what to say. Now that I can think a little more clearly, I realize that Charlie doesn't know about our past. It makes me feel awkward, on top of an already-upsetting situation.

Tim parks the car, and before I pull the handle to open the door, Charlie reaches for me. "Are you okay, B?"

To try to ease her concern, I place my hand over hers. "I'm okay. I'm sorry this was a shock to you. I thought you knew about our mom. I'm sure Beck has his reasons for not telling you, but give him a chance to explain. Don't shut him out, okay?"

She nods. "I won't. I love him—you know that. I just don't understand why he didn't tell me."

"I'm not going to assume to know what the reasons are, so just hear him out and be patient with him."

Charlie nods and leans over to hug me. "Love you, B. Text me if you need anything."

"Love you too, Char." And I mean it. Even if she and my brother weren't together, she's like a sister to me.

My brother suffered under my mother's hand a lot more than I did—physically anyway. He processes our trauma in his own way, and he would never ask for or say he needed support, but he does. He's always been my protector, and our bond is strong. We might not be twins, but I can read my brother as if we were.

He'll need us, but he'll want Charlie more. Once he's calmed down.

When we get to the lobby, I don't see my dad there, so I head up to our room.

While I wait, I take out my phone and start to search social media to see if any of our family drama made it online. I don't want that to overshadow Beck's success today. He's worked so hard for this, and getting to the national championship would be amazing.

My dad finally comes into the room, looking exhausted. "You okay?"

I nod and give him a smile. "I am. How are you? Have you seen Beck?"

I've wired myself to be okay. For him. For Beck. Not cause problems, keep the house happy, peaceful. I stuff down my anxiety so my dad and brother won't worry about me. They've had too many painful years, and they've only recently started to finally seem happy again.

Logically, I know I would never lose them, but there is a deep-rooted fear that I'm the reason why my mom drank and hurt us. I don't think she really wanted to have another baby after Beck, to be honest.

"He's going to talk to Charlie and then come up here when he's done."

"Do you know why he never told her about Mom? I know Tim and Carol have the whole story, and I assumed Casey and Charlie did too."

"I'm not really sure. I have my guesses, but you know your brother is not the best at expressing his feelings. Time's up though, and he's going to have to tell her now. She needs to understand, as hard as it may be for him," he says, walking toward me, holding his hand out to me.

I take his hand in mine and let him pull me in for a hug.

"You sure you're okay? You can tell me anything—you know that, right?"

I squeeze him hard, then remove myself from his hold. "I promise. I can't say it wasn't a shock. I haven't seen her since her parole hearing. But why didn't you tell us she got out?"

He sighs. "Honestly, I didn't want to upset either one of you, especially with everything going on with your brother, and she's not supposed to be contacting you anyway. I never would have thought she would show up tonight."

"Yeah, I mean, pretty ballsy on her part." I'm trying to be conversational about it, but on the inside, my entire body feels like it's on fire. And the tightness in my back is warning me that a panic attack could hit me soon if I don't get myself under control.

"Brooke—"

Before my dad can finish, there's a knock on the door. He walks over and looks in the peephole.

"It's Beck," he says as he opens the door.

Beck walks into the room, looking shattered. He runs his hand through his hair as he walks toward me. "You're okay?"

"I am. Are you okay?" I reach for his hand.

He shakes his head. "I'm … fuck. I don't know. Charlie is upset now … fuck." He pulls me into him and wraps his arms around me. "Everything will be fine. We'll go back to Oklahoma and forget this happened."

Forget. That's the family motto. Not forgive. Not heal.

We erase. We bury. We move on.

Or at least we pretend we do, even as the memories cling tight like they've always belonged.

I pull a deep breath in. "Right. Forget it happened."

My dad walks over to us and wraps his arms around both of us. "I'm so sorry, kids. I really am just …"

He doesn't finish, but Beck and I both know the guilt he carries with him for leaving us when we were little. He had no idea what was happening to us while he was gone.

There are questions I want to ask. *What was she doing here?*

When was the last time you heard from her? How and when did she get out of prison?

But just like I always do, I keep my mouth shut and let all my emotions boil inside. It's just a matter of time before I lose it. I just hope I can make it back home before it happens. I can't let my dad and brother see me fall apart.

If I'm not careful, I may unravel, and who will be there to save me?

CHAPTER
ONE

PRESENT

BROOKE

A GROAN and a hand squeezing my boob bring me out of a dead sleep. It was actually the deepest sleep I'd had in a long time. I'm lying on my back, cozy and nestled against a warm body. Jude Law's voice is in the background of my consciousness.

My own hand, I realize, is touching something that feels like an arm. A very hard yet soft forearm. I let my fingers skim along the skin for a moment, feeling the lines of muscle.

My eyes slowly open, and I tilt my head to the side to see Silas Arbuckle resting his head on the pillow under us both. His arm is draped across my chest, and his hand has a firm grip on one of my breasts. I gently remove his hand and blame the sleep-induced lust for the inappropriate placement.

If he were awake, I'd be mad. I have a boyfriend after all.

Ending up on this couch with him was already a bad enough decision—too much RumChata and cozy Christmas movies blurred my judgment.

If I were a wise woman, I'd jump off this couch and run for the door.

But when I take in Silas's stupidly sexy face, I allow myself to daydream for a minute about what it would be like to lie next to him every night.

I look at his long lashes, which should be illegal for a guy to have; his nose, which has a slight bend to it; and a small scar under his eyebrow. Both are probably from football injuries, I would guess. And his lips? Sweet baby Jesus. His bottom lip is a little fuller than the top, which dips slightly, creating a perfect Cupid's bow. It's unfair for a man to have such perfect features.

My gaze travels over the tattoos covering his body—from his neck all the way down to his feet. I only know that because I've seen him shirtless and in low-riding shorts. Tonight, he's wearing pajamaralls, just like I am, and one strap is unbuttoned now, so the front hangs slightly, showing half of his muscled chest.

What I would give to run my tongue over these ridges.

Stop it, Brooke. You have a boyfriend!

I first saw Silas last year, when he transferred to Walker University from Georgia. He had moved in with my brother and his other roommates, which meant I saw him fairly regularly. But I was still in high school at the time, and I felt like I was tongue-tied whenever I was here visiting because he was just that hot.

Since I'm at Walker now, I've spent more time with him and gotten to know him better as a person. Yes, he's an amazing football player, but he's a great guy off the field too. And he's really funny.

Silas shifts his body as my fingers continue to drag up and down his arm, but his hand stays firmly on my boob. His eyes flutter open, and he hits me with his blue eyes. A smirk on his face, he winks at me before slowly removing his hand from my chest.

"I would say I'm sorry, but that would be a lie." He smiles widely now.

I should get up and move away from him. I'm on the edge of the couch after all, but I can't bring myself to do it.

"Tell me the truth," he says in a deep, grumbly voice from being asleep. "Did you see my pajamaralls on the table when they came in the other day and you wanted to match me tonight?" He takes my strap and unbuttons one side, making me suck in a breath.

"Don't be ridiculous. I've had mine since October. I was just waiting for the perfect time to wear them." I huff half-heartedly.

It's two weeks before Christmas, so Charlie wanted to do an early birthday party for Noelle and have a little pajama competition, and most of the couples matched. Ace and Aston—the Griffith twins—Lily, and Arbor all had funny designs, but somehow, Silas and I both wore pajamaralls. He has caribou on his, and they're … banging. Mine are cute with a Christmas tree pattern, and I have a white crop top underneath.

"Hmm … I don't buy it. I think you saw mine and thought it would be the perfect time to let me know how much you were into me." He tips his head down, and his lips graze my shoulder, making me shiver.

"Oh, please. You wish." I start to roll to the side to get off the couch, but he holds me to him.

"You're right. I do."

He places a soft kiss on my cheek, and I shut my eyes, savoring the feeling of his lips on my skin. But then his words hit me, and I feel the blush hit my cheeks.

"You're staying here tonight, right? I can walk you home if you're leaving."

I nod. "I'll go sleep in Charlie's room with her."

"Or we could just stay here and cuddle all night." He places his hand on my hip and pulls me into him.

I lift his arm off of me and place it on his leg. "We could, but I don't think Eli would like that too much."

"Eli can suck my—"

I cover his mouth with my hand, and his tongue licks my palm, so I yank it away.

"Silas! Gross."

He chuckles. "But seriously, he's a douche. Why are you dating that guy?"

"He's smart. We have a lot in common. I don't know." I lift my shoulder. "He's the first guy who didn't want to date me to get invited to the football games or parties, so that was nice for a change."

"You've been dating the wrong kind of guys."

He studies my face, making me feel like I want to kiss him, but also wanting to get away from him before I follow through with it.

"I think it's time for me to go to bed." I sit up and stand, and my strap drop, and the front of my pajamaralls open low enough to expose my stomach.

When I look at Silas, his heated gaze is on my bare skin.

Eli doesn't look at me like this. He's the only person I've had sex with, so I don't have a lot of experience to compare, but I feel like I'm either doing something wrong—although he's very much the kind of guy who would tell me if I was doing something wrong—or he's just not attracted to me. Nothing like the heat in Silas's gaze is the way Eli looks at me, even when I'm naked.

He looks back up at my face, and our eyes connect. "I'll get the lights. Good night, Brooke."

I start to walk toward Charlie's room and look over my shoulder. "Night, Silas."

When I shut the door to the bedroom, I glance at the bed and see Charlie sleeping with her phone in her hand and my brother's face filling the screen. He's also sleeping. These two are crazy.

I can't imagine Eli and me doing something like that. He wouldn't want to disrupt his sleep pattern.

I tiptoe to the bathroom and close the door behind me softly so I don't wake Charlie. I need to get the little makeup I have on off before I climb into bed, or I'll look like a raccoon in the morning.

Once I'm done in the bathroom, I climb into bed, trying not to wake Charlie, but I must make some kind of noise because I hear my brother say, "Night, B."

It makes me smile because I miss him, and I know he feels better when Charlie and I are together. He worries about us both since he's gone.

"Night, Beck."

I roll to my side and reach for my phone on the nightstand that I plugged in earlier when it died. Not a single message from Eli. With a sigh, I set it back down and try to fall back to sleep. But every time I close my eyes, I see Silas's blue eyes staring at me.

SILAS

Did I know she was looking at me? I had a feeling she was, and I hoped she was. I was asleep, but when I felt her shift, I woke up completely. I'm a light sleeper, and then when her hand started moving up and down my arm, I had to decide if I wanted to pretend or let her know I was awake.

Brooke Linson. This girl has had me tied up for a while now. When I first met her, she was still in high school. Beautiful, but too young. Now, I can't take my eyes off of her. And every time she comes over to the house, I find reasons to be near her. Lucky for me, she's here more often than not, so I get to see her a lot, which isn't helping my mad crush on her.

Yeah, she has a boyfriend, but I don't really give a shit. I was serious about what I said to her on the couch. He's a douche, and he definitely doesn't deserve her. Not that I do either, but I'd do a damn good job of making her feel like a queen every day.

In the fall, just as we were getting deep into the season, I realized just how much I was attracted to her. She's more than a pretty face. And she's smart, which I find incredibly sexy.

It's funny because her brother is the opposite of her. Beck has been a broody kind of guy for as long as I've known him. Almost like he was carrying something heavy he never learned how to set down.

But he's a different guy with Charlie and Brooke.

Charlie is definitely the calm to his storm. And Brooke seems to keep him steady. He's very protective of them both, but in a different way with Brooke.

Over the past year of knowing Brooke, I've watched her in the small, unguarded moments. The way she listens. The way she grounds a room without trying. She carries a quiet strength that doesn't ask to be noticed, and I don't think she realizes how rare that is.

Maybe that's why I did.

I don't know where that strength comes from, only that it's there—steady and sure. And somewhere along the way, without meaning to, I started falling for her in the spaces between conversations, in the moments I wasn't supposed to be looking.

With a sigh, I shift my body and get up from the couch. I turn off the TV, the tree, and make sure the front door is locked before I make my way to my bedroom.

I undress in my room and then head to the bathroom to get ready for bed. I'm in my boxers and still sporting a semi from waking up, snuggled against Brooke, and maybe I should be a little more cautious since there are females in the house, but Charlie and Brooke are at the other end of the hall, and Bo and

Chelsea are either sleeping or still making up for lost time. It's pretty quiet now, so I'm guessing I'm in the clear.

When I get back to my room, my mind is awake, so I'll need to do some reading or something to get back to sleep. Especially because thoughts of Brooke's curvy body against mine is making it really hard to clear my head.

I slide on my glasses and grab a book from my bag—a novel I'm supposed to be reading for my English class—then pull out my phone and open the audiobook app. I hit play and flip to the page where I left off.

When you struggled to read, growing up—when the lines zigzagged and your eyes couldn't quite keep their place—you learned to use whatever tools you could.

I follow along as the voice pours into my ears, eyes tracking the page.

It should be enough to distract me.

It isn't.

My mind keeps drifting back to Brooke.

To how a woman who isn't mine—won't ever be mine, and honestly shouldn't be—has somehow taken over every spare corner of my thoughts. I can't remember the last time someone got under my skin like this.

Frustrated, I toss the book onto the floor and switch my phone to music instead. I let the songs carry me under—music about brown-eyed girls who smell like cupcakes, with lips I'd give anything to kiss.

Yeah …

It's good to dream.

CHAPTER
TWO

SILAS

IT'S FINALS WEEK, so the campus has been pretty quiet, and I just finished one for my Biomaterials class. It was fucking hard, but as a biomedical engineering major, it's a requirement. Sure, I hope to be drafted, but I also want to have a life after football.

When my dad had a heart attack when I was in high school, the pacemakers they tried wouldn't work, and it took a while to get one to fit and work properly. So, through that process, I became interested in biomedical engineering. I want to help build better instruments that are more universal and also cost-effective. The whole process and all the medical bills nearly wiped out my family's farm.

I'm still dwelling on the last answer on my exam when I walk into the house and smell something sweet. I set my backpack down, and I can hear Charlie and Brooke talking in the kitchen. They're giggling about something that I can't make out.

It's pretty common to come home to them baking or cooking for the house. We still rotate weekly for family dinner, and even though Brooke doesn't live here, she added her name to the calendar at the beginning of the school year. She's just as good of a cook as Charlie is, but her desserts, specifically her cupcakes, are my favorite.

"How are my favorite girls doing?"

They're standing next to each other, so I walk over and step between them and wrap an arm around them both. Brooke has her long brown hair in a ponytail, falling down her back. She's wearing a Walker T-shirt that is way too big for her—hanging off a shoulder, exposing a bra strap—and some loose gray sweat-pants. It's a typical college-girl look, but somehow, she makes it sexy.

"Favorite girls, huh?" Charlie looks up at me with a smirk.

"Absolutely." I drop my arm from Charlie's shoulders, but leave the other draped around Brooke. "The only ones that count. Arbor and Lily are cool too, I suppose."

"Why don't you make yourself useful and help make a salad? I'm finishing up the pork tenderloin, and Brooke needs to frost her cupcakes." Charlie elbows me in the stomach, which doesn't hurt, but I place a hand on my stomach, acting like it did.

"Okay, I gotchu." I reluctantly let go of Brooke, but I don't miss her smile when I glance down at her. "What do you need me to add to it? The usual?"

I'll admit, I wasn't much of a cook—or any help really—in the kitchen when I first moved in, but I've learned a lot from my roommates, and I'll go as far as to say I'm pretty decent now. I can work my way around a kitchen.

"Yeah, just carrots, cucumbers, and maybe some red pepper if we have any." Charlie takes a knife out of the butcher block and hands it to me.

"You got it, tiny terror."

I move to the refrigerator and start taking out all the vegeta-bles I need, lay them on the cutting board, and get to work. As I cut, I keep glancing over at Brooke as she ices the cupcakes she made. These ones are pink, and when she licks her thumb to get a smidgen of frosting off, I inwardly groan at how cute but sexy she looks, doing it.

"So, back to our conversation. Are you going to go?" Charlie asks Brooke.

She shrugs. "Yeah, I'll go. It's just been … kind of weird with us lately, and I can't really figure out why. I think he was stressed about finals, but his classes were easy for him this semester, so I don't know. Maybe he's just not really into me. It almost feels like it's an obligation for him to hang out with me."

Call me intrigued. I'm dying to hear more, and it's taking all of my self-control to keep my mouth shut and just listen.

"Well, I think you just need to talk to him honestly about how you're feeling. I learned that lesson the hard way. Don't let him play mind games with you. See how it goes tonight, but I definitely think you should have a conversation, B."

"It's just awkward, and I don't want to sound like a whiny girlfriend, especially if I'm not really sure where I want this to go, you know?" I see Brooke look over at Charlie.

"Right. Well then, I guess you need to figure out how much you care, but don't waste your time on something that doesn't work. You deserve to be happy and have someone treat you like the badass goddess you are." Charlie bumps her shoulder into Brooke's.

"Thanks, Char. Don't mention this to my brother. I don't think he likes Eli that much after the whole *no, Sint Maarten is the superior island* conversation." Brooke rolls her eyes.

Charlie winces. "Yeah, Beck was …"

"Ready to lay him out?" Brooke laughs.

"I mean, yes, pretty much. It was just the know-it-all attitude that pissed him off." Charlie smiles.

Brooke sighs. "I know, and I wish I could say that was an isolated incident, but it wasn't. I don't know why he does that. He's definitely smart, but I feel like he wants to shove it in people's faces sometimes. It's a huge turnoff, and honestly embarrassing."

"Then don't go to the game with him tonight. Just hang out with meeeee."

"No, I told him I would go, so we'll see what happens."

I clear my throat. "What game?"

"The basketball game. We play State, so Eli and a few of his friends want to go."

I had no intention of going to the game tonight, but I have a feeling that's about to change. "That'll be fun. But don't you need to study for finals?"

She shakes her head. "I took my last final today. My Thursday and Friday classes were papers, and I submitted those last week."

Charlie's phone rings before I can say anything more. "It's Beck. I'll be right back. Can you keep an eye on this tenderloin for me? I should only be a minute."

"Yeah, right!" Brooke yells after her. "Tell him I said hey."

I dump everything in a bowl, then move closer to Brooke because I want to be near her. "What flavor do we get tonight?"

She has an icing bag in her hand. "I just did vanilla cupcakes with buttercream frosting. Nothing fancy today."

I lean into her. "Can I have a taste?"

Her hand jerks, and she messes up the design on her cupcake. "Um, yeah, they'll be ready in a few." She takes her finger and wipes it around the edge, where she messed up.

I take her hand with the glob of frosting on it and pull it to my lips. "May I?"

She doesn't say anything, but her eyes are glued to my lips.

I swirl my tongue slowly around her finger, but don't put it inside my mouth. "It's delicious, just like it always is." I wink at her and smile.

"Thanks," she whispers.

"So, a basketball game. What time do you need to leave?" I try to settle back into a normal conversation with her, even though my thoughts are on spreading this frosting all over her and licking it clean.

"Oh, shoot," she says, looking at the clock. "I need to go soon to get ready. I might not be able to eat." She wipes off her finger and moves to the oven to check on the tenderloin. "It looks like it needs a little more time. I'll wait for Char to come out, and then I should probably leave."

I don't want her to go, but I also need to make plans to get to that game too. "I'll take care of this if you need to take off."

She steps back to her cupcakes, looks at me, and smiles. "Really? That would be a huge help." She pipes frosting over the cupcake she messed up, holds the bag of frosting to her lips, and squirts some into her mouth.

I hold in the groan trying to break free. Why is that so hot?

"Yeah, no problem. I'll even clean up your mess." I tug on her ponytail.

"Thanks, Silas." She sets the bag in the sink, then washes her hands. "I guess I'll see you later."

"You coming back here tonight?" I ask, hopeful.

"Oh, no, probably not. I might stay with Eli, but I'm not sure yet." She dries her hands quickly with a paper towel, then tosses it in the trash on her way toward Charlie's room.

"Great," I mumble to myself. "Douchebag."

Brooke walks back into the kitchen and grabs the mint-green Stanley that she always has with her. "Bye, Silas. Thanks again!" She smiles and waves at me as she moves toward the door.

I follow, just so I can watch her go. "See you later, Cupcake."

Her hand is on the doorknob, but she turns and looks back at me. Her mouth opens in surprise, and when I wink at her, she blushes. With an awkward wave, she pulls open the door and walks out.

The second the door closes, I get my phone out of my pocket and text Aston and Ace as I walk to Bo's room. His SUV is outside, and Chelsea's car isn't here, so I assume he's home.

> Silas: Come to the basketball game with me tonight.

Ace: What? Why?

Silas: Because I want to go.

Ace: I can't, dude. I need to study. If I don't pass this test, I'm fucked, and my mama will kill me.

Aston: He ain't lyin'. He's on her shit list right now. He has to study, but I'll come with you. I'm the good twin. I'm passing all my classes.

I pull up the basketball schedule on the school's website and see the game starts in two hours.

Silas: Pick me up at six thirty. Don't be late.

I knock on Bo's door. "Callaway, open up."

He pulls open the door, shirtless and looking like he's been running his fingers through his hair. "What's up?"

"I'm gonna hit up the basketball game tonight. You should come with me."

Bo leans up against the doorframe and crosses his arms. Bo is the kind of guy who can see right through you, and right now, he can probably read the intent on my face.

"Why?" A slow smile breaks across his face.

I look at him pointedly. "Because I'm a fan."

"Ha! Since when?"

"Since tonight. Are you gonna come with me or not?" I hold my hands out in front of me.

"This is about Brooke, isn't it?"

"You're really gonna make me say it?"

"If you want me to go with you tonight, yeah, I do want you to tell me."

"Yes, it's about Brooke. She's going with that douchebag. I overheard her talking to Charlie about him when I came home.

I'm telling you, something about that guy just irks me. He doesn't deserve her at all."

"And I'm sure Linson would want you looking out for her, right?"

"Exactly. I'm just looking out for her since he can't be here."

"Uh-huh." He sucks in a breath. "Okay, let me finish reviewing this one chapter for my exam tomorrow, and then I'll take a break and go to the game with you. Dinner almost ready? I need to eat before we go."

"Thanks, man. Yeah, I think it should be ready soon. Chelsea want to come too?"

"Nah, she has one of her big exams tomorrow, so she's locked in. I probably won't see her tonight at all."

"Okay. Aston is picking us up at six thirty."

"Fuck that. I'm driving. He's a horrible driver."

I fist-bump him. "Thanks for coming with me."

"Yeah, well, I can't let you do something stupid."

I place a hand on my chest. "Who, me? I'm offended."

"Right, but what about that time—"

"Dinner's ready!" Charlie yells from the kitchen.

"Saved by Little King. Let's go eat." I chuckle.

I shoot off a text to Aston to let him know we'll pick him up as I walk into the kitchen.

"Do you need any help?" I pocket my phone and walk toward Charlie.

"I got it. Oh, maybe just set out the silverware and napkins. I put the plates over there on the island, so you can put everything next to those. It's just the three of us since Brooke left and Casey and Noelle went out to eat."

"You got it." I grab the items and set them next to the plates. "So, tell me the truth. What do you think of this Eli guy?" I know I'm revealing my interest in Brooke, but I need to know what's going on.

She looks at me and scrunches her mouth and shakes her head. "I'm not really a fan, and she knows what my thoughts are. But it doesn't really matter what I think or what Beck thinks. She has to make that decision for herself, you know?"

"Right, but do you think he treats her well? Anytime I hear you guys talking about him, he sounds like a dick."

"Oh, he is for sure. But for some reason, she found a connection to the guy. He's her first real boyfriend, so Beck and I are just trying to be supportive and let it play out the way it's supposed to. And at the end of the day, if he's who she wants to be with, we'll all have to find a way to get along with him because we're family," she says as she cuts the pork tenderloin.

I try to take in what she's saying, and I guess I get it, but I don't like it.

"Why are you asking? You like her, don't you?" She smirks.

"I mean, she's gorgeous and fun, sure, but I'm not into her like that. I don't want some asshole fucking around with her either." I shrug, trying to act nonchalant.

Bo walks in and grabs a plate. "What are you guys doing, just standing here? We'd better eat fast if we're going to the game," he says.

I look over at Charlie, and she's leaning against the counter, smiling at me.

"Just playing a game of Bullshit, and Silas is losing."

I can't stop the laugh that comes out. I guess I'm more obvious than I thought.

CHAPTER
THREE

I SPOT BROOKE, Eli, and a few other guys sitting with them. They all look like Brads. Three-quarter zips; nice, clean-cut hair; jeans that look like they've been ironed, for fuck's sake. They probably all drink matcha too.

Essentially, the complete opposite of me. I'm covered in tattoos, and I have short hair, too, but mine always looks a little messy. And considering my physique, there's no mistaking I'm an athlete. The thing about me that they wouldn't know by looking at me is that I'm probably smarter than they are. I don't hide my intelligence, but I don't flaunt it like these dickbags. Plus, it's something I had to grow into. The confidence to accept that I was smart and not the funny, dumb kid who couldn't read in elementary school.

It wasn't that I couldn't read; I'm dyslexic, and no one caught it until I was in middle school. It wasn't a teacher, but was a coach actually. Once we figured it out, my life changed. Hours of after-school tutoring at an Orton-Gillingham reading center, vision therapy, and a shit ton of hard work paid off. School became fun, but I still wanted to fit in, so I held on to my sense of humor. But when I came to college, I became comfortable with how smart I was.

These guys though? They want you to know how smart they are. They think they're better than everyone.

"Let's sit down there." I point to the seats right above Brooke.

Bo shakes his head and laughs. "Lead the way, Romeo."

"Wait, we're going to sit with Brooke? Isn't she with that boyfriend of hers? I don't want to sit with those dickheads."

"Why do you think we're here in the first place?" Bo hits him in the chest. "Keep up, Griff."

"Oh shit," I hear him mumble behind me as I descend the stairs to the row directly above Brooke and Eli.

A few people recognize us as we walk by, and we smile and nod. Bo stops for a few selfies, but I move down the row until I'm right behind Brooke's seat. She hasn't noticed me yet, but Eli turns as I plop down in my seat, and I see him roll his eyes.

I love to fuck with this guy whenever he's around—which, funny enough, she doesn't bring him around much. Or he doesn't want to be around us. Who knows? I sure as fuck don't care.

I lean forward, in between them, and turn my face to Brooke. "Hey."

She nearly jumps with surprise. "Silas. What are you doing here?"

"I'm watching the basketball game. Huge fan."

"You are not." She leans away from the close proximity of my face to hers.

"Oh, but I am."

Eli clears his throat. "Brooke, you didn't tell me your security crew would be joining us tonight."

"They're not my security crew, Eli. I had no idea they were coming."

"Hey, Brooke. How's it going?" Bo sits down next to me and smiles at her.

"Hi, Bo." She smiles, but she looks uncomfortable as Eli gives her the side-eye.

"Little Linson! What up?" Aston holds out a fist for her to bump.

"So, you had no idea they were coming, but they intend to sit right behind us. Awesome." Eli shakes his head, irritated.

"I'm sorry, but I don't understand why it's a problem. They're my friends. You have your friends here, and I didn't care that they were coming with us."

"Actually, Brooke, I had these plans with my friends and invited you to join."

What a fucking asshole. How can she be with a guy like this?

I lean forward again, with a smile on my face, ready to tear into this douchecanoe, but Brooke catches my eye and subtly shakes her head.

"Okay, well, I thought you wanted me here because you said you hadn't seen me much this week. Sorry that I misunderstood."

Fuck that. She shouldn't be with a guy like this. She should not be apologizing to this guy.

Bo grabs my shoulder and pulls me back. "Dude, let it be. Don't make a scene here. There are eyes and cameras all around."

"I won't, but do you hear this guy?"

Bo nods. "I do, but we gotta stay out of it unless she asks for our help. He lays a hand on her though? Game over for him."

Aston leans forward, phone in his hand. "Yeah, brother, just let it ride out."

As we watch the game, my jealousy and aggravation with this guy fester. He's so condescending to her, and he's the kind of guy who's always right. Everything she says, he counters. He leaves her out of conversations with his friends too.

I know for certain that if her brother saw any of this, regardless of him wanting to let her figure this out on her own, he would be pissed. Maybe as much as I am. He's crazy protective of her, and I know Beck wouldn't stand letting someone treat his sister like this.

We're almost to the end of the first half, and if Brooke wasn't still sitting here, I would be gone. Now, I appreciate any fellow athlete, but this shit is boring. Or maybe my attention is too occupied elsewhere for me to pay attention to the game.

At least the crowd is into it. The camera guy has zoomed in on me, Bo, and Aston a few times, and we even stood up once when the crowd was cheering for us. I mean, we are in the play-offs, so it's a pretty big deal at the university.

They're doing one of those stupid kiss cameras now though. Every couple they've targeted in the crowd kisses and laughs, and then they move on. But now they're on Brooke and Eli.

She hasn't noticed it yet, but he has, and he's shaking his head and waving off the camera. When she notices his movement, she glances around, then finally up at the Jumbotron.

Her face goes scarlet, and she shrinks in her seat a little.

The crowd starts to chant, "Kiss her, kiss her, kiss her," but Eli looks like he's about to bolt.

What the fuck is wrong with this guy? How does he not realize what he has next to him?

I can't stand sitting here, watching this shitstorm. "Fuck it."

Leaning down, I reach my hand around and cup her jaw, turning her head toward me. Before she can react, I take her lips with mine. It's gentle but firm and full of intent. There's no doubt she knows I want this.

Then I pull back, and I cup the other side of her face so she can see the sincerity in my eyes. "When you're done with this guy—and you will be soon—I'll be happy to take the title." I kiss her softly again.

She pulls her head away first this time. "What? What title? Silas, oh my God," she says, shaking her head.

"Yours." Then I sit back in my seat, and the crowd goes wild, cheering.

Aston is standing and facing me, clapping.

Bo has a smile on his face, phone in hand, recording me or taking pictures of me. "That was awesome, man. I got it all on here for you. Gotta send it to Chelsea and the group chat."

I chuckle, but I look back at Brooke, and she's got one hand on Eli's arm, trying to get him to look at her. When he pulls his arm away forcefully, she leans back in her seat and crosses her arms over her chest.

Seeing her upset bothers me, and I'm sure she isn't happy with me right now, but I just couldn't help it. He was leaving her hanging, and no other guy in this place would have passed up on kissing Brooke Linson.

How does he not see how beautiful she is? Besides that, she's one of the smartest and kindest people I know. I'll never understand how he trapped her into a relationship. But I guess if he's the first guy she's ever really dated, maybe her expectations were low. I'm gonna change all that.

As I watch them, I can't help but smile because I love that I pissed him off, but more importantly, that she didn't push me away.

CHAPTER
FOUR

BROOKE

WHAT THE HELL JUST HAPPENED? An already-awkward night just became ten times worse. I cannot believe Silas did that.

I mean, if I'm being honest, everything else tuned out when his lips touched mine. It only lasted a few short minutes, but I felt the heat of that kiss all the way down to my belly.

And then what he said to me? I'm in trouble.

How can I sit here next to Eli after that? He is fuming, and I'm sure he's embarrassed by the entire thing. He likes being the center of attention when it's under his control.

This wasn't. And I'm surprised he's still sitting next to me, but he probably doesn't want to bring any more attention to us at this point.

"Eli, come on. Don't be like this. I didn't ask him to do that."

I try touching his arm again, and he turns his whole body away from me.

"Not now, Brooke. We'll discuss this later." He starts talking to his friends on the other side of him, completely shutting me out.

Silas leans to my side again, and I can't even look at him right now. I'll either kiss him or slap him. Both are strong possibilities.

"I would say I'm sorry, but I'm not. I meant what I said. I'll be here, waiting for you."

I literally cannot. My boyfriend is sitting right next to me. We're in public, for fuck's sake, but Silas doesn't care at all.

Before I can reply, the buzzer blasts, signaling the end of the first half. Eli stands up and starts moving down the row toward the stairs.

"Are you leaving?" I stand.

"I'm going to get a drink and use the restroom," Eli says, glancing my way.

Out of the corner of my eye, I see Aston look at Bo and hear him mutter, "Who says restroom?"

"Okay, I'll come get a drink with you." I follow him and his friends down the row.

"Suit yourself," he mutters, not bothering to wait for me.

When I look over my shoulder, I see Silas watching me. That boy is trouble with a capital T. And I like it. A little too much.

I turn back to watch where I'm going, and when we reach the top of the stairway, Eli doesn't bother waiting for me and takes off toward the restroom.

I walk over to the concession stand and lean against the wall, where I can see the exit to the restroom so I can watch for Eli to come out. As I stand there, I see Silas walk into the men's room.

Fuck.

I feel my phone buzz in my purse, distracting me from the potential disaster happening in the restroom right now, and I reach in and pull it out and see Charlie's been texting me in rapid-fire.

> Charlie: OMG, BROOKE! What the hell?!

> Charlie: I just saw the video. I cannot believe Silas did that! Are you okay???

Charlie: Brooke! Answer me before your brother sees it. Bo sent it to the house group chat, and Beck is still on it.

Oh shit.

Brooke: It's fine. I'm fine. Just a misunderstanding.

Charlie: Uhhhh, what am I misunderstanding? I saw Silas kiss you like y'all were in some romance novel. We'll talk about this more in detail later. I want to know everything! But are you okay? For real?

Brooke: Yes, I promise. Eli isn't though. He's definitely mad. I'm not sure if it's because Silas kissed me or because he was embarrassed publicly. I guess I'll find out soon enough. I'm waiting for him to come out of the bathroom.

Charlie: If you don't go to his place tonight, please come here. I want to know everything!

Another text alert pops up. I swipe with caution.

Beck: Brooke. What. The. Fuck?!

I navigate between my text chains.

Brooke: Beck just texted me. What should I say?

Charlie: Don't ignore him, or he'll be upset.

I have no idea what to say though. He'll either be mad at Eli or Silas. Neither option is great for me. Especially since Beck will be home soon and will no doubt be seeing Silas. Who he's good friends with!

> Brooke: Hey, big brother! What's up?

> Beck: Brooke.

> Brooke: Beck.

> Beck: Why is my friend kissing you at a basketball game?

All righty then. I'll wing it.

> Brooke: It was just a joke! All good.

> Beck: And why did your boyfriend, who was sitting next to you, let it happen?

> Brooke: Wait. Tell me which one you're more upset about, and I'll give you the answer.

My phone starts to ring, my brother's grumpy face on the screen.

"Hi," I answer cheerily.

"B, what's going on?"

I sigh. "Nothing. Everything is fine. It was just one of those kiss cams at the game, and it shot to us, and Silas just went with it, I guess."

"Uh-huh. But why didn't your boyfriend kiss you?"

"Beck, come on. I don't know. I'm fine. I'm not upset, and don't be mad at Silas either."

"Yeah, I'm not mad at Silas, although I'm gonna find out what the fuck he's thinking, kissing my sister, but we need to talk about this when I see you."

"There's nothing to talk about. All good. I can't wait to see you!"

"Brooke," he starts.

"Bye, love you!" I disconnect before he can reply.

I look over to the restroom, and I see Eli walk out, and right behind him is Silas. *This can't be good.*

As Eli gets closer to me, I notice the red in his cheeks.

"Are you okay?"

"I'm fine, Brooke. Christ. Don't make a scene more than you already have." He walks around me to get in line.

I look back toward where I last saw Silas, and he's still there, watching me. He looks like he wants to come to me, but I shake my head. And just as he looks like he's going to come to me anyway, Bo walks up to him and puts a hand on his shoulder. Bo waves to me and starts to pull Silas away with him.

I watch them go, and before they turn the corner, Silas winks at me and smiles.

After Eli gets his drink and doesn't offer to get me one, we go back to our seats. Sitting next to him now is uncomfortable, to say the least, and I'm tempted to get up and leave. But having already caused drama, I don't want to make it worse. Plus, he's my ride, and I would be embarrassed to have to call Charlie or my other friends to come get me. So, I'll sit quietly and patiently wait for the game to end.

My phone is buzzing in my purse, and I know if I don't respond to whoever it is, they won't stop. So, I pull it out and see a string of messages from Charlie and Arbor, one from my brother, and an Instagram notification from Silas.

I read Charlie's first, reminding me to come over if I'm not staying with Eli tonight. My guess is, I won't be. My brother's text says that he loves me and to text him later. Arbor's makes me laugh. She wants all the tea.

But Silas … his makes me suck in a breath. I turn my body so Eli can't see it.

Silas: Break up with him.

My thumb hovers over the keyboard, but I don't even know how to reply to this. In my gut, I know I should break up with Eli, yet there's this thing inside me that says stay. It's why I've made all the choices I have made my whole life.

My hands are starting to shake, and I can feel the tightness in my back spreading up and over my shoulders. I cannot have an anxiety attack right now. I take some deep breaths to try to calm myself down.

Five ... four ... three ... two ... one.

When I look for something to feel, I panic a little, running out of options in these bleachers. I reach into my purse and grab a mint.

As I chew on it, I barely notice the buzzer that ends the game. Eli finally acknowledges me when he stands.

"Let's go." He holds out a hand for me to take and keeps it in his as we climb the stairs.

The mixed signals make my head spin, and I feel like I can't keep up.

We make our way out of the arena and through the parking lot to Eli's car. Thankfully, his friends drove separately, so it's just the two of us in his car.

"Do you want me to take you home, or do you want to come over?"

Is he serious? He ignored me for most of the game, and now he wants me to come over?

"Well, I mean, do you want me to come over? You seemed pretty upset with me tonight and not really like you want to be hanging out with me."

"I was fine until your buddies showed up. It feels like they're always around. And I know they're your friends, but they're just a bunch of dumb jocks. I'm honestly surprised you tolerate them and spend as much time with them as you do. How do you even carry on civilized conversations with them?" He huffs a laugh.

I'm literally speechless right now. I pull in a breath and pause to think about what I want to say in response.

"Eli, you know my brother is one of those jocks you're talking about, right? And I don't really appreciate you talking about him or our friends like that. Some of those guys are as smart, if not smarter, than you and me."

"See, you always defend them like this too. It makes me wonder if something is going on behind my back."

I laugh. "You can't be serious! I've been nothing but loyal to you, and I would never cheat on anyone. Eli, I really don't understand where all this is coming from. Things started out so good between us. We've taken things to the next level by sleeping together. You know I don't take that lightly, so I'm really upset that you're insinuating that I would be hooking up with any of them behind your back. They're like brothers to me."

"Silas Arbuckle doesn't look at you like a sister. And I don't think anyone kisses their sister the way he kissed you tonight."

"Well, if you had just kissed me, it wouldn't have happened! I didn't even realize what was going on until I saw us on the Jumbotron. Do you know how embarrassing that was for me that my boyfriend wouldn't even give me a peck? I wanted to curl up in a ball on my seat."

He glances over at me with irritation written all over his face. "Listen, Brooke, I think we need to table this conversation for tonight. We're both upset, and you need to take some time to calm down."

"I need to calm down? Nice. Okay, you know what? You're right. Take me to my brother's house."

"Your brother doesn't even live there anymore. This is what I'm talking about. It doesn't make sense for you to spend as much time over there as you do."

"My brother's fiancée is like my sister. Why wouldn't I want to spend time with her?"

"I just think it's weird that you spend so much time over there with a bunch of guys when you have a boyfriend—that's all I'll say."

I can feel tears forming, and I don't want to break in front of him. I don't know why he's saying these things. I mean, it's not really a surprise that he doesn't like my friends, but he can be a jerk sometimes. Okay, maybe a lot of the time.

More and more lately, I've been questioning why I'm even

with him. I don't feel like he even likes me all that much. So, I don't know why I'm hanging on to this.

I think it's time I got real with the therapist I've been seeing and get some advice about it. I started working with the same therapist here that my brother used. I really like her, and because she knows our history, it's made it much easier for me to dive in. I haven't told Eli about any of this because I know if I told him about my past, he would definitely break up with me and probably tell everyone we know. Which I only care about because I have three and a half years to go in my program and will have to be in classes with a lot of them.

"Are you just going to sit there and pout now?" he sighs.

I rub my hands on my legs and exhale a shaky breath. "I'm not pouting, Eli. You're being intentionally cruel."

"I'm telling the truth. You just don't like hearing it."

We're turning down the street to the house, but as we get closer, I realize I'm not ready to be around Silas yet. I need some space.

"Actually, just take me to my dorm instead."

He sighs. "I wish you had told me when we passed that street a few minutes ago."

"Sorry," I mumble, even though I'm not really sorry. I have the habit of apologizing when I shouldn't.

The rest of the ride is silent. I just can't talk to him right now, or I'll cry or blow up, and neither option is comfortable for me. I shoot a text off to Charlie though, letting her know I'll call her later and that I'm staying at my place tonight. I was lucky enough to get a single room within a quad in one of the dorms. So, I'll have some peace and quiet so I can process everything that happened tonight and the things Eli said.

We drive up to my dorm, and there are no parking spots, so he just pulls to the side and turns on his hazards.

"I would walk you up, but there's nowhere for me to park. You're good, right?"

I unbuckle my seat belt and glance up at him quickly, not

wanting to make eye contact. "Yeah, I'll be fine. I'll talk to you later."

I pull the door handle, but he grabs on to my arm to stop me.

"Hey, I'm not going to kiss you tonight. I can't kiss you after that Neanderthal put his lips on you. I'll call you before I go to sleep though."

Unbelievable.

"I'm not really in the mood anyway, so, yeah, we're all set. See you later, Eli."

I push open the door so I can get out of the car. Once I'm out, I slam the door before I say something I might regret later. I think I hear him curse as I walk away, but I don't really care right now.

I wave at a few people as I walk in, but I don't stop to talk to anyone. I just want to get into my room and forget this night.

Thankfully, when I open the door to my dorm room, none of my roommates are out in the living area. All of the bedroom doors are closed, so they're likely studying. My roommates are all nice, but I don't hang out with them much. I haven't really told them much about me other than my major. If they know who I am or connected me to my brother, no one has said anything, which is good. I've struggled with genuine friendships since my brother started to become more well known.

I close my bedroom door behind me and drop my purse on my desk next to my bed. I strip off my clothes and get my pajamas on. Crossing the hall to the bathroom, I make quick work of my nighttime routine and head back to my room. Once I settle into my bed, I grab my phone from the nightstand.

Brooke: Hey, you still up?

Charlie: Yep. Call me?

I tap the Phone icon, and it only rings once before she answers.

"Hey, you. How you doing?" she asks.

I sigh, covering my eyes with my arm. "I don't know. What am I doing, Char? Everything started well with Eli, but it's just gotten … I don't know … harder, being around him lately."

"Well, I can't say that I'm all that experienced with dating. You know I've only had two boyfriends, and I'm marrying my first. What I can say is that Eli reminds me a little bit of the guy I dated at Chandler before I transferred here. He was really full of himself, and looking back, I realize he got off on putting me down. Like it made him feel better about himself or something. It was a total change from how Beck had treated me, so I knew it wasn't exactly right, but I was still messed up over your brother that I think I just tolerated it." She pauses. "But, Brooke, don't waste your time on someone you don't even really like being around. I know you were excited when you first met him, and you have similar interests and whatnot, but that doesn't carry a relationship. And I was a little nervous when you told me you were going to sleep with him, but that wasn't my place to say anything. You had to make that choice."

"Yeah, I know. It's like I know all of this logically, but I can't exactly make myself break up with him. You know I don't like to hurt people, although I'm not sure he'd be all that disappointed if I ended it. It's almost like he lost interest after we started having sex. And when we do, it feels very mechanical. It makes me feel like maybe he isn't that attracted to me and we're just doing it because we're a couple. Is that stupid?"

"No, it's not stupid. You're saying a lot about what you think he thinks or feels, but you're not saying anything about how you feel. You know you're allowed to have an opinion on this relationship, right? You're part of it too. He doesn't get to make all the calls here, B." She scoffs.

"No, I know. Urgh. I don't know why I'm like this."

"Have you talked to your therapist about this at all? I feel like some of these pieces of what you have told me are connected to the bigger picture of your past. We don't have to dig deep tonight, but I think you need to talk to her about Eli the next time you have an appointment. Be really honest about how you feel about him and why you're hanging on to this relationship."

"You're right, and, yes, I have an appointment with her next week, just before Christmas. You're staying on campus and driving home for Christmas Eve? Are y'all staying at your house or mine? I know Beck only gets a few days off."

"Yeah, you can come stay at this house for sure. Beck will fly into Oklahoma City and come directly here. I think we'll spend one night here, then head home, but I'm not sure if we'll be at your house or mine. Not that it really matters since they're right across the street." She laughs. "Casey will only be home for Christmas Eve because they'll need to be back here at practice. Bo and Silas will both be here too, obviously. I'm pretty sure Chelsea will be staying around, and Noelle is going home ahead of Casey to spend a few days with her family, but will be back the day after Christmas."

"Y'all are going to the bowl game in Houston, right?"

The football team has made it to the playoffs this season, but we have to make it through two rounds of bowl games before the big show.

"Yes, for sure. Are you and your dad coming with us? I thought you were."

I nod even though she can't see me. "Yeah, I think so. I'll probably just ride home with you and Beck because I do need to be here for my appointment on Monday. Maybe I'll just stay home after Christmas and have my dad bring me back here after the game."

It might be good to spend some time with my dad too. He's all alone now with Beck and me gone. I know he's busy with work, but I hate to think of him sitting at home by himself night after night. Even if the Kings are across the street, it's not the same as living with someone.

"Okay, just come stay here then until we leave."

"Oh, wait, where will I sleep though?"

She giggles. "I'm sure Silas wouldn't mind you sharing his bed with him."

"Charlie, that kiss caused enough problems for me. Can you imagine if I slept in his room? Eli would definitely break up with me. He was pissed about that kiss."

"Well, hopefully, it taught him a lesson. But I have to ask, did you feel anything when Silas kissed you?"

"I felt it everywhere," I whisper, but I'm not sure why. No one can hear me.

"I love that for you. I know the situation is complicated, but, B, you have to admit, it was fucking hot! I'm going to send you the video Bo posted in our group chat. I was cheering, and I wasn't even there." She laughs.

"He came in before you called and asked if I'd talked to you at all. I think this is more than a crush for him. I suspected it when we went to the rodeo in the fall, but I see the way he looks at you and tries to be near you whenever you're over. And don't think I missed that you were cuddled up together on the couch at Noelle's party."

I groan. "You think everyone's noticed that we fell asleep on the couch together?"

"Oh, yeah, babe. We've all noticed. I was waiting for him to make a move, but I never would have thought he would do it in front of your boyfriend. He's got balls. I loved it!"

"Well, his balls caused some drama for me tonight. In more than one way." I sigh. "Eli is pissed, and what's worse is that I can't stop thinking about it either."

"Sounds like you have some decisions to make, sister. Beck is calling, so I'm gonna let you go. I'll check in with you tomorrow, or just come by when you're done with your exam. Love you, B."

"Love you too. Tell Beck I said hi, I'm okay, and I love him."

"Will do. Byyyye!" She hangs up before I can reply.

I set my phone on my chest and shut my eyes. I wish I had

what Charlie and Beck have, but I don't think I'm going to find that with Eli. I guess I just don't know how to navigate this relationship stuff yet.

My phone buzzes, and I lift it to see a text come through from Charlie. I open the video and zoom in on Silas and can see him mouth, *Fuck it*, right before he swoops in and kisses me. At the time, the kiss only felt like seconds, but watching it, I guess it lasted a little longer. I trace my lips with my finger, and I swear, I can almost feel his lips on mine while I watch.

I play it a few more times, then save it to my phone.

Just as I'm about to plug in my phone, another Instagram message from Silas pops up. I swipe it open and bite back a smile.

> Silas: Sweet dreams, Cupcake.

I debate answering him and decide to give him something since I didn't respond earlier. But really, what would I have said to him telling me to break up with my boyfriend?

> Brooke: Night, Trouble.

> Silas: Ooh, I like that. 😊

I close out our message and scroll through my feed. Silas already follows me. I don't really post much, so there are only a few photos, mostly family pictures and one or two with Beck after they won the championship game two years ago.

I pull up his profile and decide to follow him back. His profile looks a whole lot different than mine. His is basically a thirst trap, but also features some of his game footage. He really is an incredible player to watch. I heart a few of the game reels and a few pictures on his grid. There are no pictures with girls, which is a relief. Although I know he hasn't been celibate since he's been here—or even this year. I've seen a few girls come out of his room the next day, and I didn't like it.

I'm sure he sees me liking his posts, and I like knowing that he knows I'm cyberstalking him. He's definitely ignited a spark tonight. But the question is, what am I going to do about it?

When I finally plug my phone in, I realize that Eli never called, and I feel … relieved.

CHAPTER
FIVE

SILAS

WHEN I'M on the field, I become a different person in the sense that I can shut all the noise in my head out and lock in on one thing. Getting the ball. It's my job, as a cornerback, to make sure the best receivers on the opposing team don't score—or even get the ball in the first place. And I need to make the big plays, big tackles, and if I'm lucky, I can grab a few interceptions.

We're one game away from the national championship game, and with the holidays and anticipation of bowl games, it's easy to lose focus on what we're working toward. But not me. This season is important for me. I'll either stay here one more year or declare for the draft. It'll really all depend on how I play in the next two games.

Sure, I've had a great season, and I'm what is considered to be a lockdown corner, which means I'm an essential player on the team but also the guy quarterbacks want to avoid. Other teams design plays just to move around me. And I might be one of the best, but I also need to consider what teams are looking for a talent like me and if that need is likely to pay off for me now or in a year from now.

Our practice for the day just ended. It's our last before we head to Houston for our game tomorrow. The defensive coordinator worked us hard today, and I should sleep well tonight. The tight end that I'll be covering for during this game is fast, and I fully anticipate that he'll make me work for every move I make. That's okay though. I'm up for the challenge. Hungry for it even.

When I make it to the locker room, the music is blasting, and most of the team is already undressing and getting ready for showers. I set my helmet on the hook in my cubby and start to pull off the rest of my pads and toss my practice jersey into the laundry bin.

Bo comes into the locker room last, just like he always does. He's one of the hardest workers I've seen on the field. Always the first one on and the last one off.

As he walks by me, he whips me with his towel. "Well, Romeo, have you talked to Brooke since the basketball game?"

Casey's at the cubby next to Bo's, and his head whips up at the mention of Brooke. "Yeah, tell me how that all happened. I only saw the clip Bo sent out in the group chat, but haven't been home yet to get all the details."

"You gossip like a girl, King. Has anyone ever told you that?" I laugh.

"Fuck off. Brooke is like a sister to me, so I want to know what happened."

"Well, our boy here laid one on her when her asshole boyfriend left her high and dry with the kiss cam." Bo laughs.

"Seriously? Gah, I hate that guy." Casey shakes his head. "I wish she would just break up with him. The whole thing reminds me of Noelle's ex in a way, minus the cheating part. I don't think Eli has it in him to cheat on Brooke, but I guess I could be wrong."

"Yeah, he doesn't seem all that into her, at least from what I've seen anyway, but I agree; I don't think he'd cheat. If Silas has any say in the matter, she'd be on his arm instead," Bo says.

"Caught on to that, too, a while ago. But let me ask you, Silas, does Beck know you're into his sister?" A wicked smile spreads across his face.

"Beck is on the group chat, so I know he saw the video," Bo chimes in again.

"I'll have to ask him what he thinks about it." Casey pulls his phone off his shelf.

"I love that you guys are talking about this in front of me like I'm not here," I mumble.

But I can't lie; I've watched the video a few hundred times at this point. Okay, maybe not a hundred, but close.

"Speak up then, man. Talk to us." Bo nudges my shoulder.

Before I can answer, Casey dials up a FaceTime call with Beck.

Great.

"What's up, brother?" Beck answers after three rings, the sound of a treadmill running in the background.

"Hey, not much. Just wanted to see if you caught that video of Arbuckle kissing Brooke." Casey looks at me and winks.

I flip him off and shake my head.

"He in there with you?" Beck's deep chuckle could be a good one or a bad one. "Well, I mean, I don't love seeing one of my buddies kissing my little sister, but from what Charlie said, Eli was being a dickhead, so I forgive you, Arbuckle!" Beck shouts.

I walk over to Casey so I can fit into the frame. "Sup, Linson? Look, I wish I could say that I'm sorry, but I'm not. That guy is the worst, and if you had seen the way he was talking to her and blatantly ignoring her—even with me, Callaway, and Aston there—he was still an asshole. And I gotta tell ya, she never looks happy when he's around or when I hear her talking to Charlie about him. I'll spare you some of the things I've heard, but he doesn't deserve her."

He's nodding, and he doesn't look real happy, but I don't think he's mad at me. "Did you say anything to him?"

I look down, but lift my eyes to the phone. "I put the pressure on him a bit in the bathroom before we took off, but didn't lay a hand on him, like I wish I could have."

"Is that why you took off after them at the half?" Bo asks me.

I look over at him and nod. "Yeah, I originally wanted to just make sure she was okay, but then I saw him walk into the restroom and couldn't help but follow him."

"What did he say, or did you start it?" Casey asks.

"I asked him how it felt to see his girl kiss a real man. He got all red in the face and told me to fuck off. But when I told him to treat her better or leave her alone, he spun around on me and got in my face. Which, honestly, just wanted to make me laugh, but I was too curious to hear what he had to say." I chuckle. "So, he told me that I needed to step off—his words—and that me and my jock friends were interfering with his relationship with Brooke. And I couldn't hold in the laugh by then, so I crowded up to him and told him if I ever saw him or heard of him disrespecting her again, he would be getting a visit from me on his nerd farm."

"He doesn't live on a farm. I think he lives on campus," Ace joins in from out of nowhere. Kid can be stealthy when he wants to be.

We all turn to look at him to see if he's fucking with us, and, nope, he's not.

"What? Am I wrong?"

Casey punches him lightly in the shoulder. "Bro, we know he doesn't live on a farm. Silas was just trying to make him mad."

"Ah, gotcha. Yeah, I hate that guy." Ace shakes his head and walks to his cubby station.

"Well, thanks for that, Arbuckle. I appreciate you looking out for her, but, hey"—Beck pauses—"don't fucking kiss my sister again."

I look him dead in the eye, knowing what I'm about to say could hurt our friendship, but I'm gonna risk it anyway because she's worth it. "If she wants me to kiss her, you and nobody else would be able to stop me." I wink to lighten the blow, but he knows I'm not joking.

He sighs and shakes his head. "All right, assholes. I need to run. I'll see you in Houston." The call drops before any of us can respond.

"Welp, it's your balls on the line, Arbuckle. What are you gonna do now?" Casey asks.

"I've already told her to break up with him, so I feel like it's pretty clear to her that I'm into her." I shrug.

"Never assume they know, brother. Sometimes, these girls need to see it clear as day. Don't make her guess, and I'll fuck you up if you play games with her too." Casey points at me, smiling.

Bo takes hold of my shoulder. "You should probably see how it goes over the next few weeks. Hopefully, she'll come to her senses on her own. But we need you ready to play now. Worry about your girl problem later, yeah?"

"No, you're right. I need to stay locked in right now and figure this out later."

"She's going home for a few days, so you won't even see her until after the game anyway." Casey turns back to his cubby and starts packing up his gear. "I'm gonna grab a snack, then head home to shower. See you guys later."

Brooke going home is probably a good idea for both of us. I don't want her to feel awkward, being around me now. She needs to figure out her relationship with Eli on her own, and maybe the space will give her that clarity.

But maybe my checking in with her from time to time wouldn't be a bad thing.

After I left the field, I got an email alert from one of my professors, telling me there was a problem with my submission for my final grade. It didn't transfer completely to the portal, and it needed to be done before five p.m., which didn't leave me a lot of time to get it done. So, instead of going home and resubmitting it, I swing by the library, settle in at one of the study tables, and get my laptop out of my bag.

I've just put on my glasses when I look up and see Brooke walking by.

I whisper-shout to her so I'm not totally disrupting the other students, "Brooke!"

She stops and looks around, and I wave to her to catch her attention. When she just stands there, I think maybe she might still be upset about the kiss. But then she walks over to the table and pulls out the seat across from mine.

"Silas." She drops her backpack on the floor, then leans in, resting her arms on the table. "What are you doing here? Didn't you have practice?"

I nod. "Just got done, but I need to submit an assignment that didn't make it through, and I would have missed the deadline if I had gone home first. Speaking of, don't move. Let me just send this out real quick."

As I'm typing a note to my professor, I can feel her watching me, so I glance up and wink at her. It's a little dark in here, but I swear she blushes.

"Okay, done. So … what are you up to? Aren't you done with finals?"

"Yeah, I am, but I remembered I had a book I needed to return before break, so I ran over here to get it done." She tilts her head, still studying me.

"Do I have something on my face?" I pull off my glasses and run my hand over my face.

She laughs lightly and shakes her head. "No, nothing on your face. I just didn't know you wore glasses. I've been around you for, like, what, a year and a half ? And I've never seen you wear them."

"Oh, yeah. I don't have to wear them all the time. I just put them on when I'm studying or reading."

I debate on telling her about my dyslexia. I'm not embarrassed by it or anything, but I'm just not sure I want to get into a whole conversation about it right now. Truth is, the glasses help to contrast the numbers and letters and also help with what my eye doctor calls visual stress.

"It's funny that I've never seen you do either one with how often I'm over at your house." She smiles.

I shrug. "It's hard to focus in the house when people are coming and going, so I usually study in my room."

"Makes sense." She leans back in her seat, dropping her hands into her lap. "So, you ready for the game?"

"I'm always ready, Cupcake." A smile spreads across my face. I like that she's asking about the game.

"Good. I'm excited for y'all. I think you guys can win the whole damn thing." She crosses her arms.

"Me too. We've got a strong team, and we're really vibing this year. I love these guys."

She nods and smiles. "Yeah, it seems that you all have really good chemistry on the field, but you actually like each other too."

Then we just sit there, looking at each other, smiles on our faces. I have questions just dying to spill out, but I just said in the locker room that I would give her space. But, damn, the waiting is gonna be hard. I want to walk around the table, pick her up, and walk right out of here. Then take her to my bed and fuck her all night. I mean, can't help it. She's drop-dead gorgeous with her long brown hair, dark brown eyes, and pouty lips. And her body … it doesn't quit. Curves for days, and I want to learn every. Single. One.

She pulls in a deep breath. "Well, I guess I should probably go." She places her hands on the table in front of her and stands.

I stand with her. "I'll walk you out. You heading to your dorm or our house?"

"I'm going to the dorm tonight. My dad will be here before lunch to get me. I was going to wait for Beck to get here and ride home with him, but my dad wants to do some last-minute Christmas shopping and needs my help. But we'll be at the game." She picks up her bag and slings it over her shoulder.

"Can I walk you to your dorm?" I slide my computer in my bag quickly and pull the straps over my shoulders.

"Uh, I'm not sure that's a good idea." She grimaces.

"Why not?" I walk over to her and nudge her arm with my elbow.

"Silas." She looks at me incredulously.

"Is this about the dickhead?"

We start walking toward the exit of the library.

"Eli?" She rolls her eyes. "I mean, a little bit, yeah."

"Okay, how about I walk you to Lindsey Street at least?" When we get to the door, I walk ahead and hold it open for her.

She looks up at me and smiles. "Fine, but you aren't crossing with me."

"All right, Cupcake."

I hold out my arm for her to take, and she shoves it away.

"Don't push it, Arbuckle," she says, laughing.

I touch my chest with my hand. "I'm nothing but a gentleman."

"Right." She smirks.

"You'll see." I wink at her.

"Okay …" She adjusts the strap on her shoulder. "So, will your family come to the game, or will you get to see them at all over break?"

"My parents are supposed to come, but my siblings won't come."

"You have a big family, right? Kind of like Archie's?" She looks up at me.

I nod. "I have seven siblings. I'm lucky number eight."

"All boys?"

"Nope. I have two sisters, who are like bonus moms." I chuckle, thinking of my bossy sisters.

"So, you're close with just them or all of them?"

"Well, we're all pretty close in age. One of my brothers and my older sister are Irish twins." I lift a shoulder. "I guess I'm closer to a few of them than others. My older two brothers are married with kids already. I also have a brother in the Navy, but the rest are near home and work on the farm."

"And your family has a produce farm? I'm sorry. I can't remember what it is."

"We harvest wheat mostly, but we also grow rye. All for commercial use, like breads, cereals, and that kind of stuff. I'm not really involved, but I've done my time, working on the farm." I laugh.

"I would imagine it's a lot of work."

"Yeah, it is. I hated it when I was a kid, but as I got older and started training, I used it as an extension of my conditioning. It definitely helped with my upper body strength. We have machines that handle the really heavy lifting and, of course, separating the seeds out, but I've spent many hours in the barn, moving bales after the seeds are removed."

"That's really interesting. In one of my classes this semester, we had to write about weather patterns and how they affect agriculture in our region." She looks at me and smiles.

"Weather is a gift and a curse in that world. It can determine whether or not you'll make good money in a year."

A guy on an electric scooter comes out of nowhere, cutting far too close. I barely have time to register it before instinct takes over.

I grab her around the waist and pull her back against me, turning us just enough to get her out of the way. Her body fits easily into the space I make for her—soft curves under my hands, warm and very real. My fingers sink in for half a second longer than necessary, reluctant to let go.

She exhales sharply, one hand braced against my chest. I can feel the rise and fall of her breath, the subtle press of her hip against mine as the world rights itself again.

"Hey, asshole! Watch where you're going," I yell out to him.

"You okay?" I ask her, keeping my arm around her.

"I'm fine. Thanks for saving me from a scooter disaster." She leans into me slightly.

"Happy to be your knight in shining armor anytime."

I wink at her, and she shoves me away, making my arm fall.

"You're too much, Silas."

I don't want to be too much. I want to be her everything.

"Here's where we part ways. I guess I'll see you in Houston." She leans forward and slides her arm around my waist, surprising me. "Good luck and be safe out there, okay?"

Before I can react to her half hug, she draws her arm back and jogs across the street. She turns around when she reaches the other side and waves.

I hold up my hand in response and then wait for her to get farther down the pathway toward her dorm. Then I cross the street and stay a decent distance behind so she won't necessarily see me if she turns around, but I'm close enough that I can make sure she gets to her dorm safely.

Once I see her walk in the door, I turn and start to make my way home.

I'm not even ten steps in when I feel my phone buzz in my pocket. I pull it out and see a message from her on Instagram.

> Brooke: Thanks for making sure I got to my dorm safely. 😊

I can't help the laugh that slips out.

This girl. I think she might like me too. She just doesn't want to admit it. Yet.

CHAPTER
SIX

BROOKE

I WASN'T LYING when I told Silas I was leaving today, but what I didn't tell him was that I also had my appointment with my therapist today. My dad will be here to get me before lunch, which will give us plenty of time to stop at some stores on our way home. And I'm honestly looking forward to it. For multiple reasons really. I need some time with my dad, but I also feel like I need some time away from campus and Eli.

There's five minutes till my appointment, and I'm hustling to reach the door. I hate to be late. It makes me anxious. I just couldn't make myself get out of bed this morning, and I'm normally an early riser. Maybe I slept in because I knew I needed to dig deep in therapy today, and was subconsciously avoiding it.

I swing open the door and run up the stairs, and when I reach the top, I see my therapist, Kaitlin, standing at the door, waiting for me with a smile on her face.

"It's okay for you to be a minute late, you know?" she says.

"My need to be on time might not be a habit we will be able to curb." I huff as I reach her.

She places a hand on my shoulder. "Come on in. I want to hear about what you've been up to."

"Well, get ready. I have some things to unpack with you today."

"Ooh … that's good!" Kaitlin moves to the chair she usually sits in and picks up a small notepad.

There's a brown leather couch in the room across from her chair, so I take a seat and remove my crossbody and set it on the table between us. I take a few deep breaths just so I can breathe to talk. My brother got all the athletic genes for sure. I work out, but running at lightning speed across the oval, like Beck can, is not in my wheelhouse.

"So, tell me how your finals went. Did you have any attacks?"

"No panic attacks, thankfully. They went well. Pretty easy, to be honest. You know I enjoy writing, and two of my classes were essays, so I actually had fun with those. One was on the correlation between shifts in geographical patterns and the severity of tornado activity, particularly the eastward shift of Tornado Alley." I fold my hands together because I tend to wave my hands around while I'm talking as a nervous habit.

"That does sound interesting, Brooke. I would love to read it when you get it back from your professor." She makes a note on her notepad.

"Yeah, of course. But, yes, everything went well. I'm ready for a break though." I shake out my hands when she nods to them and sees me squeezing them so tight that my knuckles are turning white.

"What are your plans for the break?"

She makes another note on her pad. I wonder what she writes on it. I wish I could see it one day.

"Uh, well, my dad is picking me up before lunch today, and then we'll take care of some holiday stuff. Beck comes home tomorrow, but he's coming here first to get Charlie. Then I guess Christmas at my house or the Kings' or both. After that, we'll all head to Houston to watch the game." I start to twist my hands again because now I'm thinking about the fact that I'll be watching Silas play too. "Oh, and we're going to Chicago to watch Beck's game between Christmas and New Year's."

"Busy then. But that's really good for you to spend time with your family. Get some downtime from school. You've been working hard this semester, and honestly, you've adjusted very well to school and being away from your dad."

"I think I had to. I mean, Charlie and Casey being here helps. It might have been harder for me if I didn't have them." I reach for my bag to grab a mint.

"In what way?" she asks.

"Well, because it's difficult for me to fit in, I guess. I'm not really comfortable making friends." I shrug. "I mean, all my friends here are Charlie's friends or were my brother's friends and teammates, so I knew them all before I got here. I don't really have any friends outside of that circle."

"That's true, but that doesn't mean you couldn't meet people. What about Eli? You met him on your own. How is that going?"

"Yes, I did, but that was because we met in class. And he made the first move." I crunch my mint and swallow. Starting to feel anxious because this is the big thing we need to talk about.

"And things are going well with him?" She has that stupid pen poised on the pad again.

"Actually, not good at all. And I'm not really sure what to do about it now. I don't think we're a great match. It's really hard for me to talk to him too. I just …" I know what I'm about to say isn't going to paint him in the best light. "He can be kind of mean, in the sense that he talks down to me. And the worst part is that I just sit there and take it. I'm staying with him, and I can't figure out why I can't walk away."

"So, he's condescending to you?" She points her pen toward me.

"Yes, he is. But I also wonder if he even really likes me as a person. Like, I don't understand why he's with me, you know?"

I hold out my hands in front of me. "He hates my friends. Makes comments about the guys being dumb jocks, knowing who my brother is and how I'm associated with them." I drop my head back on the couch. "I don't feel like I can really be myself with him either. When I'm at Charlie's, it feels like home. Everything is just easy, so I feel like I can relax and be myself. But when I'm with Eli, I feel like I have to perform. Does that make sense?"

"Tell me what you mean by perform." She motions her hand toward her body. "That's an interesting word to use."

I sigh. "That I feel like I have to look a certain way, talk a certain way, and never be disagreeable, or he belittles me. Despite the fact that I'm just as smart as he is. Like, if I challenge him in any way, he'll punish me by ignoring me. Like he's done this week actually."

"What happened this week?" Kaitlin tilts her head, watching me.

I clear my throat. "Well, he asked me to go to a basketball game with him, but I don't think he really wanted me to come or expected me to say yes. I didn't realize his friends were coming with us. I thought we were going to be spending time together, but he ignored me when we got there." Then I meet her gaze. "Some of the guys from the football team showed up and sat behind us. And, long story short, the kiss cam happened, and Eli refused to kiss me, so one of the football guys did, and … as you can imagine, it made Eli pretty mad."

"That sounds uncomfortable and confusing," she says evenly. "Especially since you went into the situation with different expectations. What emotions came up for you in that moment—before Eli reacted?"

"At first, I think I was just shocked. Like, it took a minute for my brain to catch up to what was happening. And then Eli was upset, which just irritated me more than made me anxious. I didn't want to cause a scene either. So, I guess in a different situation or different circumstances, I would have had a panic attack, but because it was someone I knew, I didn't. I'm not really sure."

"So, familiarity played a role in how safe your body felt in that time," she says. "Does that feel accurate to you?"

"Yes, for sure."

Silas's face pops in my mind, and all I can see are those blue eyes and that sexy smirk he wears.

"That's important," she says. "Have you thought about whether your sense of safety was situational, or whether it was connected to *him* specifically? In other words, do you think you would've felt the same way if it had been someone else?"

"All the other guys I spend time with have girlfriends, or most of them anyway, so that would have been really awkward."

"So, this particular person doesn't?"

"Not that I'm aware of. I've never seen a girl hanging around long. And never anyone he's introduced to us. Come to think of it, it's been a while since any girls have come around. Maybe earlier in the school year."

She makes a note. "Do you think he has feelings for you?"

"I mean … maybe. He definitely flirts with me, and he's really sweet and funny."

"Do you have feelings for him? You're smiling," she says, raising her eyebrows.

Shit.

Instead of answering right away, I grab another mint from my bag.

"Silas is a friend. And, yes, he's extremely attractive, and I might have had a crush on him, but that was before I came here. I mean, it's not like anything would ever happen because he's friends with my brother." I bite down on my mint, breaking it in half.

"And yet he kissed you in public. In front of your boyfriend."

"Right."

She lets that sit for a beat. "How did your night end with Eli?"

"I was supposed to go to his place, but the whole night changed into something that just upset me, so I went home instead. I thought about going to Charlie's, but Silas lives there, too, and I didn't think I was ready to see him yet."

"Did you enjoy that kiss?"

"Yes," I whisper.

"I'm guessing this is one of the guys that Eli doesn't like. So, my next question to you is, do your new feelings or realizations, or whatever you might call them, about Eli have anything to do with Silas?"

"I don't think directly. Eli has been acting this way since we slept together. And even that isn't great. I am new to all of that, but he doesn't make me feel confident in what I'm doing. It's like we do it, and then it's over. There's not even a whole lot of lead-in to the main event, if you know what I mean." I can feel my face heat.

"I know what you mean, yes." She laughs lightly. "Maybe he also lacks experience, and he's insecure."

"I'm not so sure about that, but either way, it doesn't feel like we're compatible in and out of the bedroom. So, I just don't know what to do about it. I hate confrontation. I hate hurting people's feelings. And I hate that I'll have to see him if we break up. I won't be able to avoid him. Since we're both Atmospheric and Geosciences majors, I'll see him at the weather center often." I clench my fists and cover my eyes.

"I can see why you would think that would be awkward, but do you think you would feel worse or better staying with him? Compromising your own happiness because you don't want to hurt his feelings? Respectfully, it doesn't sound like he cares about your feelings, or if he does, he doesn't know how to maturely express them."

"No, I know he probably doesn't care about my feelings. I don't even know how to approach this though. He's my first boyfriend. I almost wish he would just break up with me so I didn't have to do it." I laugh humorlessly.

"Do you love him or even like him? You're talking about him and what he might think or feel, but what about you?"

I shake my head. "No, I don't love him. I thought maybe I might, and that's why I had sex with him. But I know I don't. And it's getting to the point where I have to force myself to be excited to see him because I'm on guard about what he might say to hurt my feelings or how he might just be a jerk in general."

"Well then, Brooke, I think you have your answer, don't you?" She closes her pad and sets it on the table.

I shrug, then nod.

"Whatever decision you make regarding Eli, you have to do what makes you happy. But also make sure you're prepared for a potential panic attack after or even before. Use your steps. Try to stay grounded and clear. You're still taking Zoloft, right?"

"Yes, I am."

"And you feel like that's still helping with your anxiety?"

"I do. I mean, it's there, but not as severe." I shake my head. "I'd like to try to stay on the low dose if possible."

"I'm okay with that as long as you're doing well on it. But, Brooke, even if you did have to move to a different dosage, there's nothing wrong with that. You have a genetic predisposition, and there isn't anything you can do to change that. But you can manage it, and you are." She stands. "Our time went fast today. Do you want to schedule an appointment for when you come back after break?"

"Yes, please." I take my phone out of my crossbody, and we schedule our next appointment.

"Brooke, whatever you decide with Eli, it will be okay. He will be okay, and more importantly, you will." She smiles gently.

"Thanks, Kaitlin. I know all of this logically. It's the emotional pieces that I struggle with, but you already know that!" I laugh.

"Have a good break. Enjoy your time with your dad and brother. And hey, maybe do something spontaneous, again.

Might be good for you." She walks to the door and holds it open for me to leave.

"Not sure about that, but thank you. Same to you." I laugh and walk down the stairs and outside the building.

My phone is still in my hand, and I look down at it and just stare. Like it's going to give me some kind of answer or something. Then it buzzes with a text from Eli.

> Eli: You haven't texted me all week. Are you going to keep ignoring me? All break? Don't be childish, Brooke.

And there's my answer. If he was really concerned about our relationship or just wanted to let me know he was thinking about me, he could have reached out sooner too.

> Brooke: I'll be leaving around lunchtime. Do you have time to come over?

I know he does because he's done with exams and he isn't leaving to go home right away.

> Eli: I have about thirty minutes. I'm meeting a few people for lunch.

> Brooke: That's fine. I'm walking to my dorm now. See you soon.

Deep inhale in, exhale out.
I can do this.

I'm just finishing packing my last bag when there's a sharp knock on the apartment door. Thankfully, my roommates have already left, so I won't have an audience for this.

Before I pull the heavy door open, I take a deep breath. When he knocks again, I open it to see Eli standing there, looking somewhat irritated, but also like he's trying to be happy to see me. Or maybe he just needs to use the bathroom. I can't really tell, honestly.

"Hey," I say shortly.

"Hello, Brooke. So, what have you been up to? I thought I would hear from you at least once before break." He walks in and takes a seat on the couch.

"I've been finishing up for the semester, as you know. And just getting ready to go home for break. You could have called me too. After the game, you told me to take a few days to *calm down*, so I guess I wasn't sure what the timeline was on that." I sit down on the loveseat across from him instead of beside him.

"And have you?" He holds his hands out.

"Have I?" I prompt.

"Calmed down?"

He smiles, trying to look … I don't know. Charming? It might have worked on me early on, but not anymore.

"I've been calm, Eli. You were the one who wasn't. So, you tell me." I sit back and fold my arms across my chest.

"That's not cute, Brooke. You know what I mean." He shakes

his head and shifts his gaze away, like he just can't stand to look at me.

"I'm not sure that I do know, but I also don't really care anymore. Can I ask you something?" I lean forward and rest my elbows on my knees. "Do you even like me? Want to be with me?"

"What kind of question is that? Don't be stupid. Of course I like you. I'm with you, aren't I? I'm here to see you before you go."

I huff a laugh. "Okay, so you call me stupid and, in the next sentence, tell me you like me? Maybe I am stupid because that doesn't make sense." I feel my skin flush from my neck to my face.

"You don't cause drama," he says. "You're chill. You understand my schedule. You don't get mad about little things … until now."

"These aren't little things," I say quietly.

He waves that off. "You know what I mean. You don't need a lot. You're low maintenance."

My stomach sinks.

"And you always know how to read the room," he adds, like he's helping his case. "You don't embarrass me—well, except for this recent episode."

"So, you like that I don't take up space," I say.

"That's not what I said."

"It is," I reply. "You like that I make your life easier. That I don't ask for much. That I smile and let things go."

He shifts, uncomfortable now. "I like having you, Brooke. I like knowing you're there."

There it is.

Five … four … three … two … one.

Five things I can see. Two buttons on Eli's shirt are unbuttoned. Two bags are sitting in the hallway. One person I see in my mind when I close my eyes and it's not the man in front of me.

I look behind him.

Four things I can feel. The soft cotton of my leggings. The rough carpet under my feet. The coarse fabric of the couch. My skin, warm and soft.

Three things I hear. Eli calling me stupid. The whirling sound of the refrigerator. People talking in the hallway.

Two things I smell. The strong scent of Eli's cologne. The unlit candle sitting on the coffee table.

One thing I taste. I can still taste the sweet, minty taste of Silas's kiss. Even days later.

Breathe.

"Brooke, what is all this about? You know I don't think you're stupid. These questions you're asking are stupid though. Where is this coming from?" He smacks his hands on the couch on either side of his body.

I exhale.

Then I nod slowly. "You don't actually like *me*. You like having me around."

He doesn't answer.

And somehow, the silence says everything.

"Eli, I think you should leave. And I think you should lose my number." I stand up.

He stands and puts his hands on his hips. "Are you serious right now? Are *you* breaking up with *me*?"

I nod and purse my lips. "Yep, I sure am." As soon as the words leave my mouth, I know I've made the right decision.

"Okay, whatever. You're not worth the headache."

He storms to the door, yanks it open, then lets it slam behind him.

And I watch him go.

A wave of relief flows through my body, and for the first time in my life, I've done something completely for me, despite how Eli may feel. And I like it.

CHAPTER
SEVEN

BROOKE

THE WEEKS after my breakup with Eli blur together in the way they only ever do during the holidays.

Walker won and advanced to the national football championship, set for January in Las Vegas.

By the time we got home, Christmas was already pressing in—tree lights, family dinners, and me pretending everything felt normal.

A few days later, we were back on a plane, this time to Chicago to watch Beck play the weekend after Christmas. Beck won and had a great game personally as well. He's on track to be the best rookie running back of the year. I'm so proud of all the hard work he's put into his football career and excited to see it paying off.

Tonight is New Year's Eve, and we stayed close to Beck's condo. The Kings—minus Casey—are in Chicago, too, holed up in a ridiculously bougie hotel across the street from Beck's. I opted to stay with Charlie and Beck instead, tucked into the extra bedroom Beck insisted on when he bought the place, just in case Dad or I ever needed it.

Which feels fitting somehow.

A new year.

A full house.

And the quiet sense that something is shifting, whether I'm ready for it or not.

We walk into his place after dinner with the family, and I honestly don't think I can sit around until midnight and watch Charlie and Beck be all in love and kissing and celebrating the new year. They're getting married this year, and I'm happy for them, but I'm fresh off a breakup, and even though Eli was a jerk, I might be feeling a little sorry for myself that I have no one to share the night with.

"I think I'm just going to go to bed. I'm pretty tired, and I'll let you guys spend some time alone since we're leaving tomorrow," I say, motioning over my shoulder toward my room.

"You sure? I got some of that pink champagne you girls like to pop right before midnight." Beck walks over to me and wraps an arm around my shoulders.

"Yeah, I'm gonna take a shower and maybe read or something." I slide my arm around his waist and pull him into me for a side hug.

Charlie walks over to us and wraps her arms around both of us for a group hug. "I have almost all of my favorite people here tonight. I'm a lucky girl."

"Almost all? Boss, I'm your very favorite." Beck kisses her forehead.

"Duh, of course. I do miss Casey though. This is my first New Year's Eve without him. Kind of feels weird." She pulls away. "Maybe we can FaceTime him right before or after?"

"Whatever you want, baby. I'll admit, I miss him too. I haven't spent the holidays without him since we moved to Oklahoma, come to think of it. We've been together a lot of years." Beck removes his arm from my shoulders and steps away, making my arm drop back to my side.

"Maybe y'all can work out a holiday schedule or something when he gets drafted, so you won't have to be apart next year." I squeeze her shoulder as I walk by her.

"We'll just have to see where he is, I guess, but, yeah, that would be ideal." She reaches for my hand before I get too far from her. "And you'll be here in Chicago with us celebrating, of course."

"Obviously. Where else would I be?" I laugh, but inside, that makes me feel a little sad. It would be better if I had someone with me, and we could all spend the holidays together.

"Maybe with your next boyfriend's family. You never know!" she calls after me.

"Next boyfriend?" Beck asks.

I turn back to them, and Beck is standing with his hands on his hips, head tilted, and looking at me like he's confused.

"Babe, she and Eli broke up before break." Charlie smacks him lightly on the chest.

"No one told me." He looks at her, then me. "You okay?"

It's sweet of him to ask, and I really do think he cares, but I don't want to get into my relationship issues with him.

"I'm fine. I promise."

I smile so he doesn't worry about me. Although I know he will. That's just how he is. He's my protector.

He nods, and his brow furrows. "Okay. Well, good night. If you need anything, you know to help yourself."

"I should be good. Seriously." I turn to finish my walk to my room.

"Wait! Let me give you another hug before you go to bed." Charlie hustles over to me and wraps me in a hard hug. "I love you, B. Happy New Year. I just know it's going to be the best one yet."

I nod and look over her shoulder at my brother. He has a soft look on his face, and it almost brings a tear to my eye. Beck looks and acts tough, but he's really a softy.

"Love you more. And, yes, it's going to be a great year. Wedding countdown officially begins!" My voice pitches in excitement. I am happy for them, and I don't want my little pity party to dampen the vibe.

Beck walks over to us. When I let go of Charlie, she steps back, and Beck pulls me in for a hug. "Love you."

I smile into his shoulder. I've really missed him. It was one thing when he was away at college, a few hours drive, and I saw him almost every weekend during football season, but with him in Chicago, I don't see him nearly as much as I would like.

"Love you, big brother." I step away and walk backward. "Good night, you two. See you in the morning."

"Night," they say together.

When I get into the room, I take a quick shower, and once I'm done with my nighttime routine, I grab the book I've been reading off the nightstand before I pull back the covers. The cord hanging over the side of the table reminds me I haven't looked at my phone in a few hours since everyone I talk to is here, but I'm sure it needs to be charged.

I pick up the small bag I brought and take out my phone. I scan my notifications, mostly from Instagram friends and their party posts, but I also see one from Silas. I won't deny that butterflies float around my belly.

When I open the message, it's a phone number with a phone emoji. That's it.

> Brooke: Who am I supposed to call?

Not even a minute goes by before he replies.

> Silas: Me.

I haven't talked to Silas since he followed me home from the library. I didn't get a chance to see him after the game in

Houston either. He's liked a few of my posts and posts that Charlie tagged me in, but that's it.

I close out of the app and pull up my text messages. I'm not just going to call some random number without testing it first.

Brooke: Silas?

Silas: Yes …

Brooke: Prove it.

I am not prepared for what happens next.

Silas: *photo*

It's a selfie of Silas, sitting in his bed, shirtless, sweatpants low on his waist. The band of his boxers is sticking out. A book is resting next to him. Oh, and he's wearing his glasses. It's basically my own personal porn.

"Sweet Jesus." I shake my head as I zoom in a little closer at the outline of his dick. It's large, even covered. There is absolutely no mistaking its size.

My phone rings, startling me, and I nearly drop it.

"Hello?" I say quietly. I don't want Charlie or Beck to hear me.

"Brooke," Silas says in his deep, grumbly voice.

"Hi, Silas." I smile, and I'm sure he can hear it in my voice.

"Are you alone? Is this a good time?" he asks.

"Yeah, we got home from dinner a while ago. I'm just getting ready for bed."

"You aren't going to wait until midnight?"

"Nah, I'm tired." I don't want to tell him I don't see the point since I don't have anyone to share it with. That sounds slightly pathetic.

"I'm pretty tired, too, and I can't drink right now, so I've just been hanging out in my room since dinner," he says, and it sounds like he's stretching.

"Casey and Noelle are there, right?" I ask.

"Yeah, they're here, and so are Bo and Chelsea. I think she was thinking about going to Florida, but changed her mind. She didn't want to be away from Bo or something." He chuckles.

"Ah, yes. That makes sense." I settle into my bed and lean against the propped pillows.

Neither of us says anything for a beat, and then I hear him huff out a breath.

"So, I finally got your number. I'm not gonna lie; I'm feeling like we might be friends now." He laughs.

"Silas, we've been friends. Just not texting or calling friends." I smile.

"Well, I couldn't exactly ask anyone for your number without raising suspicion, could I?"

"Yeah, I guess not," I say quietly. "Are you excited for Vegas?"

"Fuck yes. I can't wait to get there and just get it done. I think we're ready, and Callaway is on fire right now."

"He's playing well for sure. But you all are. I'm so happy for y'all. It's an exciting time. When we won the national championship a few years ago, it was pure chaos on the field afterward. I can only imagine what it must be like for you guys."

"I can't wait to experience it. Bowl games are one thing, but winning the whole damn thing … yeah … I might even cry." He laughs, but I think he might be serious.

These guys get pretty emotional at the big games. All their hard work and sacrifices they make—and honestly, that the families make too—feel worth it.

"Some guys do cry. I was crying when we won. Seeing Beck that happy was really emotional for me."

"Did Beck cry?" He laughs. "I can't see him crying. About anything."

I giggle. "No, he didn't. I don't think I've ever seen him cry. Even when we were little. He tends to hold his emotions close to his chest. Maybe not with Charlie, but in general."

"I can see that. You're coming to Vegas, right?"

I nod even though he can't see me. "I am."

"Good. I'm glad." He clears his throat. "So …"

"Yes?" I singsong.

He chuckles. "Fuck it. I'm just gonna ask. Have you talked to Eli since you've been on break?"

I'm honestly surprised he's asking. I did leave that day, so I really only told Charlie, and she and Beck were a day behind me, so it sounds like she didn't tell anyone, including my brother, that we broke up.

"No, I haven't." I sniff. "We actually broke up before I left."

"Before you left? Were you broken up when I saw you at the library?"

"He came over on Friday before I left, and we broke up."

He huffs a laugh.

"What?" I ask.

"Did he break up with you, or did you break up with him?"

"Why does it matter?" I laugh dryly.

"Because if he broke up with you, he's a bigger idiot than I thought. But if you broke up with him, well, that's pretty fucking fantastic." He barks out a laugh.

His laugh makes me smile.

"I broke up with him."

He pulls in a breath. "Good. He didn't deserve you."

"Thanks, Silas. That's sweet of you to say." I look at the time and see it's three minutes to midnight. I breathe in. "It's almost midnight."

"Yeah, it is."

We're both quiet for a minute.

I break the silence first. "I guess I'll let you go. We're leaving in the morning, so I should probably get some sleep."

"Can you hang on until midnight?" he says quietly.

If I looked at myself in the mirror, I would probably see pink in my cheeks. "Okay. I can wait."

"I have a confession to make." His deep voice sounds even deeper.

"Oh? Tell me. Or maybe I don't want to know." I try to act like I don't care, but I so do.

"I wish I were with you tonight. I wish I could kiss you at midnight instead of being on the phone with you. I'll settle for this. For now. But, Brooke?" He pauses.

"Yeah?" I breathe.

"Next year, when the clock strikes midnight, it'll be my lips you kiss. I promise you that," he practically growls.

I'm literally speechless as heat flows through me at the thought of kissing him again.

Fireworks startle me out of my haze, and I look at the time on my phone. Midnight.

"Happy New Year, Brooke," he says softly.

"Happy New Year, Silas," I reply with a whisper.

I can't sleep. After we hung up, I tried reading my book, but I couldn't stop thinking about him.

With a huff, I get out of bed and head to the door. Maybe a cup of chamomile tea will help me relax and get some sleep.

It's dark in the hallway, so I assume Beck and Charlie are in bed for the night. When I reach the kitchen, I grab a mug out of the cabinet and fill it with water. I don't want to wake them with boiling water, so I just use the hot-water option on the fancy coffee maker Beck has.

I settle in on his couch with my mug of tea and look out at the city skyline. It makes me really think about how quickly Beck's life changed. He barely had a minute after the draft before they sent a plane for us and we came up here. Beck moved here that weekend, for the most part.

Makes me wonder about my own future. And who I'll be sharing it with. I hope I can find someone I love like Beck and Charlie love each other.

"What are you doing up?" My brother's grumbly voice carries to me.

"Hey," I say, smiling.

"Can't sleep?" he asks as he walks into the kitchen and grabs a water from the fridge.

I shake my head. "No, I just can't seem to turn off my brain tonight."

"You thinking about Eli?" He settles on the couch next to me, spreading his arm along the back.

I take a sip of my tea and shake my head. "No, not at all." But I also don't mention my phone call with Silas.

"That's good. I gotta say, I'm a little disappointed you didn't tell me that you broke up with him." He stretches out his legs and props them on the coffee table in front of the couch.

"Sorry, I just … I don't know. Everything was just so busy between traveling and the holidays. It didn't really seem that important, you know?" I shrug.

"But are you okay? Do you want to talk about what happened?" Beck takes a sip of his water. "Wait. It doesn't have to do with that kiss between you and Arbuckle, does it?"

Oh God. I clear my throat. "Beck, no! Nothing to do with Silas." *Liar.* Not completely anyway. "There's honestly not much to say. I think his behavior was pretty self-explanatory. You don't have to worry about me. I'll be fine." I look down at the tea in my mug.

It's not that I want to keep anything from my brother or don't want to tell him what happened, but I meant what I said. I don't want to be a bother or a worry to him.

"Brooke, look at me," he says patiently.

When I do look at him, his eyes are soft.

"I will always worry about you. That's my job as your big brother. But I don't want you to hide things from me because you think I'll be upset. I want to be there for you. Help you through whatever is going on, and also be there to support you and celebrate the good things too. I mean, in my opinion, this breakup deserves a party, but maybe you're not there yet." He tilts his head and smirks.

I can't help but laugh. "No, it's a good thing, and I probably should have done it sooner. I guess I just have a hard time … I don't know … hurting people. Although he wasn't hurt. Not in the way you should hurt when something with someone you cared about ends. I think his ego was more bruised than anything. And maybe he was a little angry that he wasn't the one to do it."

"Well, you're a natural pleaser." He lifts a hand and gestures to me. "You don't like to upset people, for sure. And not to sound like I know everything, but since I'm more in tune with my feelings now"—he chuckles—"you aren't responsible for other people's feelings or behavior. The only thing you can own is how you handle it. And if someone or something makes you unhappy or hurts you, it's okay to walk away."

"No, I know." I shake my head. "I mean, I know I'm not responsible for other people, but I don't like to be a problem or cause drama."

"Okay, but, B, you have never in your life caused problems for anyone. You are the kindest and most selfless person I know. You are always thinking of everyone else and making sure we're happy. But I want you to be just as happy. You are your only priority. Just like me, Dad, Charlie, and anyone else you feel like you need to take care of—we are responsible for ourselves. Although I take ownership of Charlie too." He winks at me. "Not really, but you know what I mean. You can be considerate and want to take care of people, but not at the detriment of yourself. I know he was your first real boyfriend, but the few times I was around him and from what Charlie told me, he was a total asshole. I tried to keep my mouth shut because I didn't want to interfere, and it was rough. I hoped you would figure it out on your own. And, look, you did because you're a smart girl." He smiles at me.

"Woman," I correct him, smiling.

"Don't remind me."

I swat at him.

"I'm kidding. I know you are a woman, and I know you can take care of things on your own, but that doesn't mean it's easy for me. I've protected you your whole life." He reaches over and squeezes my shoulder.

I nod. "I know, and I'm really lucky to have you as my big brother."

"I have an idea." He sits up and drops his feet to the floor. "When we go to Vegas, I think you should let loose. Do something you wouldn't normally do. Have fun. Like *real* fun. Without worrying about anyone but yourself. If it makes you happy, do it."

"I don't know about that. I usually just follow along with what everyone wants to do. Not that I'm complaining. Y'all are fun. But I don't really see myself going wild with ideas on my own." I laugh half-heartedly.

"I mean, I don't want you to get hurt in any way, but it's okay to have fun. To do things that you like or might want to try."

"Who are you right now? Don't act like you're some adventurous guy either." I poke him in the shoulder.

"I didn't say I was, but I also don't do things that don't make me happy. I have everything I could ever want though. A beautiful woman, who will be my wife this year. My dream career. And an awesome father and sister. Oh, and friends who will be around for a lifetime. My cup, little sister, is full." He stands. "I want the same thing for you. But first, you need to find what makes *you* happy." He points at me.

"Okay, Dr. Phil. I'll think about it."

"Ha! Dr. Phil. Speaking of, are you still seeing Kaitlin?"

I nod. "Yeah, I just saw her before break."

"Keep up with it. It's really helped me. And Dad's going now too. Did he tell you that?"

No, he hasn't told me, and I feel a little hurt that he hasn't. "He didn't mention it, but I'm glad he's going too."

My dad and brother may know that I go, but they don't really know about my anxiety attacks. Like the severity of them. It would worry them too much.

"Me too. All right, I'm heading back to bed. You getting tired yet?" He holds out his hand to help me up. "I'll sit with you longer if you want."

I take his hand and let him pull me from the couch while I keep a firm hold of my tea. "I think I can probably get some sleep. My tea should kick in soon."

He wraps me in a hug. "I love you, you know."

"I know. And I love you too."

When he pulls back, he touches my shoulder. "Think about what I said about Vegas. We won't let you do anything too crazy, but I think you should have some fun and step outside your comfort zone, you know?"

"Okay, we'll see. Funny, but Kaitlin said the same thing." I laugh, walking into the kitchen to set my mug in the sink.

"Great minds think alike. You should listen to us. See you in the morning." He waves over his shoulder.

"Night," I say quietly.

Me, let loose in Vegas? I can't even imagine it.

SILAS

THE CLOCK IS WINDING DOWN, and we need to get the ball back. It's third and six, and the crowd noise is deafening. Their offense needs this conversion in order to win, but we're gonna be ready for them.

I look over to the sideline at my defensive coordinator, Ty, and he calls a *cover two trap boundary corner*. Which means this is all me. My adrenaline is pumping, and I'm hungry for this win. I'm not here to just cover; I'm here to hunt.

I'm aligned press-bail on the receiver, which gives me inside leverage. I stay focused in on him. My heart is pounding but controlled. My eyes are focused and unwavering.

Our safety over the top shows deep half, making their offense see a soft spot in our line. Then our nickel creeps in toward the direction of the box, hinting we might go for the blitz. We want to make their quarterback think he's got an easy-out route to his receiver.

When the ball is snapped, I give a half-step bail, just enough to make the quarterback think I haven't read their play and make him believe he has time. But then the receiver releases to the outside, just as I thought. I'm watching the quarterback though and see that he's watching the receiver, but my eyes are locked in on his shoulder and not the receiver.

At three steps, I see the receiver snap into the five-yard out in my peripheral vision. Then the quarterback fires off a missile confidently. As he releases it, I plant hard off the inside of my foot and take off, directly into the line of fire.

I get to the receiver before the ball reaches him and stretch my arms through the catch point, but my helmet knocks the ball out of his way. I shoulder the numbers on his jersey, knocking him on his ass. I jump up and hold my hand out to the receiver.

"Not your day, Evans," I heckle.

"Fuck you, Arbuckle." He swats my hand away and stomps off toward his bench, head hanging.

I run back over to my sideline as our special team unit takes the field for the punt return. Bo is ready to get back on the field, anxiously shifting back and forth on his feet, but smacks my helmet as I walk by him.

"Good job, man. You got this for us."

"Just here for a little huntin'." I laugh as I take off my helmet, and it makes him laugh and shake his head.

I stay right on the front line instead of going to the bench as our offense heads onto the field.

The clock is down to a minute thirty-five, and if we don't make a move here, we could lose the game. The ball snaps to Bo, and he hustles out of the pocket and launches the ball to Casey. King reaches above his head and jumps up to grab the ball. As soon as his feet hit the ground, he takes off running right into the end zone.

The offense rushes down the field, and I see Casey flexing in front of one of the cameras, which makes me laugh my ass off.

I yell out, "Fuck yeah!"

We go for the two-point conversion, and one of our running backs takes it home, securing our win.

The clock is almost down to zero, and there's no time for

them to receive the ball, so I drop my helmet from my hand and run out to the field with my team as red and white confetti falls from the ceiling all around us.

Our media person tugs me and Casey away and tells us we have interviews and leads us over to the reporters. As we answer their questions, someone hands me a shirt and hat that say *National Champions, Walker University*. I tug the shirt on and get it over my pads, the best I can, and put the hat on my sweaty head.

As soon as we wrap up the quick interviews, I move toward the stage where the field crew is setting up for the trophy ceremony. Teammates grab me along the way for a handshake or, in some cases, a hug. Some guys are, in fact, crying, but not me. I'm fucking ecstatic! We did it.

My parents find me just as I'm about to walk up to the stage, and my mom has tears in her eyes.

"Silas! Oh my word, son. That was just amazin'. I'm so proud of you. I wish your brothers and sisters were here to see this, but you know they're all watchin' it on the television." My mom leans in and hugs me, even though it's a little awkward with all my pads on.

"Thank you, Mama. I couldn't have done any of this without you and Dad. This belongs to y'all too. Bring it in, Dad." I laugh, pulling my dad into our hug too.

"Silas, I have no words. I'm just so proud of you and your team. You've worked so hard for this. This is going to change your life, son. I just know it." My dad pats my back as he pulls away.

"Thanks, Dad. I love you guys." I reach up and straighten my hat that got crooked in our hug.

"Holy shit. Is Callaway proposing to his girl?" someone behind me shouts.

I look up and around for Bo, but I don't see him until he pops up and lifts Chelsea in his arms. The guys that are around him rush them.

"Mom, Dad, stay right here. I'll be back," I say over my shoulder as I walk toward Bo and Chelsea.

"We'll be right here!" I hear my mom shout.

When I reach them, I push through and smack Bo on the back and then hug Chelsea. "Congrats, you two! I'm so happy for you."

Bo starts to say something, but his parents come up and interrupt him. I don't stand around, waiting, but Chelsea mouths a thank-you to me before I turn back to my parents.

I noticed Chelsea in the stands with the Kings, Linsons, and Noelle's family, which means Brooke has to be around here somewhere. Just as I start to look for her, Coach calls us up to the stage.

Coach gives the first speech, then hands the microphone off to Bo. After Bo says a few words, he gives it to Casey, who keeps it really simple with a thank-you to God, his family, and Noelle. He starts to hand it to me, but is interrupted by the presenter.

"This year, the Defensive MVP goes to Silas Arbuckle. He had three tackles and a forced fumble, contributing to Walker's strong defensive showing with three sacks and six tackles for loss. Well done, Silas." He presents me with a small glass trophy that's heavier than it looks.

I step up closer to the microphone. "Thank you. I'd like to thank God and my family first and foremost. And our defensive coordinator, Coach Ty Haines, for his excellent planning that put our defense in a position to succeed." I lift up the trophy.

"Yes, Walker has one of the best defenses in NCAA football. Congrats to you all for a fine performance this season." He leans into me, making me step away from the microphone.

I don't really hear anything else after that because the cheering is overpowering the speakers at this point. When I step off the stage, I look for my parents and finally spot her. She's standing with her brother and dad behind the Kings. Beck has his arms wrapped around Charlie from behind while Brooke's arm is looped with her dad's. She's got a huge smile on her face, and I don't know that I've ever seen her look happier.

She must feel me looking at her because she glances over at me, and our eyes lock. I lift my hand in a wave. Instead of returning it, she lifts onto her toes and whispers something to her dad, then releases his arm and starts to walk toward me.

"Congratulations, Silas!" she says, wrapping her arms around my neck as I wrap mine around her waist. "I'm so excited for you. You had an incredible game! Your last play had me jumping up and down." She laughs, then releases me, but my hands stay on her hips.

"Thanks, Cupcake." I lean in and speak near her ear so she can hear me over the noise of the crowd. "I'm glad you came. You coming out later to help me celebrate?" I say, brushing my lips across her cheek.

I feel her shiver in my hold.

"Yep!" she squeaks. "We'll meet everyone after the team stuff. I think they already have a plan in place for where to meet, right?"

"I'll go wherever they tell me to. I'm ready to celebrate though, and I would love it if you were there." I drop my hands, but I don't move away, and neither does she.

"Okay, then I guess I'll see you later." She points to someone behind me. "Looks like you have people waiting on you, Trouble."

"Ha! See you later, Brooke." I wink at her and place my hand on her shoulder. I slide my hand down her arm, then squeeze her fingers before I release them.

I don't miss the smile and the pink in her cheeks as she walks away.

Today, I got the trophy.

Tonight, I'm gonna get the girl.

Before the elevator doors open, I can feel the music vibrating. XS Nightclub is known for its exclusive parties with celebrities and athletes. It's a rooftop deck overlooking the Vegas skyline, with a covered section I need to walk through to find my friends. I've never been to or seen anything like it. I'm way out of my comfort zone here, but I want to celebrate with my boys, and I really hope Brooke is here.

I fist-bump a few of my teammates as I make my way through the crowd. Girls slide up to me and wrap their arms around my waist, congratulating me, but there's only one I'm looking for.

I spot my friends hovering near the dance floor, but not dancing. Casey is usually one to get out there and dance, but he's tipping back a beer and then speaking animatedly to Bo. I think we're all still on an adrenaline high and ready to celebrate.

And then I see her.

She's dancing with Chelsea—who's wearing a white sash with *Bride-to-Be* on it—along with Charlie, Noelle, and a few of my teammates' girlfriends.

Now, I've played in stadiums that hold over ninety thousand screaming fans. I've been plowed down by three-hundred-pound linemen, but nothing comes close to seeing Brooke on the dance floor. She just about knocks me on my ass.

Short silver dress.

Backless.

Catching the lights in the room like it was made just to ruin me.

She throws her head back, laughing at something Noelle said. Her long brown hair swings as she dances, and her hips move like they know exactly what she's doing.

Driving me wild.

Hypnotizing me.

As if she senses me in the room, her eyes meet mine across the club, and she smiles softly. Then it spreads into something wicked. Almost like a challenge.

Game fucking on.

Beck walks by me and hands me a beer. It's not lost on me that I'm standing here, staring at his sister, and he's the one who hands me a drink.

I shake my head slightly and smile.

"Cheers, man. Hell of a game." Beck leans in closer so I can hear him over the noise and taps his bottle to mine.

I tip back my beer and nod. I should be here in the moment. Celebrating our national championship with my team. Soaking in the chaos of the club. "Thanks, Beck. Glad you could make it to the game."

"Wouldn't have missed it. Come on. Let's go over to the rest of the guys." He starts walking.

I follow behind, but my eyes find Brooke again, and I watch shamelessly as she sways her hips to the music.

As we reach our group, the music gets louder, and Casey clamps a hand on my shoulder. "Dude"—he leans in close to my ear—"are you alive? What took you so long to get here? I thought you were coming over right after dinner."

"I walked my parents back to their hotel so I could say good-bye. They're taking an early flight out," I reply.

"That was nice of you, Boy Scout." He nudges me with his shoulder and laughs. "Come on. Let's go dance with the girls. I can't get anyone else to go with me." He starts to move closer to the edge of the dance floor.

He doesn't have to tell me twice. Not that I'm much of a dancer—well, okay, I can move a little bit—but I'm dying to get closer to Brooke. And as we reach them, she's all I see. Silver dress flashing in the lights; skin shiny, like she's a little sweaty from dancing; and her mouth parted slightly as she watches me move toward her.

"You're staring," she says when I reach her.

"Well, you're wearing that." I gesture to her body. "I don't really have a choice."

She giggles. "I didn't know the nation's MVP cornerback got so easily distracted. Don't let anyone find out."

"Only distracted by you, Cupcake."

Her eyes sparkle, and I'm a half second away from pulling her into me and kissing the hell out of her.

"Don't worry; I won't tell anyone." She smiles softly and then bites her bottom lip.

Okay, yeah. I gotta lay my lips on her tonight. I don't even fucking care that her brother and everyone else are standing behind me.

She reaches for my hand in a bold move and starts to pull me in further on the dance floor. "Dance with me."

Brooke is usually a little quieter and reserved, and I've never seen her take control of a situation like she is now. I gotta say, it's a huge fucking turn-on.

We make it through the crowd as "I Can't Feel My Face" by The Weeknd blasts through the speakers, and she takes my hands in hers and sets them on her hips, then slides her hands up my chest. My grip on her tightens possessively. Like they know they belong on her body.

"People are watching us." She glances over my shoulder, and there's a wicked gleam in her eyes. "And those girls over there" —she nods—"look mighty jealous."

I tip my head back and belt out a laugh. "I don't fucking care who's watching us right now." I lean in close to her ear. "All I can see is you."

"Good," she says in my ear, sending shock waves straight to my dick.

Yep, he's awake.

"Confidence looks good on you." I pull her closer into me. "And so does silver."

Her hands wrap around my shoulders, making her tits brush against my chest. There's no way she can be wearing a bra in this dress. She absolutely knows she's torturing me.

We dance until sweat slicks my neck, and our bodies are molded together. Restraint feels like a punishment right now.

As the song changes, she leans in closer to my face, as if she wasn't close enough already. I can feel her breath on my jaw, on my lips.

"I think I need to get another drink."

When we walk by Casey and Noelle, Brooke grabs her arm. "We're going to get a drink. Do you want to come with us?"

Noelle leans in and nods, but I can't hear what she says over the noise. She and Casey follow us over to our friends, who are now standing around high-top tables, drinks in hand.

"This turn into a different kind of party?" Casey points at Chelsea's sash when we get close.

Bo tips his head back and laughs. "No, the girls thought it would be fun."

"So, you're not off to a chapel to elope tonight?" Casey asks.

"Not tonight, brother. I want to give her the wedding of her dreams. When she's ready, of course." Bo tips his bottle toward Chelsea.

"I mean, it's not a bad idea. I wouldn't mind running down to one of those places. Save a lot of time and money." Beck shrugs.

"Beckham Linson!" Charlie gasps. "I'm not missing my moment. I have my dress, and everything has already been ordered. We aren't eloping. My parents would kill me!"

"She's not wrong," Casey chimes in, smiling. "Our parents wouldn't want to miss their only daughter getting married. They love you, brother, but I think even my dad would want to lay you out."

"It was just a joke. Sort of." He pulls Charlie into him and kisses her.

"So, are we going to stay here or move on to somewhere else?" Ace pops over to us, and it's pretty clear he's hammered.

"I'm not going anywhere else. If I leave, it's going back to my room. With my girl." Casey swings his arm around Noelle.

"Hey, Ace. Where did Archie and Emma go? I thought they were going to come out with us tonight," Charlie asks.

Ace shakes his head. "Had to take off. Something with Lainey. I'm sure she's fine since she is staying in my parents' room. They probably just wanted to take advantage of a kid-free night. I swear they still can't keep their hands off each other. Kinda surprised she's not pregnant again." He chuckles.

"Can't say I blame him. I'm ready to head back to our room as soon as the boss here says the word." Beck wraps his arms around Charlie from behind.

She leans her head on his shoulder and twists her head to look at him. "We can go whenever you're ready."

"Wait! Y'all are leaving? You can't leave yet." Brooke walks over to Charlie. "You told me we were going to live it up tonight. And you," she says, pointing to her brother, "told me to let loose this weekend while I was in Vegas. And now y'all are bailing on me?"

Charlie wraps her arms around Brooke. "Sorry, B. You should totally stay out all night if you want. I fully support that. And honestly, you shouldn't waste a dress like that. You're a total baddie."

Now, wait a second. Over my dead body will Brooke be going out without me at this point. In my mind, she absolutely wore that dress for me.

"Urgh, you suck." Brooke wiggles out of Charlie's hold and turns to Noelle. "I guess you guys are leaving too?"

Noelle starts to shake her head, but Casey covers her mouth with his hand.

"Sorry, babe." He looks at Noelle, then back to Brooke. "But, yes, we'll be heading back too. I'm ready to fuck my beautiful girlfriend into next week. We've been apart now for a few days, and I can't wait another minute."

"Casey, ewww!" Charlie screeches while Beck belts out a laugh.

Noelle pulls his hand away from her mouth. "Oh my God, Casey King! I cannot believe you just said that." She hits him in the stomach with the back of her hand.

He leans in and takes her mouth with his.

When he pulls back, Noelle looks at us, glassy-eyed. "See you all tomorrow!"

"Sucker," Brooke grumbles.

"All right, well, I'm out. If y'all are leaving, I'm gonna go find Aston and see if he's up for sticking around or maybe hopping to a few other places. We need to spread the Griffith love all around. Equal opportunity and shit." He taps fists with us guys and then quickly hugs the girls.

When he gets to Brooke, he holds on to her a little longer than I'd like. "If you want to hang out with us, let me know. You don't have to leave because they are."

Oh, fuck no.

"I got her." I step in behind her, glaring at him.

He gives me a shit-eating grin and runs his hand down her bare back. It's like he wants to be punched. "Let me know if you change your mind, darlin'."

She laughs and pushes him away. "I'm not sure I'm ready for the kind of fun you guys get into."

Bo picks Chelsea up in his arms. "We're gonna head out too. We'll see you guys in the morning. Maybe."

As he walks away, Chelsea leans her head back. "Bye, everyone!" She waves, laughing.

"I have an idea. Why don't you and Silas go hang out for a

while? Or stay here and dance some more." Charlie grabs Brooke's hand and lays, I assume, Brooke's phone in her palm.

Brooke looks over her shoulder at me, the confident girl I danced with fading just a little. "Do you feel like staying?"

I nod. "Yeah, I'll stay here with you."

I wouldn't dream of leaving yet. And if I have my way, she'll be coming back to my room with me tonight. I won't say that in front of everyone though.

"That's a great idea. Arbuckle can keep an eye on you and make sure no one tries to spike your drink or something," Beck says, handing her a credit card and her ID, then wraps her in a hug.

He looks at me over her shoulder. "Make sure she has a good time?"

When he pulls away from her, I wrap an arm around her waist and pull her into me. "Absolutely. I got her."

I reach my hand out for him to shake, and he takes it and pulls me in for a bro hug. "Keep her safe."

"I got her."

"Boss, let's go." He holds out his hand for Charlie to take. "Night, fuckers."

"Bye, everyone. And, hey, congrats, guys. You all were amazing today," Charlie says before they walk away.

"Hey, wait for us. We'll walk out with you." Casey clamps a hand on my shoulder. "See ya, man. B, have fun." He winks at her.

Noelle hugs Brooke and says goodbye to us quickly as Casey ushers her away to join Beck and Charlie.

"And then there were two." She looks up at me and smiles. "Do you want to stay here or move on?"

"It really doesn't matter to me, as long as I'm with you." I kiss the top of her head.

"Okay, well, I think I'm done dancing. I'm too young to gamble, and I think it's too late to see any shows. I guess we could walk around and maybe get a late-night snack." She turns to face me, holding up Beck's credit card and her ID.

"Yeah, that sounds fun. But put the card away. You won't need it. I got you covered."

"I don't really have anywhere to put it though." She runs a hand down her body.

Fuck me.

"I'll put it in my wallet for you. Just remind me to give it back to your brother later. Let me have your phone to hold for you too." I take it from her hand and pull out my Ridge wallet from my front pocket before tucking the cards in.

When we get into the elevator, she grabs my hand and twines her fingers with mine. I squeeze her hand lightly and look at our reflection in the mirror on the doors. She smiles, and I return it with a wink.

The doors open on the ground level, and it's almost just as loud as the club upstairs. Machines are ringing, people are calling out numbers, and there's cheering coming from the direction of the casino. I even see some of my teammates as we walk through. I nod and wave, but don't stop to talk. I'm done sharing Brooke tonight. I have no doubt they're wondering what I'm doing with Beck's sister though. Especially with our hands linked.

"Where should we go?" she asks when we stop walking outside the hotel.

"Honestly, I don't really know. This is my first time in Vegas." I look down the street.

The neon and noise create the kind of electricity that makes stupid ideas seem … like good ones.

"Same. It's getting late, and the only things I think I can do are go back to the club or a different one. Oh! We could try that Ferris wheel." She smiles and tugs on my hand.

"Okay, we can head that way and see if we can get on."

I signal the valet, and he walks over to us. "Can you get us a car to take us to the Ferris wheel?"

"Yes, sir." He nods and jogs away, then waves down a car with an Uber sign in the window. He directs the car toward us and opens the door for us when it stops. Before he closes the door, he instructs the driver. "Take them to the High Roller." Then he looks at us. "Have a good night."

I take out some cash and hand it to him. "Thanks, man."

"My pleasure. Come back and see us. And, sir, congratulations on your win tonight." He nods, then closes the door.

"That was nice of him." Brooke scoots closer to me once the car pulls away.

I smile down at her because she's just so fucking sweet.

"Oh shoot. I gave you my phone right?" She drops her head back on the seat.

"Yeah, it's in my pocket. Do you need it?" I pull it out of my pocket and hold it out to her.

"Nah, I'm good right now. I doubt they want to hear from me anyway. I'm sure they're … busy." She looks at me.

"Probably, yes. But they know you're with me, and I'm not gonna leave you on your own, so they aren't likely worried about you." I place a hand on her knee.

"Right." She giggles. "I hope we can get tickets. I would love to see Vegas in a broad view."

"Well, looks like we're about to find out." I point to the wheel out the window.

"Go ahead and scan the QR code on the back of the seat to pay," the driver tells me.

I pay quickly, then open the door, holding my hand out to Brooke to help her get out of the car. Her dress is short, and no one needs to see anything but me.

When we get to the ticket counter, there's only one other couple in line. The woman is wearing a wedding dress and a long veil. The guy is dressed in a casual suit, but it's clear they just came from their wedding. Made even more obvious when the bride starts flashing her ring at the attendant.

"How cute!" Brooke claps quietly. "Congratulations!" she

yells out after them, and they turn around, smiling and waving to us.

We step up to the attendant. "Can we get two tickets? And is it possible to get a private car?" I ask her.

"Yeah, we're pretty dead now. Most people are at the clubs or burning their money in the casinos by this time of night." The receipt pops out of the slot, and she hands it to me. "Enjoy the ride," she says dryly.

"Thank you," Brooke says.

The couple in front of us gets into their car. They're holding champagne flutes, and the groom has the bottle in his other hand.

"We should get some champagne." I nod to them, then look around to figure out where they got it. I spot a bar close enough that I can run over and get us a bottle. "You stay here. I'll be right back."

"Okay." She smiles. excitedly.

They only have a large bottle left, so I take it, along with two flutes. I rush back to her just as our cart arrives. No one is on it, so we walk right in. It's a lot bigger on the inside than it looks from the outside. It's like a round bubble, with two red seats on either side, glass around the whole thing, music playing in the speaker system.

"Oh my God! Silas, look at this!" She holds out her arms and spins in the middle. "This is amazing! I can't wait to move so we can see the lights. Did you know that the Las Vegas lights can be seen from space?" She rushes over to one of the windows, not waiting for my answer.

I can't wipe the smile from my face. Seeing her happy like this just makes me fall for her even more than I already was. I'm not really sure where to put the champagne, so I set the flutes on one of the seats and pop open the bottle. Luckily, it doesn't explode when I open it.

After I fill a glass for her, I walk over to her and hand it to her, then fill mine. "Cheers." I tap her flute with mine.

"Cheers," she replies. "And congratulations on an amazing season, Silas." She holds her glass out to me and tips it slightly toward me.

"Thanks, Cupcake. It was pretty fucking epic, if I do say so myself." I smile smugly.

I set the bottle down next to me, then step in closer to her. "So, tell me, Brooke Linson, what was your favorite play in the game today?"

She takes a long drink of champagne.

"Easy there." I chuckle. "It'll hit you before you know it."

"Sorry. It's just good. I like this much better than the drink I had at the club." She dabs the top of her lip with her tongue.

I clear my throat. "Yeah, it is pretty good, but it can go to your head fast."

"That's okay. I hardly feel the drink I had earlier anymore. *Viva Las Vegas*, right?" She lifts up her flute again, then takes another drink.

"Okay, but don't blame me when you wake up with a headache." I chuckle.

"I promise I won't." She loops her other arm through mine. "Hmm ... so my favorite play of the game ... I guess it's a toss-up."

"A toss-up between what?" I nudge her with my shoulder.

"You have to admit that Casey's game-winning touchdown was incredible." She looks at me through her long lashes.

"Agreed. Definitely a key moment." I nod. "And the other one?"

She untangles her arm from mine, turns her body to face me, and takes another drink. "You. That last drive when you stopped them. I was amazed by how you could see the play coming. How do you do that?" She places a hand on my chest.

I love that she's comfortable with touching me tonight.

"A lot of practice." I smirk, then take a drink from my glass.

She nods and narrows her eyes. "Right. That makes total sense."

We both start laughing, her hand falling from my chest, and then finish off our drinks.

"You want more, or are you done?" I lift the bottle.

"Sure. Why not? I mean, my brother and Charlie did tell me to have fun, so …" She holds her glass while I pour.

"But seriously, I'm really glad you came to the game. Even if it was just to see Casey." I wink.

"I mean, of course, I wanted to watch him. He's like my brother. But I couldn't miss seeing the best cornerback in college football play his final game."

Whoa. I guess I haven't really thought about that part. I've been soaking in all the celebration, and it hasn't hit me that this was my final game as a Walker Stallion.

"Fuck. Yeah, it was my last game."

"Goes fast, doesn't it? I remember watching Beck's final game last year. It was bittersweet, knowing he was done because that meant our lives would change again when he got drafted, but we were also excited for the next chapter."

"Has it been hard for you all, as a family, to be apart? Or are you used to it?" I guzzle more of my champagne.

"Used to being apart, but also hard because we can't just get in the car and be there in a few hours." She shrugs. "So, what are your plans? I assume you're declaring for the draft."

I nod. "I am. Coach told us earlier this week that those announcements can be made now that our game is over. I haven't officially signed with an agent yet, but I'll probably go with the guy Archie uses. He's Beck's agent too, right?"

"Scott? Yeah, that's Beck's agent. He seems to have a monopoly on the Walker roster, but I think he reps Archie's brother Aiden too. The one who plays hockey."

"Oh, right. I kind of forgot there's another one. I've only met him once, I think."

"Probably. He isn't around a bunch. Not at Walker anyway. Their season is so long." She turns back to the window.

"I am a little jealous that they can throw down." I laugh.

"There have been a bunch of guys I wish I could have clocked over the years."

"I bet," she says, then taps on the glass. "Look! You can see everything now."

"We're definitely up pretty high." I turn my head and look around the globe.

"Are you afraid of heights?" She spins around and places a hand on my shoulder, looking concerned.

"I am. I think you should hold me," I say seriously, but I can't hold it and start to laugh.

She pushes the shoulder she was touching and starts to walk away, but I grab her hand and pull her into me.

There's a small ledge in the middle of the glass, large enough for me to set our glasses on. So, I take hers out of her hand and set it next to mine.

"You're too much," she says as she wraps her arms around my neck.

"So I've been told." My hands go around her waist, and I pull her in so our chests are touching. I can feel the soft skin on her back, and I'm tempted to run my hands right under the fabric and grab her tight ass.

"Have you been told that you were too much? I was only joking. I think you're pretty great." She stumbles over her words, and I can tell she's starting to feel the champagne.

"I mean, yeah, but I'm not upset about it. Don't you worry about me." I kiss her forehead.

"Silas," she whispers.

"Yeah, Cupcake?"

"Are you ever gonna kiss me again?" She runs her fingers up my neck and onto my cropped hair.

"You want me to kiss you?" I take one of my hands from her waist and cup her jaw.

"Yes," she breathes.

"I'll kiss you again when you admit that no one kisses you like I do." I lower my head toward her mouth.

"Well, my experience is limited …" she teases.

"Is that right?" I know she hasn't had many boyfriends, but I have no idea how many guys she's kissed, and the thought of her kissing anyone but me pisses me off.

She leans in closer, eyes on my mouth. "No one kisses me like you do."

The words barely leave her mouth before I drop my mouth to hers.

When she sighs against my lips, I deepen the kiss, sliding my tongue into her mouth. No rush, just certain that this is exactly what we should be doing. My thumb on my other hand is absentmindedly tracing circles on her hip, making her melt into me. She rises up on her toes and holds my head in place, like she's afraid I'll pull away too soon. Not a fucking chance.

She tastes sweet, like the pink champagne, and I can't get enough.

When she moans, I kiss her so deep, hungry. The kind of kiss that steals your breath.

Then she matches my rhythm, like my kisses are only meant for her. Making me feel like my control is slipping.

My hand falls from her face, and I slide both hands under her ass and lift her so her pussy is cradling my dick, which is straining painfully against my zipper. When she rolls her hips against me, it's my turn to groan, breaking our kiss.

"You're gonna kill me, Cupcake." I rest my forehead against hers.

"I don't want to kill you. I want to kiss you." She says it so softly that I'm not sure I heard her correctly.

"I don't want to keep going when I can't finish what we're starting up here." I brush my nose against hers.

"Okay, yeah, you're right." Her hands cup my face. "Will you dance with me?"

I kiss her lightly on the lips and lower her enough so her feet touch the ground. "I would love to."

She keeps her arms around my neck, and we sway to Elvis

Presley singing "Can't Help Falling in Love," which is honestly just too fucking coincidental. I'm head over ass falling for this girl.

I tip her chin with my finger and kiss her soft and slow this time. I want her to feel the sincerity in my kiss.

We're so lost in each other that it barely registers that we've stopped moving until the song changes to some one about a sports car.

I pull away just enough that our lips are still brushing. "I think our ride is over."

"Okay," she says, running her hands from my head down to my neck.

"What do you want to do next? Are you hungry?" I trail my fingers up and down her back. "We're in Vegas, so whatever your inner desires are, this is the place to do it."

She looks out the window, and I follow her gaze to see the newlyweds walking down the ramp to the exit.

"I have an idea."

"Lay it on me." I bend my head to kiss her neck.

"Let's get married."

CHAPTER
NINE

SILAS

WE MADE it to the clerk's office just as they were locking the doors. Luckily, the guy was a football fan and recognized me, so he ushered us in, and we were the last couple of the day to get a license.

Then we stopped to get me a new shirt since I didn't want to get married in the one I had on, since it was too casual compared to her dress. But Brooke assured me my jeans were fine, so I changed in the car.

She watched.

The white wedding chapel we found smells like roses, champagne, and bad decisions. And, yeah, this might be crazy, but I've never felt surer about anything in my life.

I go all in on the ultimate package—everything except the Elvis impersonator. Brooke chooses a pink bouquet, soft and bright against her silver dress. I opt for a bow tie, looping it around my neck with hands that are steadier than I expect them to be. There's a photographer. Two chapel employees agree to be our witnesses without blinking. Like this happens all the time.

Maybe it does.

Elvis may not be in the building, but we still get to choose the song we walk down the aisle to. It feels right, considering it's partially responsible for how we ended up here in the first place.

Thank God for Ferris wheels.

The music starts. Brooke laughs as she walks down the aisle, enjoying herself and the absurdity of the moment, surrounded by neon lights. I'm having way more fun than I should as well.

Brooke finally stands in front of me in her silver dress, holding the small pink bouquet that she must have gotten before walking down the aisle to me. Her cheeks are flushed, and she's looking at me like she's trying to decide if this is insane or fun. Maybe both. Probably both.

The officiant, who's wearing a gold suit, smiles at us like he's been doing this all night. "Rings?"

I look back at Brooke, and we both start laughing. "Uh, we didn't get that far."

"That's not a problem." He waves to a woman standing off to the side, and she walks over to us, holding a velvet tray. Yep, totally normal.

"Pick one you like," I say to Brooke.

Her hand hovers over the tray. "Hmm … this is tough. They're actually all kind of pretty. Simple but pretty." She plucks a plain gold band and hands it over to me. "Your turn."

"I'm easy. This one works." I hand Brooke a thick, solid gold band.

"Okay, now that we have the rings, let's get started," the officiant says, clearing his throat.

Our eyes meet, and there's no hesitation when I take her hands in mine.

The officiant steps forward like he's about to deliver a sermon *and* a headline.

"Dearly beloved, who wandered in off the Strip because the doors were open," he booms, "we are gathered here today at this fine establishment of love, luck, and legally binding decisions to witness the joining of these two souls."

Brooke bites her lip. I swear she's trying not to laugh.

The vows are short, but surprisingly meaningful for a spontaneous wedding.

Brooke laughs softly as I slide her ring on her finger. But I don't miss the tremble in her fingers.

"You okay?" I tilt my head, looking at her.

She nods quickly. "Yeah, I'm good. We're really doing this. I mean … wow."

Something possessive and real makes my chest tighten.

I run a finger down her cheek to her jaw. "You're so beautiful. And mine."

She leans into my hand and blushes. "Yours."

When it's my turn, Brooke slides the ring on my finger, pausing to look at my face. "No backing out now."

I laugh because making light of any situation is what I do. And in this case, it's safer than admitting I'd run through a brick wall for her right now. "I got this. I thrive under pressure."

She snorts. "Maybe, but this isn't a fourth-quarter interception opportunity."

I shake my head and smile. "Nah. This is much better."

The officiant interrupts our flirting. "By the power vested in me—"

Holy. Shit.

Husband.

When he says I can kiss my wife, I don't even wait for him to finish speaking.

I wrap my hand, the one with my ring on it, around her neck and pull her in for a kiss. Everything disappears as we get lost in each other. And when Brooke drops her bouquet, she winds her arms around my neck, and this time, she deepens the kiss, slipping her tongue inside my mouth.

The officiant taps on my shoulder. "Hate to disturb, but we have another couple waiting."

We pull apart reluctantly.

He gestures to a couple behind us—who honestly look too blitzed to be getting married, but who am I to judge?

I look back at Brooke, and she starts to laugh.

"Oh my God, Silas. We really did that." She covers her mouth with her hand.

I grin. "Follow-through is one of my strengths."

She pushes my chest. "I knew you were trouble."

"You married me though." I hold up my ring finger.

Her smile softens. "Yeah, I did, husband."

We leave the chapel in a limo that was somehow just sitting outside. Like it was an Uber limo or something. Who cares? My wife is sitting in my lap.

"Oh, Silas. They have more champagne." She leans forward and taps on the divider. "Sir, can we have the champagne back here?"

He lowers the glass just enough for us to hear him. "Yes, ma'am. That's for all my guests." He raises the glass, and it's just us again.

Brooke wiggles off my lap and scoots over to the bar. "This one looks good." She holds up a bottle.

"Sure, that's fine. I gotta admit though, I don't know a whole lot about this stuff." I take it from her hand.

The cork pops, and she holds two flutes in her hands. "To the top, husband."

"Yes, wife. Your every wish is my command." I smirk.

"As it should be. Now give me a kiss." She puckers her lips and leans in.

I set the bottle in the cupholder next to me, cup her face, and kiss her fully on the mouth.

When I pull away, her eyes are still closed, and she sighs. "Best night ever."

"I hope you're saying the same thing come morning." I chuckle.

"Of course I will." She hands me a glass. "To my husband."

"To my wife."

We both take a drink, and when she spots the button to the roof, she practically bounces. "A moonroof! We've gotta stand up. Come up here with me."

I laugh, but pull my body up and through the window. Her hair is blowing behind her, and she's looking around at everything with awe.

I wrap an arm around her waist and tuck her in close to me. "You happy?"

"So happy. I mean, this is seriously, like, the best day ever. For both of us!" She tilts her head up for a kiss.

When the limo stops at a light, people honk and wave at us. I swear this city never stops moving.

Brooke leans across the roof and yells to them. "We just got married!" She waves her hand out in front of her, and I can't help but laugh. "And my husband just won the national championship! He was even the MVP!" She points to me, and I smile and wave.

More horns honk, and our driver starts to move again.

When Brooke sways from the motion, I wrap my arm around her waist. "I got you."

She looks up at me. "I just want to be clear … I expect a real wedding night."

If my dick wasn't already semi-hard from her sitting in my lap, it would be now.

"Okay ... and by that, you mean?" *Why the fuck am I asking this question? Oh, right—because I do actually care about her.*

She grabs my shirt and pulls it, making my body bend down to her. "I mean, I want to fuck my husband."

Never in a million years would I have expected those words to come out of her mouth. But she's on a roll with the surprises tonight. And her confidence is a huge turn-on.

A wicked smile spreads across my face. "I can make that happen."

"I guess we probably shouldn't stay at the same hotel as the team, right?"

"Probably not. I don't really want my wedding night to be paid for by my athletic department." I pull out my phone. "Let me see what I can find available."

I scroll through my phone and find some kind of luxury suite at the Bellagio. I book it, then crouch down and tap on the divider. "Can you take us to the Bellagio instead?"

"You got it," he replies.

Brooke comes down and shivers. "It's getting a little chilly now." Her head tips back as she finishes her glass of champagne. "More, please."

I fill her up, then finish off my glass and refill my own. We're celebrating after all.

The ride is pretty fast, but in that short time, we've managed to finish off the bottle.

When the driver pulls up in front of the hotel, he exits the car and comes around to open our door.

"Thanks, man." I step out of the car, slide him a few hundred-dollar bills, and then hold my hand out for Brooke.

"Thank you so much for the ride. It was so fun!" Brooke smiles at him as she takes my hand.

"My pleasure. Congratulations." He nods and shuts the door.

"Oh, and make sure you make a wish in the fountains tomorrow. Have a good rest of your night."

"I wonder how many people he's had in his limo. I bet that guy has some stories." I look at Brooke, and she nods.

"Right? Probably a lot of famous people." She giggles.

We walk through the doors to the hotel, and we see Ace, Aston, and a few of the other younger guys walking out.

"Yo! Little Linson! Arbuckle! What are you guys up to?" Ace picks Brooke up in a hug. Then Aston gives her a hug.

Ace holds out a fist to me, and I reluctantly bump it. Not because I don't love the guy. I do, but he's trying to get under my skin with Brooke tonight. And also, I want to get up to the room. I've waited a long time to have this woman look at me the way she has tonight. I want to hold her, kiss her, and make love to the girl of my dreams.

"We're just hanging out, driving around and stuff." Brooke shrugs.

"Together? Just the two of you?" Aston asks.

Fucker.

"Uh-huh," Brooke mumbles.

It's time to take matters into my own hands. Brooke isn't drunk, but tipsy enough that the truth serum is in full force, I suspect.

"We'll see you guys later." I bend down slightly and lift her over my shoulder, holding her dress down with my forearm so she doesn't flash the whole lobby.

"Ahh, Silas!" She laughs as her head pops up, and she yells to the guys as we walk away, "Okay, I guess we're going. Bye, guys! Make good bad decisions! I want to hear all about them tomorrow!"

"Say cheese, Little Linson," Ace calls out.

I feel her laugh against my back, her body bouncing as one arm braces around my shoulder and the other shoots into the air for the picture.

"Cheese!" she shouts, and it's so fucking adorable that it almost hurts.

We're halfway through the lobby when Ace audibly gasps.

"Holy shit," he yells after us. "You guys get married?"

I turn my head just enough to see him standing there, mouth hanging open, phone still raised in his hand. I frown, trying to figure out how the hell he put that together—until he flips the screen around.

Sure enough, there's my bride on it. Draped over my shoulder. Beaming. And very clearly flashing the wedding band on her finger.

Well. Shit.

"*What happens in Vegas* energy?"

"Later." I shut him down.

Ace laughs under his breath. "You're insane. I need details."

"Just pretend we were never here."

Ace lifts both hands. "Fine. I'll save my spiral for daylight."

"Smart choice." I turn with Brooke still over my shoulder and a prayer that Ace will keep his mouth shut.

Once we're near the check-in desk, I put her down and instinctively wrap an arm around her waist.

"Welcome to the Bellagio. Do you have a reservation?" the clerk asks.

"Arbuckle." I pull out my wallet.

"Ah, yes, the Premiere King suite." She taps away on her keyboard. "Do you have a card you want to use for incidentals, or is the one you used for the reservation okay?"

"That works. Use that card." I pocket my wallet again since I won't need it.

Brooke takes my hand in hers. "The Premiere King suite? Isn't that expensive?"

"Don't worry about it. I've had some lucrative sponsorship deals. Plus, I'm smart with money." I wink at her.

She smiles. "I can't wait to see it."

"Here you are, Mr. Arbuckle. Your room number is on the

envelope. You'll take the main elevator to the thirty-first floor. We hope you enjoy your stay here at the Bellagio." She slides an envelope to me.

"Thank you," Brooke and I say together.

As we walk to the elevator, hand in hand, I look at her face. "You okay? We don't have to do anything. We can just hang out or even go to sleep if you're tired."

She looks up at me with heat in her eyes. "I meant what I said earlier, husband."

"I'm just making sure. And just to be clear on my end"—I lean down so people walking around us can't hear me—"I can't wait to get that little dress off and devour every perfect inch of your body." I kiss her cheek.

She shivers.

I push the elevator call button, and we step in. And I watch the buttons light up as we climb.

Within minutes, we're on our floor. When the doors open, I place my hand on her lower back and lead her out first.

"What's the room number?" she asks.

"It's 3149."

"49! That's your jersey number! How funny!"

"Oh shit. I guess it's meant to be, huh?" I wink at her.

"Here it is." She points to the plaque on the wall next to the door.

I scoop her up into my arms, and she wraps her arms around my neck to hold on. I tap my key against the keypad, and when the lock beeps, I open the door, then push it closed with my foot once we're inside.

The room is quiet compared to the busy street below. Lights glittering through the floor-to-ceiling windows.

"This is so pretty, Silas. Thank you for doing this." She turns my face to hers and kisses me.

When she pulls away, I set her on her feet. "Anything for you."

She studies me for a minute. "You really mean that, don't you?"

"Hell yeah, I do." I kiss the tip of her nose.

She smiles as she kicks off her shoes. "Ahh, that feels so good. I don't understand how women can stand to wear heels. I mean, I know they look good, but my feet hate me right now."

She turns to face me, and we stand there for a second, the *wife* and *husband* settling between us.

"Well, you said you wanted the title," she says lightly. "Guess you could say this escalated quickly." She holds up her hand and twists her ring.

I can't help but laugh as I step closer, crowding her space until her back touches the window. "Maybe not the one I had in mind originally, but the meaning of it is all the same. I'm yours, Brooke." I brush my knuckles down her cheek.

Her breath hitches when my hands find her waist. "To think it all started with a kiss cam."

"Nah, for me, it started way before then," I murmur, dipping my head to kiss her slower this time. Like I'm not in a rush. Because we have all night.

Her fingers slide into my hair as mine trace the curve of her back, following the smooth line of skin the silver dress doesn't cover.

She breaks the kiss and exhales against my mouth. "Silas, we're really married."

I smile, my lips brushing hers. "We really are."

"How ..." she starts. "I mean, how long ago did it start for you?"

"Hard to say an exact time. I guess you could say when we went to the rodeo in the fall, I was pretty certain you were meant to be mine, but I had an obstacle in my way. Your douchebag ex-boyfriend." I lean in to kiss her again. "So, let's just say that I've wanted this for a really long time."

I unzip her dress as I look into her eyes, gauging her response as the fabric falls and silver pools at her feet, leaving her standing there, naked, except for a tiny piece of fabric covering her pussy.

"Goddamn. You are so fucking beautiful; it hurts."

She looks up at me, heat in her eyes. "So, are you saying this wasn't just a spontaneous decision for you?"

I kiss one corner of her mouth. Then the other. "No. If anything, I think it was long overdue."

"It wasn't spontaneous for me either. I … haven't been able to stop thinking about you."

She crashes her mouth to mine, reaching for the buttons of my shirt, working her way down quickly. When she reaches the last one, she pushes my shirt off my shoulders, and I shrug out of it, letting it drop to the floor near her dress. She pulls on the button of my jeans, then works the zipper down.

I push them down and step out of them, leaving me standing in front of her in my boxers.

"Good God. You think I'm beautiful? This"—she waves her arm in front of her—"is unreal."

"Trust me, it's very real."

I grab my dick over my boxers and squeeze it. Her gaze drops to my hand, and her breath hitches.

"And very much yours."

She steps in closer and runs her hands up my chest, then back down, tracing the lines of my muscles. It tickles a little, and goose bumps break across my skin.

"You ticklish?" She grins.

"Maybe." I grab her wrist when she scrapes her nails down my side. "Playing dirty."

Her smile falls slightly, and she tries to pull her hand away, but I don't let her.

"I want you to touch me, Brooke. Even if it tickles."

She shakes her head. "It's not that. I just … I'm not very experienced, so I don't know if you're expecting me to be some kind of siren in bed." She hides her face in her hands. "I don't want you to be disappointed."

"Hey." I take her wrists and pull her hands away from her face. "The only expectation I have for tonight is to make you come as many times as I possibly can."

"Really?" she says breathily. "I don't think I've ever done that before."

"You've never come?"

Nope, not even gonna finish the thought.

She shakes her head. "I don't think so. At least not like how I've read about or how I've heard other girls talk. Maybe I'm doing something wrong. And I have zero experience with blow jobs because Eli didn't like to give oral so he didn't think it was fair to expect me to do it." Her head falls back. "God, this is getting embarrassing. I can't stop talking. Let's just forget I said anything. Carry on with making me come." Her arms slide around my waist, and she pulls me in closer.

I rest my forehead against hers, and my voice is low and gentle as I say, "We don't have to do anything you don't want to do. Just tell me if you want me to stop."

Her smile turns wicked. "Don't you dare stop."

I lift her in my arms and carry her to the bed. And when I lay her down, I kiss her without rushing. Our kisses turn heated, and I want to savor every second I have her in my arms.

I pull away from the kiss and move my body to the side of hers. My erection is damn near painful at this point, twitching against her thigh. I take one of her breasts in my hand, squeezing.

She turns her body slightly to the side, and we kiss again, hands exploring. Her fingers wander down my stomach, and when she starts to slip her hand inside my boxers, I pull my hips back and break the kiss.

"I want your hands on my cock more than you can imagine, but I want this to be all about you first." I place a kiss on her shoulder. "And I'm dying to taste your pussy."

With my eyes on hers, I move down her body, taking a minute to suck a nipple into my mouth, pulling her thong off as I go, and lying between her legs, peppering kisses on the soft skin of her belly. I toss the thong over my shoulder. Then I wrap my arms under her legs and spread them wide so I can take my time. I drop kisses on the inside of her thigh, and just before I get to her center, I suck on the delicate skin, making her buck her hips.

I release my hold and look up at her. "Don't move your legs."

She nods and bites down on her bottom lip.

With one of my hands, I spread her, and she's just as perfect as I imagined. "Look at you. You're soaked. Marrying me make you wet, Cupcake?" I don't wait for an answer.

At the first stroke of my tongue, her hips start to rise again, so I lift my head and set my other hand on her mound.

"Here's what I want you to do. I want you to grab on to my head and push my face into this pretty pussy. And I want you to hold it there until you come. Do you understand?"

"Okay," she whispers as she takes hold of my head with her hands.

Tentatively, she pushes my head back down to her center.

I can tell she wants me to take charge, and I will. But I also want her to learn what she wants and feel like she has some control. Most importantly, I want her to understand that I don't just want her to feel good; I need her to feel everything.

As soon as she stops pushing and holds me in place, I get to work.

I run my tongue up and down, tasting and teasing her. Then I take her clit between my lips and suck hard, making her gasp. When I release it, I swirl my tongue around it to soothe the sting.

"Silas, do that again." She's practically panting.

I groan against her clit and continue licking and sucking. Then I move my hand from her mound and slide a finger inside her tight pussy, pumping in rhythm with my tongue.

"Oh God, Silas. I can feel it." Her hips start to rock against my face.

I release her clit with a pop. "That's a good girl. Give it to me. Soak my face with that sweetness."

I pump my finger in and out faster, then add another finger and scissor them to stretch her a little more. I'm a big guy, and I don't want to split her in half the first time we fuck.

She's tightening around my fingers, so I know she must be getting closer.

I suck, lick, and swirl my tongue around her clit as her moans get louder.

Brooke's hips are grinding and rocking against my face as her orgasm hits. "Silas! Fuck. Don't stop."

Not a fucking chance.

Now, my hair is cropped short, but she somehow manages to grab hold of some on the top and tugs as she reaches her peak. A shot of pain rushes through me and nearly makes me come too.

I can barely breathe, but I don't stop until she releases her hold on my head.

When I do, I kiss my way back up her body and settle between her legs, grinding my dick against her center. I kiss her lips gently, but then she grabs my face and deepens it, slipping her tongue inside my mouth. She sucks on my tongue and rolls her hips. I can feel her pussy soaking my boxers.

When she pulls back from the kiss, she's breathless. "Silas, that was …" She laughs and shakes her head. "I know for certain that's never happened before."

"Is it bad that that makes me happy?" I run a finger over her lips. "I want to be the only one who's ever made you come."

She kisses the tip of my finger. "Okay, that works for me. But I think we need to get those boxers off, so we can, you know …" She says, blushing.

"Fuck?" I smile wickedly.

"Yes, that." She moves her hands from my face to my neck, then down my back.

"Take them off then."

I don't move from between her legs, but I twist my body

enough for her to reach between us and tug my boxers low on my thighs. When she can't reach further, she tucks her foot in between my legs and pushes them the rest of the way. Then I kick them off my feet.

When I roll my body back over hers, her silky cunt hugs my dick.

"I don't mean to rush, and I'm all for making this last all night, but if I don't get inside you soon, I think I might explode."

She giggles. "We don't want that. Do you have condoms?"

"Fuck. I don't. I didn't really plan on getting married and fucking my bride this weekend." I kiss her lips. "Let me call down and have them bring me a box."

"They can do that?" she says, surprised.

"Yeah, Cupcake, they can." I wink and start to roll off of her, but she wraps her legs around my waist.

"Silas, can we try it without a condom? I've never done that before, and I know it might sound stupid, but I feel like I want to do that with my husband."

My already-hard cock leaks with pre-cum. "Are you sure? Are you on birth control?"

She nods enthusiastically. "Yes, I'm on the pill, and Eli always wore condoms. The first few times, he even wore two. But we don't have to if you don't want to."

"Oh, I definitely want to. But don't mention Eli again right before I fuck my wife," I practically growl. "And just so you know, I haven't been with anyone since the beginning of September, never without a condom, and I got tested after that last time."

"Okay," she whispers. "So, no condom then?"

"No condom." I lean down to kiss her, and it's wet and dirty and full of heat.

She slips her hand between us and takes my cock in her hand, stroking it up and down. "Good God, you're so thick and massive."

"Don't worry, Cupcake. You can take it." I smooth a hand over her head. "But if it hurts at all, you have to tell me."

She nods. "Okay."

Her hand moves up to the tip, and she squeezes once, then moves her hand back down and positions the head of my cock at her opening.

Holy fuck.

I take her mouth with mine, peppering soft kisses as I push in slowly. Being bare inside her steals the breath from my lungs; her pussy is warm, overwhelming, and far more intimate than I expected. My body shivers as I take in the sensation. It's a first for me, too, and damn if I nearly lose the breath in my lungs from how good she feels. My hips still. She feels like heaven.

I groan when she tightens around me. "You're taking me so good, baby. Relax."

She tips her head back, moaning as I hit deep. "I feel so full."

I push up onto my elbows and frame her face with my hands. "You ready for me to move?"

Her hands run down my back. "I think I'll die if you don't."

Our mouths smash together, and we let the feeling of our bodies coming together carry us where words don't need to follow.

Without breaking our kiss or our rhythm, I take hold of her thigh and put her leg over my shoulder. The stretch makes me reach even deeper inside her.

Our pace gets faster with every thrust of my hips, and when I feel her walls clench around my dick, I break the kiss. "Come for me, Cupcake. Claim my cock. Claim your husband."

"Ah fuck! Silas! I'm coming!"

I remove her leg from my shoulder and drive into her, hard and fast, as she comes. My orgasm erupts, nearly stealing my breath.

"Goddamn. You feel so fucking good, baby," I pant as I paint her inside with my cum.

"Silas," she says breathily, "I don't think I'll be able to move tomorrow."

"That's okay. I can carry you." I press a soft kiss to her lips.

"It was the husband line that did it for me, you know." This time, she kisses me.

"Huh?" I lift my head to see her eyes.

"When you said to claim my husband, that's what tipped me over." She smiles and runs her hand up the back of my head.

I kiss the tip of her nose. "Oh, yeah? I'll remember that, baby."

CHAPTER
TEN

BROOKE

I WAKE up to sunlight streaming through the windows and the weight of an arm thrown lazily over my waist. I feel a little disoriented, so I just lie there, staring at the ceiling, cataloging the evidence—his steady breathing against my neck, his thigh tucked between mine like he belongs there, the faint ache in my body that makes heat curl low in my stomach.

Vegas.

Silver dress.

The High Roller.

A wedding chapel and the ring on my finger.

The man next to me.

My husband.

Silas.

The panic starts to rise as I think about the implications of what we did. I try to ground myself before a full-blown panic attack takes over.

Pulling in a slow, deliberate breath, I begin.

I can see five different colors in the painting above the couch

—soft blues, a muted green, a streak of gold I hadn't noticed before, cream, and charcoal.

Four. The feel of the sheets against my naked skin. Silas's leg draped over mine. My lips puffy from kissing last night. The delicious soreness between my legs from multiple orgasms.

Three. People closing doors in the hallway. The hum of the air conditioner. The sound of Silas breathing.

I inhale again. Deeper this time. The tightness in my chest eases, just a little.

Silas shifts beside me, the mattress dipping under his weight. I turn my head, and when he opens his eyes, he smiles—slow and unguarded, like he was already awake and just waiting for me.

Two. The smell of sex still lingers in the air and the fading smell of Silas's cologne.

"Hi," he says, voice gravely from sleep. He takes my hand and places it on his heart.

One heartbeat. It's not something I can taste, but it grounds me nonetheless.

"Hi," I say, quietly. The panic dissipates the longer I look into his eyes.

"You, okay?" He leans up onto his elbow, and the hand that was resting on my waist moves up to my face, and he tucks a piece of my hair behind my ear.

The gesture is so sweet it almost makes me want to cry.

I swallow the lump in my throat and nod. "Yeah, I'm fine."

"Fine?" He shakes his head. "No, talk to me." He studies my face like he can see inside my soul. "You're freaking out about last night?"

I try to sit up, but he pulls me down and leans over me.

"I'm just processing." I try to look away, but he cups my jaw, keeping my gaze on him.

"Makes sense. Getting married is pretty life-altering."

"I can't believe we were so reckless last night," I say, covering my eyes with my hands.

"Going bare might have been wild, but—" he starts.

I drop my hands, panic crashing in all at once. "I'm talking about getting married. I've never done anything against the rules. Out of order. I keep waiting to wake up and find out this was all just some crazy dream."

Silas reaches for me, gently pulling my hands into his. His mouth curves into that easy, maddening smile.

"If it is," he says softly, "don't wake me up."

He laces his fingers through mine, grounding me, and the ring on my hand catches the sunlight, flashing like it's proud of itself.

"Silas," I whisper, "everyone is going to lose their minds." I suck in a breath. "My brother is going to be so upset—and he might actually kill you." I gasp as another thought hits. "My dad …" My eyes sting.

"Brooke, baby"—his voice stays steady, calm in a way that almost makes me more emotional—"it'll be okay. I'll talk to your dad and your brother. They know me. And they know I won't hurt you."

He presses a kiss to my cheek, warm and reassuring.

"There will be no talking to anyone," I blurt. "We have to go get an annulment."

I start to sit up, already spiraling, but he brackets me in with his arms.

"We're not gonna do that." He hovers over me and starts to pepper kisses on my cheeks, then moves to my lips.

"No?" I swear this man has the ability to make me lose all sense.

"Nah. First, I'm gonna kiss every inch of you, all the way down to that sweet pussy. Then you're gonna hop on and ride your husband until you come. And when you've taken all that you need from me, we'll go downstairs and meet our friends for breakfast before we get on the plane and go home."

"Silas," I barely get out as he begins kissing my neck, sucking hard on a spot right below my ear, making me hiss.

Then he licks the sting with his tongue and continues down to my breasts. His palms cup my breasts in his hands. Then he circles one of my nipples with his tongue and pinches it with his thumb and forefinger. His other hand wanders down my stomach to my center.

"How can you be so calm about this?" I ask. "You have so much going on. I'm just starting school. I just turned nineteen, for fuck's sake. How would we even stay married?"

"Because we're both consenting adults."

He kisses the inside of my thigh, slow and deliberate, like he knows exactly what it does to me.

"Because while I may have a wild reputation," he continues, his mouth curving with quiet confidence, "I happen to be a catch. Handsome. Generous. Fully capable of taking care of my woman for as long as the earth keeps spinning."

He nips my skin lightly, just enough to make me gasp.

"And because you're allowed to start making decisions based on what feels right for *you*—not what looks right to everyone else." His thumb traces a calming line along my leg as he looks up at me. "So, tell me, Brooke, does this feel good to you?"

When his middle finger slides in between my lips, I can't help the moan that slips out of my mouth. The brush of his finger against my clit makes me circle my hips, looking for more.

"Yes. It feels … unbelievable."

"Stay with me, baby."

He continues down my body until he meets his finger and sucks my clit into his mouth. His finger enters me while he continues to suck. I thrust my hips up again, and it's not enough. I want more.

I grab his head and pull on his hair, forcing him to look up at me. "Silas, I want you to, uh …" I stutter because I'm almost embarrassed to say this out loud.

"Tell me what you want." He turns his head and kisses the inside of my thigh.

"I want you inside me," I all but whisper, my face no doubt

turning red. My confidence from last night is dimmer in the bright Vegas sunshine.

"Anything you want, it's yours." He moves his body beside mine.

"Okay, so then …" I gesture to my vagina.

He drops his head back and laughs. "You are the cutest fucking thing in the world."

He shifts his body and takes hold of my waist, and the next thing I know, I'm straddling him.

"I want you to ride me." He slides his fingers up my torso and grabs my breasts in his hands.

I swallow down my nerves because I've never been so exposed, and I'm not sure I know exactly what I'm doing. I'm starting to understand that maybe Eli and I had a pretty bland sex life. I mean, I suspected it, but I didn't really know.

I clear my throat and try to form a coherent thought before I blurt out how inexperienced I am in all this. Again. "I'm not really sure what to do."

"Cupcake, I've seen you on a mechanical bull, and I saw you move those hips last night. You know what to do." He rocks his thick erection, and it parts my folds, the head of his cock hitting my clit.

I shake my head just a little. "Okay, but I want you to feel good too."

"Oh, baby, I'm dying for this. Now sit that pretty pussy on my cock." He circles my hips for me over him. "Lift up and take my dick in your hand, then feed it into your pussy, nice and slow."

I mean … I might just come from him talking to me. Jesus, the mouth on him.

But I am a pleaser, so I do what I was told and take his dick in my hand and position him at my opening.

"That's it, baby," he groans.

I sink down on him and brace my hands on his chest. I take

in our skin and how plain I am compared to him. The ink on his body tells a story. And I want to know all of them.

He's just so pretty; it almost hurts to look at him.

"You're so tight. You've gotta start moving, or I might blow with you just sitting on me, staring at me with those gorgeous eyes of yours."

I smile at the compliment and lean down to kiss him, bracing one of my hands on the mattress. He tilts my head with his hand and deepens the kiss, thrusting his tongue into my mouth. Our tongues tangle, and my hips start to move on their own.

Up.

Down.

The friction of our bodies moving together feels so good; I almost can't bear it. I break the kiss to catch my breath as the tension builds. "Silas," I moan.

"That's it, baby. Take it all." He stops moving his hips, but holds on gently to my waist.

I sit up and put my hands on his chest again, and we hold eye contact while I roll my hips slowly. "Why are you stopping?"

He doesn't answer, but he skims my body with his fingertips, making me shiver. The way he's touching me, along with the rock-hard cock inside me, tells me he's enjoying this. And when he smirks at me in that stupid-sexy way of his, I know this is a challenge.

"Don't you dare stop, Silas. Move with me."

"Come here," he says, wrapping his arms around my waist and pulling me down to him. "I want you to own this. Own the way this makes you feel."

With the way he's holding me, our chests are touching, and the brush of his skin against my nipples is heightening every-thing. I bring my arms up on either side of his neck and hold his head in my hands as I rock.

He takes the back of my head in his palm and brings my face down to his, searing me with his kiss.

I'm so lost in our kiss, the way he feels inside of me, that I barely notice when he releases my head and grabs hold of my hips, taking control. He's so deep, and our gazes hold as I edge closer to my orgasm.

"Do you feel what you're doing to me? I can't get deep enough."

Sweat starts to dampen my skin as we move faster and faster. I can barely catch my breath when I come so hard that I practically forget my own name.

"Silas," I pant.

"Fuck, Brooke. I can feel you pulsing around my cock." He pushes up into me as I come, and then he holds my hips in place as he comes.

I pretty much collapse on his chest, and he wraps his arms around me, stroking up and down my back.

"I'm just sayin', married sex is pretty fucking awesome," he rumbles under me.

I smile, and even though it was my idea to get married, I have to face my brother soon, then my dad, and I have no idea how I'm going to explain this. Not to mention, Silas and I still need to figure out what *this* is.

CHAPTER
ELEVEN

BROOKE

AFTER WE REALIZED that neither one of us had any fresh clothes–and we don't have time to go to our rooms at the other hotel–Silas ran down to the hotel shop while I showered. I'm not in panic attack mode. Yet. But I can't help but run through the events of last night through my head again now that I'm alone and can think without his ridiculously sexy body distracting me.

Was this the craziest thing I've ever done? Hands down. However…my brother and my therapist both said to have fun in Vegas, let loose and all that. So…I did.

Oh my god. What have I done?

I stop pacing and walk over to the window looking out over the Strip and pull in a deep breath to steady myself.

While I admittedly have feelings for Silas and have definitely been attracted to him for a long time, this wasn't exactly in my plan.

What's even crazier about this though, is that when I brought up the annulment, he was like 'nah'. Well not in those words exactly, but not in a rush to do it. Like he really wants to be with me, and see how it goes.

And I kinda want to too.

I start to pace again and he opens the door to the room, smiling.

"I found some clothes for us." He has a Bellagio sweatshirt for me, a t-shirt for himself, and some shorts for both of us. "We better hurry if we want to get there in time."

I nod, and shake myself out of my thoughts.

We dress quickly, and make our way down to the lobby.

Now, as we make our way out of the Bellagio to the Marriott, the hotel we were supposed to be at last night, I'm still trying to figure out what I'm going to say, and how I'll explain this to my dad and brother.

"You okay, Cupcake?" Silas has my hand in his as we walk out of the hotel.

"Honestly? No. I'm just trying to work out in my head how to tell them."

I look up at him. I don't want to make him feel bad or think that I regret what we did last night because I'm not sure that I do. But this is a lot to take in, and knowing I have to explain it all is making me a bit sick to my stomach.

He stills, his movements gentle as he cups my cheek. "Listen, Brooke. I don't want to cause you stress over this." His thumb brushes just beneath my eye. "I know you didn't marry me for love. Hell, you didn't even know how good we'd be together in bed until after." A quiet smile tugs at his mouth before fading. "But I can't explain it perfectly, other than this just ... feels right to me." His voice drops. He's honest in a way that makes my chest ache. "I'm truly happy. Right here. In this moment."

He exhales slowly and continues, "If you want to grab a car and ride down to the courthouse and get this annulled before anyone knows, I'll do it. I swear. I'll only do it if it's what *you* want—not because you're worried about what your dad will say. Or your brother. Or your friends. Or your professors. Or me." His eyes search mine. "What do *you* want?"

It's a loaded question.

What do I want?

I want my dad not to lie awake, worrying that his daughter married a football player on a whim in Vegas and threw her life away for a man he doesn't know. I want my brother not to lose his mind and take it out on Silas. I want to be the perfect daughter—the one who follows the rules, gets the good grades, doesn't cause a ruckus, and keeps her family calm.

But what I also want is to feel alive.

I want to feel free.

I want to be a little reckless for once in my life.

And surprisingly … I want to stay married to Silas.

Even if it's just for a little while longer.

I let out a breath. "I want you."

His smile is beguiling as his brows rise. "I can handle talking to your dad and brother if you want."

He's so sweet. Truly. I guess if I had to pick a guy to elope with, Silas is a great one.

I shake my head. "I have to do it. It would be nice to have you with me though. I'm not sure I'll have the nerve to bring it up at breakfast though."

"We can even keep it between us for a while if you need time. Whatever you need, just say the word."

He starts to pull me toward the Bellagio fountains, where the water is splashing and dancing. "Our driver told us to make a wish before we left, so let's go do that, and then we can get over to the hotel."

"I don't think we have time."

"Nope, we have to. And I doubt we'll be the last ones there anyway." He snickers.

"Okay," I say softly. "I have no idea what I'll wish for though. My mind is all over the place."

He reaches into his pocket and pulls out a five-dollar bill. "Shit. I don't have any coins."

"I don't either. I mean, you have my ID and card."

He has my phone in his pocket too. I almost forgot it in the room because I was so distracted.

A man and a woman with three kids walk by us, holding out quarters, excited to make wishes.

"Excuse me." Silas holds out a hand.

The family stops and looks at us.

"Hi," the woman says, smiling.

"I forgot to grab some coins before we came out here. Do you happen to have a few extra for me and my bride?"

"Oh, how sweet. Did you just get married?" She looks over at me and takes in my outfit, confused.

"Last night, but we were told to make a wish for luck before we left."

The husband digs into his pocket. "I have a half-dollar coin, but not two. Will that work?"

Silas looks at me. "Yeah, that would be great."

He holds it out to us, and I take it in my hand.

Silas tries to hand the man the five-dollar bill, and the guy waves him off.

"Nope, keep it. My wife and I were married here ten years ago. Great memories for us." He looks at his wife and smiles. "Congratulations to you both."

"Yes, congrats!" the wife says before chasing after her kids.

"Thank you," we call after them.

Silas and I look at each other and smile as we watch them try to keep their little boy from climbing over the rail.

"Let's just stand here for a minute and let it come to you." He leads me over to a spot that's not too crowded.

"Do you know what you'll wish for?" I look up at him.

"I do." He winks, then turns me and takes both of my hands in his. "Are you superstitious?"

I shrug. "A little, I guess."

"Just close your eyes and take in some deep breaths. Clear your mind and think about what you want in life right now. Or maybe a long-term goal."

He leans forward and kisses me softly on the lips.

I keep my eyes closed after he pulls his lips away and focus on the sound of the water and the faint sound of the music accompanying it.

Nothing is coming to me, but standing here, enjoying the moment, is calming me down a little.

"Okay, wife. Are you ready to make that wish?" He slides his arms around my waist and pulls me into him.

My arms move around him, and I link my hands together on his lower back. When I rest my head on his chest and take in the safety of him, I feel calmer.

"We only have one coin, so we need to toss it in together." He pulls away and reaches for my hand, turns it, and lays the coin in the center.

"Okay, so let's hold hands and do it?" I cup the coin so I don't drop it.

"Let's do it." He moves his hand under mine, and his fingers cross with mine, so I'm still cupping the coin, but we'll make the toss together.

As we stand side by side, hand in hand, I look over at Silas and see him already watching me.

"Three, two, one." He counts us down.

I close my fingers around my palm so the coin doesn't fall out too early, and we pull back our arms and when we swing forward, I release the coin and we watch it soar through the air, as I make my wish.

Once we see it plop into the water, he turns toward me. "You make a wish?"

I nod. "I did."

"Good. Me too. But don't tell me." He chuckles. "Or it won't come true."

"I won't tell you." And I won't because I want it to come true, and today, I might believe in a little superstition.

When we walk into the restaurant at the hotel, I see my brother and Archie sitting next to each other first. Kind of hard to miss Archie because he's so big. And loud.

Silas squeezes my hand again. "Go in guns blazing or …"

I reluctantly let go of his hand. "Well, I don't really want to announce it to everyone at once. I think Beck should know first, don't you?" I look up at him.

"Yeah, that would be the smartest move." He places a hand on my lower back as we walk around a few tables to reach our group.

Chelsea sees us first and waves. "Hey, guys!" She motions to two empty seats next to her.

Silas walks over, but I stop to hug my brother and Charlie quickly.

"Hey," I say, trying my best to swallow down the nerves.

When I get to my seat, Silas is standing behind my chair, waiting to push it in once I sit.

"Arbuckle, the gentleman," Casey says.

"Damn straight." He pushes me in, then taps fists with Casey.

Noelle leans around Casey since she's on the other side of him. "So, what did y'all end up doing last night after we left?"

Silas places his arm over the back of my chair. "We went to the Ferris wheel and got a limo to drive us around to see some Vegas lights."

I pull my hands from the table and into my lap, absentmindedly twisting my ring around my finger.

"Oh, how fun!" Charlie says from across the table, next to my brother.

"Yeah, it was a lot of fun."

"When did you get back last night? Wait, why are you both wearing Bellagio clothes?" Charlie points.

Fuck.

"Well—" Silas starts to say, but Archie interrupts.

"Where the hell did you two come from?" He's looking behind us, so I turn and see Ace and Aston walking toward the table in the same clothes from last night.

"Dude, it was fucking epic." Ace pulls a chair from the table next to us and sets it between Archie and my brother.

Aston also pulls a chair over, but he settles next to Emma, and he quietly hugs her.

"Good Lord, Aston. You smell like a distillery." She pushes him away gently.

"Lay off my wife, fucker." Archie playfully knocks the back of Aston's head.

"Ow, asshole," Aston mumbles.

"Okay, back to me." Ace points at his chest. "So, after we left you losers, we went to Spearmint Rhino."

"Isn't that a strip club?" Archie asks.

"You bet your ass it is, big brother." Ace grins wide.

"How the fuck did you get in? You're not twenty-one yet," Archie asks him.

"We have our ways." Ace winks at Archie and then looks around him to Emma and smiles.

She just shakes her head and laughs. "Let me guess. The Griffith charm?"

"Don't you know it?" Aston chimes in.

"Now, darlin', that Griffith charm worked on you, didn't it?" Archie pulls Emma into him and leans his head down to kiss her.

"Maybe a little." She pinches her fingers together, smiling.

"Okay, so tell us more, but can you spare us the details of that little visit to the Peppermint Club?" Charlie laughs.

"Spearmint Rhino," Aston corrects.

Ace pipes in, "Oh, come on. But that was one of the best parts of the night." Ace holds his hands up. "You don't want to know about how Honeyy, with two *Y*'s, gave Aston a lap dance, and he practically came in his pants?"

"Fuck off. I did not." He shakes his head, but he's smiling.

"Okay, maybe not, but, dude, it was so hot. I was mad jealous."

"Anyway"—Aston shakes his head—"after that, we hit up a few more clubs, but I honestly don't remember a whole lot."

"Don't worry, brother. I got pictures. I think," he says, pulling out his phone. He barks out a laugh. "Aston, look at Ramirez trying to climb that horse statue."

I'm listening, but I'm also watching my brother. He's just calm and smiling. Watching the Griffith twins being, well, them.

Silas leans in subtly. "You doing okay?" he whispers.

I turn my face just enough so he can hear me. "Yeah."

But I'm not, and he knows it.

His hand covers both of mine under the table, and he softly brushes the knuckles on one of my hands with his thumb.

The twins are still regaling us with tales of their night, and I'm half listening to what they're saying until Ace yells out, startling me, so I look at him.

"Holy fucking shit!" He's leaning forward in his chair, holding his phone with both hands.

"What?" Charlie tries to lean over Beck to see.

Ace looks up at me and Silas and points a finger at us. "I totally forgot. You guys got married last night!"

"What?!" Casey yells and looks over at us.

When I look back at Ace, he's holding his phone out to my brother.

Oh God. What are they looking at?

Beck takes the phone from Ace.

This is not good.

Charlie leans into him and gasps, "Oh my fucking God, Brooke!"

"Okay, now, let's tone it down a little." Silas brings his hands to the table and holds them out in front of him.

"Tone it down?" Archie laughs. "Brother, you just blew shit up."

"Brooke," Beck says deeply.

I swallow. "Yes?"

I don't know if I can do this right now. Not in front of everyone.

"Do you want to tell me why Arbuckle has you over his shoulder and you're flashing your hand, which has a goddamn ring on it, looking like you just hit the jackpot in the casino?" He's not yelling, but he's definitely not happy.

"Linson, maybe we should talk about it somewhere more private." Silas wraps his arm around my shoulders, and I watch my brother track the movement.

"Oh, you do, do you?" Beck tilts his head and raises his brows.

"Okay, so let's back up a second." Charlie takes the phone from my brother. "Silas, I knew you liked her, but this? Is it a joke?"

Silas shakes his head. "Fuck no, it's not a joke."

"At what point in the night did this happen?" She holds the phone out toward us, and everyone at the table leans in to see it closer.

Kill me now.

I cover my face with my hands and lean on my elbows on the table.

"Oh fuck. She does have a ring," Casey whispers.

Silas puts a hand on my back. "Uh, well, we got married after the Ferris wheel. But this particular moment, we had just gotten to the Bellagio and happened to run into Dumb and Dumber here." He waves a finger between Ace and Aston.

"You motherfucker. I told you to keep an eye on her, not fucking marry her!" Beck smacks the table.

"You know what? I feel like this is a conversation the family should have first, so maybe let's just enjoy breakfast and celebrate your win yesterday," Emma chimes in, trying to calm down the tension.

"I agree." Chelsea nods.

I look around the table, and there's a mix of shock and fake smiles aimed at us.

Beck's chair scrapes across the floor, and he stands and starts to walk away.

Charlie jumps up at the same time I do. "I got him, B," she says with an apologetic smile, then hands Ace his phone.

Archie is leaning toward Ace. "You're such a dumbass."

Someone clears their throat.

"Well, I guess we have a few things to celebrate then, huh?" Bo laughs, trying to change the tone. "A national championship, my and Chelsea's engagement, and apparently Brooke and Silas's nuptials."

"Yes," everyone awkwardly says at once.

Noelle gets up from her seat and walks over to mine. "Congratulations, Brooke," she says, hugging me from behind.

I tilt my head toward hers. "Thanks."

"Okay, so once again for those of us who are still a little drunk," Aston asks. "I knew you had a thing for her, but dude, this is real?"

"It's real," Silas says assuredly.

"I had no idea you guys were even, like, a thing," Archie says.

"Baby, it appears that this is a shock to everyone." Emma leans over and kisses Archie's cheek.

"Okay, well"—Casey slaps a hand on Silas's shoulder—"just

know, if you hurt her, you'll have more than Beck to worry about." He squeezes. "But, hey, congrats!"

"I'd never hurt her," Silas says.

The waitress comes over to us before anyone can say anything else and takes our orders.

When she asks me what I want, I don't answer, my nerves too jumbled, so Silas orders something for me.

Bo directs the conversation back to Ace and Aston, and they continue to tell us about their night while we wait for our food. I don't hear any of it over the pounding in my head.

Silas reaches in his pocket and pulls out my phone. "Do you want to call him or text him?"

I nod, taking the phone from his hand. "Thank you."

"Remember, I'm right here. I won't leave you to handle this on your own." He kisses the side of my head.

I pick at my food when it arrives, and then my phone buzzes.

> Beck: Come to room 1456. Dad's on his way over.

I might actually start crying.

> Brooke: Okay, be there in a few.

"Beck?" Silas asks.

"Yeah, he wants me to come up." I show him my phone.

"Then let's go." Silas pulls out his wallet to get money out.

"You guys leavin'?" Archie asks.

"Beck just texted," I say as I stand.

Silas stands with me, holding my chair.

"You two go take care of that. Breakfast is on me," Archie says.

"Thanks, Arch," I say softly.

Silas nods to him. "Appreciate it, man."

"Not a problem." He leans back in his chair.

We wave behind us as we start to leave the dining room.

Silas wraps an arm around my shoulders. "It'll be okay, Cupcake. I'll be right there with you."

I nod, but I can't answer because I'm not sure him being there with me right now is a good idea.

CHAPTER
TWELVE

SILAS

OUR WAY UP to Beck's room is quiet, but I haven't let go of her yet. Her body is tense, so I rub my thumb along her hand, trying to calm her. I'm not sure if me opening my mouth right now would make her feel better or worse.

The elevator dings, and the doors open. She steps out, and I put my hand on her lower back.

"Maybe I should go in by myself," she says, looking up at me.

I tilt my head to the side and look at her. "I'm not letting you do this alone. But I kinda need to know how we're approaching this."

"I have no idea," she whisper-yells. "On one hand, if I say it was a mistake and we were just goofing around, they'll never trust me again and just continue to baby me forever."

"It wasn't a mistake," I cut in.

She smiles shyly at me. "I didn't mean it that way. I'm sorry. I just ... God, this is all too real now."

"Brooke, I thought I'd made it clear to you last night and again this morning, but if I need to keep saying it until you believe it, I will." I run my hand up her back to her neck. "This, for me, didn't just happen overnight. I've had feelings for you for a long time now. And I abso-fucking-lutely took my shot to spend some time with you, not just last night, but any night before."

"Okay, so maybe we don't say it was a mistake then?" She stops walking and turns to face me.

"I think"—I wrap my arms around her waist and pull her into me—"we should be honest. You can't tell me you haven't thought about being with me before last night. So, I really don't think this was random on your part either. Am I wrong?"

"I definitely thought about seeing you naked before. Getting married? Well, that never crossed my mind. This isn't about us hooking up or even dating. We got married, Silas. They're going to ask questions we don't know the answers to yet." She puts her hands on my biceps.

"Then that's what we say. We don't have all the answers yet."

"I can't believe you aren't freaking out about this." She looks at me, eyes roaming over my face.

I shrug. "I don't know. I'm just … fuck." I turn my head from side to side, trying to figure out how far I should take this right now. "I'm happy about it. Is the timing ideal? Nope, but as far as I'm concerned, I've won the whole fucking house. Any man would be lucky to be with you, but I"—I poke my own chest—"get to call you my wife. So, I don't see how that would be bad in any scenario."

"You're gonna make me cry before we even get in the room." She tips her head back.

"I don't ever want to make you cry, Cupcake." I brush my thumb under her eye, catching a stray tear.

"You're right though. I have thought about you for longer than I should admit. If I'm honest, it was never just about how good you'd look naked."

"I know." I lean down and kiss her softly.

I can feel her phone buzz between us.

"We'd better get in there, or he might come looking for me." Brooke pulls away. "Now's your chance to back out."

"No way. Let's do this." I take her hand and place a kiss on her ring finger.

When we get to the door, Brooke barely knocks before it opens, and her dad, Ryan, is standing on the other side, looking none too happy.

"Brooke Delilah Linson, you'd better have a good explanation for this." He backs up and holds the door open for us to enter.

"Hi, Dad," she mutters as she walks by him.

Beck is sitting on the bed, leaning forward, hands on his knees. The look on his face though … if I wasn't a big guy, I might be shitting my pants about now. I think the only thing keeping him in place is the hand Charlie has on his back.

"Hey, guys," Charlie says with a cautious smile.

When the door to the room slams, Brooke flinches, and the room feels a bit smaller.

Ryan sits in a chair. He leans back and crosses his arms over his chest. "Well, start talking."

I take Brooke's hand in mine and squeeze it gently, prepared to step in if she needs me to. If I could feed her the strength to do this, I would.

"Well, Dad, Silas and I got married last night."

Beck sits up. "No shit. We know that part. We want to know *why* the fuck you would do this."

"Beck," Ryan glares at Beck, then watches us, no doubt studying every move and expression.

"Because we care about each other." A little sass comes out, and I have to bite back a smile.

"That's cute, and it would make a great Hallmark card, but that's not gonna cut it with me," Beck snaps.

And … I've had enough.

I step forward in a protective move on instinct and feel every eye in the room on me. "Let me explain the situation clearly. For starters, in case you forgot, Brooke is an adult." I let that settle in for a second. "And I know this might look like we did this on a whim—"

"Well, we did do it on a whim," Brooke interrupts and places a hand on my back.

"Okay, valid. But, sir …" I turn to face Ryan because I don't owe Beck any explanations. Yes, he's my friend, but he knows me, and I'm not some fuckup. Ryan though? I need him to hear the sincerity of my words. "I understand that this looks like a rash decision, but I've had feelings for Brooke for quite a while now."

Charlie pipes in, "That is true. He's been pining since at least September."

"Not helping, Boss." Beck turns his head to look at her.

"Sorry. I was just trying to validate what he's saying. I saw it." She shrugs her shoulders.

Ryan stands again, pacing. "Okay, fine, you care about her, but walk me through last night and why you two thought it was a good idea to get married. Liking someone, having feelings, is a stepping stone to developing a relationship, kids."

"Dad, Silas and I are both intelligent people. We understand all that," Brooke says.

"So, tell me. Every detail." He stops pacing and places his hands on his hips.

I grimace, hoping he doesn't see because I'm sure he doesn't want to hear about how I gave his daughter multiple orgasms last night and at least two this morning.

Charlie sees it though and smothers a laugh with her hand.

"Seriously?" Beck glares at her, and she glares back.

"Excuse me. Don't look at me like that." She nudges him.

"Babe, I'm struggling to sit through this. This is my baby sister."

"See, that's the problem. I'm not a baby anymore, and I think you guys forget that sometimes. You can't always protect me from things that may or may not hurt me." The sass is back in

Brooke's voice, which is starting to turn me on, and now is not the time for me to get a hard-on.

"Okay, you two. Back to the point. Brooke, start talking." Ryan waves a hand in the air.

So, Brooke starts talking and lays out the course of our night for him, minus the naughty parts. And by the time she's done, I can tell by her tone that she's tired, so I wrap my arm around her waist and tug her to me.

"You're telling me this was your idea, Brooke? You weren't pressured? This wasn't just an extended adrenaline rush from winning the game?" He says the last line, looking at me.

I shake my head. "No, sir."

"No, Dad. Silas didn't pressure me. If anything, I pressured him."

"Well, it didn't take but a minute to answer you, so trust me, Cupcake, I wasn't pressured." I can't help but place a kiss on her temple.

"Aww," Charlie sighs.

Silence stretches while Ryan looks between me and Brooke.

His gaze settles on me. "Silas, do you understand what this means for you? I assume you're entering the draft this year, right?"

"Yes, I am. But I don't see how any of that will change the way I feel. And if anything, having Brooke by my side will make it easier. She also knows what to expect from this lifestyle, so I feel like we can both make adjustments when we need to."

"Right, but she just started college. You don't expect her to leave all of that behind and follow you, do you?" he asks me.

"Dad, he's not asking me to give anything up." Brooke twists and takes my arm from her waist and wraps hers around mine, like she's protecting me or something. It's so fucking cute.

"Brooke"—Beck drags a hand down his face—"you skipped dating. You skipped the engagement. You skipped every normal fucking step of all of this."

"Well, I mean, I don't think anyone can say I'm exactly normal." I try to make light of the moment.

"Not funny." Beck rolls his eyes.

"I am pretty funny actually, but this isn't a joke to me." I turn to face Ryan, and I reach for Brooke's hand. "Sir, I'm not asking for your blessing after the fact. I'm asking you to judge me on what I do next, how I treat your daughter."

"And what is it you plan to do?" He crosses his arms over his chest again.

"I'll protect her," I say immediately. No pause. No hesitation. "She will always be my priority."

Beck's jaw tightens, but I keep going.

"And as far as my career and hers, that's between us to figure out, but I will never let the rough parts of mine touch her. Ever. She comes first."

Beck steps forward, not directly in my face, but close enough that his following question feels like a challenge. "What if she changes her mind?"

The answer is already on the tip of my tongue.

"Then I'll support her." My voice stays steady. "In any way she needs. Even if it costs me." I don't blink because I mean it—because my loving her doesn't mean owning her, even if walking away from her would tear me apart. "I'll fight for her, yes. But I won't trap her."

That does it.

Beck exhales a long, tired sound, and his shoulders slump, the fight draining out of him. "You realize if this goes sideways, I'll never forgive you, right?"

I nod once. Then I hold out my fist, offering it without bravado. "I would never expect you to. But I promise I won't hurt her."

He stares at my hand, noticing the ring on my finger, then closes his eyes and shakes his head, but knocks his knuckles to mine.

Ryan watches us and sighs long and hard, in a typical parental way.

"Brooke, you've never made a spontaneous decision in your life. I think that's almost more surprising than you getting married." He stares at her, with a mix between the reality that she isn't a little girl anymore, maybe, and a little pride that she made a big leap.

"I'll piggyback on what my son said. You hurt her, I won't call first. You understand?"

"I understand."

"He's serious, Arbuckle. And I'll be with him," Beck says.

"I know, but I am too." I look at Beck, then at Ryan.

"So, what's going to happen next? Is she gonna move in with us?" Charlie asks.

Brooke's head snaps toward me, her eyes widening just a fraction. "I—" She laughs softly, but it doesn't quite land. "I haven't even thought of that."

Her fingers twist together, knuckles whitening before she seems to notice and forces them to relax. This was supposed to be a whim. A story. Something unreal enough to laugh about later. And now it's turning into logistics. Rooms. Houses. A *life*.

"We haven't talked about it yet," I say carefully. "But I want her in the house with me, if that's what she wants." I look at Brooke as I say it, giving her space, giving her the out I promised.

Her throat bobs when she swallows. For a beat, I can see it all cross her face—the weight of it, the speed, the fact that a single night of fun has led to questions that sound permanent.

Then she exhales.

Her shoulders drop just a little, and she gives me a small, steady smile. Not carefree. Not reckless.

But real.

"Yeah, I guess that makes sense. Would be kind of hard for you to move into the dorm," she says to me.

"I mean, you could not move in together and maybe do the whole dating thing. Just a thought," Beck mumbles.

Brooke shakes her head. "No, I think moving into the house feels right. And don't worry, Beck; I'm sure Charlie will keep you informed on how things are going."

Charlie nods. "Pretty much, yep."

The girls look at each other and smile.

"What about the combine next month? I know you'll get invited," Beck asks.

I nod. "I'll be training, just like I would if we hadn't gotten married."

"That's not what I mean. Or, well, I guess, part of it. You'll be gone a lot for training, then a week for the combine. It was hard on me and Charlie, and we'd had years of being together."

"Yeah, but it was hard on you guys because you didn't like being apart." Brooke points her finger and waves it between Beck and Charlie. "Silas and I will find what works for us, but it'll be a lot easier if y'all can let *us* do it together."

"Okay, so then you'll move in with us when we get home and work through things as they come. But if I can say something?" Charlie stands now. "As hard as it is for Beck and me to be apart, I can't imagine starting a relationship when he was going through the draft process. So, I'm not saying this to scare you, but you need to be honest with each other about how you'll deal with it." She wraps Brooke in a hug.

"We will." Brooke looks at me, eyes a little watery.

Ryan clears his throat and looks at his watch. "We need to start packing up, kids. We'll all miss our flights if we don't get moving. Brooke, I'll meet you back in our room."

"Okay, Dad. I'll be there in a bit."

He taps his watch with his finger. "Not too long." Then he walks out the door.

"Yeah, everyone, get out. I want to spend my last thirty minutes with my girl. You guys really fucked up my timing."

"Beck, stop." Charlie rolls her eyes.

Beck hugs Brooke then. And when he pulls back, he meets my eye. He's no longer tense and slightly hostile. More like measured, assessing.

"Take care of her, Arbuckle." He holds out a hand.

I shake his hand. "Always."

Charlie hugs me next. "We'll see you at home."

"Bet."

Brooke reaches for my hand, and we walk out together. The floor I'm on with the team is just below where we are now, but we take the elevator down wordlessly.

As soon as we get into my room, she practically sags into my chest. "Well, I guess that could have been worse."

I kiss her head. "I'm still alive, so I'll take that as a win." I chuckle.

She tilts her head up, meeting my eyes. I tuck some loose hair behind her ear, then cup her face with my hands.

"Thank you."

"For what?"

"Helping me through that. For not caving to the pressure."

"Pressure? Ha! Babe, that was nothing. I'm the youngest boy in my family, my ass has been handed to me more times than I can count, and I go up against some of the biggest and baddest guys in college football. This was a walk in the park."

"Well, when you put it that way …" She giggles.

"Listen, I married you. I may have made the decision lightly but I take my commitments seriously and this is very real for me. I wasn't lying about that. I'm not going anywhere." I take her mouth in a deep, searing kiss.

When she breaks it, we're both a little breathless, and I'm a whole lot turned on.

"This just got very real." She takes my shirt in her hands and pulls. "I'm someone's wife. I have a husband."

"Yeah, you do. I'm one lucky fucking bastard." I kiss her again.

"I'd better go so we don't miss our flights." She walks to the door.

"Let me walk you to your room." I pull open the door.

"No, it's just around the corner. You need to pack up and meet with the team."

"Okay, but I'm watching you until I can't see you anymore."

She lifts up to kiss me, then pushes my chest. "Go. I'm fine."

I watch her walk away, but just as she's about to turn the corner, I call out to her, "Hey!"

"Yeah?" she says, turning.

"I'll see you at home, wife." I wink at her and can't help the huge fucking smile that spreads across my face.

"Bye, husband. I'll see you at home."

Yep, luckiest asshole alive.

BROOKE

THE PLANE HUMS beneath my feet as we level out somewhere over the desert. The cabin smells like recycled air and stale coffee, making me feel sick to my stomach. Not to mention the fact that my dad hasn't said a word to me since we sat down.

He's just staring at the back of the seat in front of him. The book on his lap hasn't been opened, and the travel pillow, which he always uses, is still attached to his carry-on under the seat. His silence is definitely intentional. My dad has always been a *think before you speak* kind of guy, and I have a feeling he didn't say everything he wanted to say today because we had an audience with Beck, Charlie, and Silas in the room.

I force my gaze from him and look out the window and see Vegas disappearing into brown nothingness. My reflection in the glass is faint, but I can see my messy ponytail needs to be adjusted. And when I lift my hand, the sunlight catches my ring. I shift uncomfortably, wanting to shield it from my dad's view.

"Do you remember the summer you played soccer and wanted to quit?" my dad says quietly.

I nod slowly. "Yeah. I was around ten, right?"

"Yes, exactly ten." He nods. "When I asked you why you wanted to quit, you looked at me with your little hands on your hips and told me you didn't love it anymore."

"I think we can agree that I was pretty bad at soccer."

"I don't know that I would say you were bad, but it definitely wasn't a strength." He inhales deeply. "My point is, you weren't comfortable being bad at something that you once loved."

I'm not really sure where he's going with this. "Dad, what is it you're trying to say? Because I'm not finding a connection."

"It's because you don't want to see it."

He turns toward me, no longer angry and not even disappointed, just thoughtful.

"Brooke, I'm not saying you've made a mistake here, but I do think you made a very spontaneous decision in a very exciting moment in time."

He tries to take my hand, but I pull it away.

I drop my head forward and look at my hands in my lap. Looking at my ring.

"I wasn't drunk. I wasn't pressured." I huff a laugh. "Hell, it was even my idea."

"Don't you think maybe you just got swept up in the moment though? That's what I'm trying to say."

"I appreciate you, Dad, and maybe if we'd had this conversation before yesterday, I might have agreed with you. But Silas seems to want to make a go of this, and I'm not afraid of trying."

"I believe that." He watches me. "But your good intentions don't protect you from consequences."

Consequences. Interesting word choice.

"Brooke," he says, "his life is about to change, honey. Fast. There will be expectations put on him that can be overwhelming. Do you think you're truly ready for all of that?"

Silas's face pops into my mind. He sounded so sure of us. And when he told me he wasn't going anywhere, I believed him.

"Yes, I think I am." My voice is not as confident as it was this morning.

"And what if he decides that he needs to put football first?"

"Did you have these same conversations with Beck? Or with Beck and Charlie?"

"It's not the same, and you know it." He sighs, rubbing a hand over the back of his neck. "You've always been so centered —anchored really. And I don't want you to lose yourself. Or what *you* want."

He hesitates, then presses on. "And don't forget your own dreams. Ever since you were a little girl, you've wanted to be a climatologist. What does this mean for your future plans?"

"I'm still getting my degree," I say quickly.

"I know." His voice softens, but the worry doesn't fade. "I also know what it's like to fall for someone who's the life of the party. I know how easy it is to lose yourself in someone else's orbit—and then wake up one day, wondering how your life ended up on a road you never meant to take."

He gestures vaguely, like he's trying not to sound accusatory. "It was a big weekend. The game. The celebrations. I can see how you might've gotten swept up in all the … frenzy."

My stomach tightens.

I look down at my hands, at the ring catching the light, suddenly very aware of how permanent it looks.

"Dad," I say quietly, "I didn't marry him because he won a game or because we were caught up in the excitement."

I lift my gaze, forcing myself to hold his eyes, trying to summon the confidence I felt yesterday—before doubt started creeping in from every direction.

"I married him because of who he is when the noise dies down. And Dad, I've had feelings for him for a while. The feelings…didn't happen overnight."

"I believe you feel that because it's who you are. You see people with depth. I just think that a lot of change is about to come that boy's way. He's entering a career that rewards selfishness. And I'm not saying that to be mean; it's just the truth. I'm very proud of your brother, but he's a man I know and raised. I don't know Silas in the same way as I know my own son."

"So, you think he'll change," I say.

"Honey, I think everything will change." He reaches over to take my hand, and this time, I let him. "I'm just not sure where all this leaves you. And if I were a betting man, I would give this two months, tops. In fact, I'll even get the annulment paperwork ready for you, so when it happens, you'll be prepared."

"Dad, that's not fair. You don't know what's going to happen. And I'm not fragile. I can handle it. And it's not like I don't know the kind of dedication it takes to be a professional athlete."

He shakes his head. "I don't think you're fragile. I think you'll allow yourself to endure more than you should. Like you always have."

Well, that hits deep.

A bump of turbulence interrupts us, and I grab hold of the armrests.

"Are you okay?" my dad asks.

"I'm fine. The bumps make me nervous when we fly."

He pauses, then starts to say something, then stops again. Takes a deep breath and exhales slowly.

"Do you love him?"

The question lands gently, but it hits hard.

I open my mouth, ready with something safe. Something practical. Something that keeps everyone calm. But nothing comes out.

Because love isn't supposed to happen like this. It's supposed to be slow. Earned. Measured in dates and time and certainty. Not in one reckless night that somehow turned into *everything*.

Except …

He makes me feel safe. Not in a grand, dramatic way, but just because he's there. My mind stops racing because he isn't asking me to be anyone other than who I already am.

He listens. Really listens. Not to respond, not to fix—just to understand.

He asks what *I* want—and means it.

He's the calm after the panic.

"I think I could. I know I care an awful lot about him. But I'm not sure I can define those feelings yet."

"I think he's in love with you, but loving someone isn't the hard part. It's the *staying* amid all the challenges and changes."

I try to swallow down the lump in my throat.

"Silas hasn't hesitated once, Dad."

"And neither did you, from what it sounds like." He smiles.

"So, you're saying the hardest parts are coming."

"Of course they are. Everything's fun in Vegas. Heck, a college campus makes life seem pretty easy. All your friends and obligations in one place. Wait until the combine and the graduation and your dreams and where those take you. It will make your relationship strong. Or it will break."

I close my eyes and rest my head back. I understand what he's saying, and I do think we can get through the next few months together.

But …

What if my dad is right?

Fear starts to creep in. I picture the training. The long distance. Being the one waiting patiently and understanding. Not fearing Silas intentionally hurting me, but maybe the thought of being left behind. Or worse, me falling harder.

"Look, maybe I'm wrong. The time I've spent with Silas over the last few years, he seems like a really good kid. But you're my daughter, and I don't want to see you put your life on hold for a weekend romance. You want to finish school, you want a career. I also think you should ask yourself whether you're prepared to fight for space in someone else's world."

My chest tightens, and my breaths become shallow. Because I don't know the answer.

We don't say anything else the rest of the short flight home.

But as the plane begins its descent, my father squeezes my hand once.

"One final thought," he says. "You're not stuck. You're allowed to choose yourself. You have your own path."

I nod.

Because the farther we get from Vegas, I'm starting to wonder if he's right. Except what happens in Vegas doesn't stay in Vegas. I'm going home with a husband and a father who's betting our relationship won't last.

CHAPTER
FOURTEEN

BY THE TIME I get home, it's just after dinner. I texted Brooke on my way from the airport to the field house. She should be at the house by now with some of her things. I told her to wait for me to help her, but she never replied.

Bo pulls his SUV into the driveway, and as soon as he parks, the front door opens, and Chelsea comes running out of the house.

"Yay! You're home!" She leaps into his arms.

"Hey, Lucky. You miss me already? It's only been a few hours." He nuzzles her neck.

I grab my bag out of the back and walk toward the door, kinda wishing that my wife had met me at the door like Chelsea did. But as soon as I walk in, I'm hit with the sweet smell of cupcakes. I set my duffel bag by the door and turn the corner to see Brooke in the kitchen, bent down and pulling a muffin pan out of the oven. She's wearing a gray sweatshirt and little black shorts.

"Hi." I walk over to her and slide my arms around her waist from behind, then place a soft kiss on her neck.

She shivers just enough for me to notice. "Hi," she squeaks. "Did you have a good flight?"

I don't let go of her as she sets the pan on the top of the stove. "Yeah, it was fine. I'm so happy to be home though. Did you get everything you needed from your dorm?"

She turns in my arms, but she doesn't touch me. She's not looking me in the eye either.

I'm not sure if she's feeling awkward or shy now that we're back and reality has set in.

"Um, yeah. Charlie helped me get a lot of my clothes and personal items. There are a few things I still need to grab, but nothing urgent. My roommates were definitely confused, but I just told them I would be staying with Charlie for a while. I guess I need to contact student housing and let them know, but I'm not really sure what to say. And I think my dad prepaid for this semester, so I hope he can get that money back."

Her dad.

"How did the flight home go? Did he say anything to you about us?"

She laughs dryly. "He did. Surprisingly, he wasn't angry. I think he's just really shocked by the whole thing. Just like everyone, I suppose."

I put my finger under her chin and lift to meet her eyes. "Are you okay?"

She bites her bottom lip and nods. "I am. It's just now, we're back, and I'm moving in. You leave in a few weeks for the combine. You'll be training all the time. I just ..." She pauses.

"Brooke, we have a lot to talk about for sure. But I still don't regret anything that we did last night."

"I can't believe that was last night. It all feels like a whirlwind." She shakes her head and looks away, making my hand fall.

"You're telling me. I won a national championship yesterday and got married. If you had asked me last week if I thought any of this was possible, I would have said yes to the championship, but marrying you … only in my dreams."

She finally breaks into a smile. "Stop. You didn't think about marrying me."

"Maybe not in the way we did, but I definitely wanted you. And if you need me to reassure you, I will happily do it. Right here. Right now."

I take her ass in my hands and lift her, and she wraps her legs around my waist.

"Smells good in here," Bo says as he and Chelsea walk in. "You make us cupcakes, Brooke?"

I keep her in my arms and walk us away from the stove, and then I set her on the island, but I stay between her legs.

"Yes, I did. I made the ones you like with the chocolate fudge swirls." She turns her head to watch him take one out of the pan. "They just came out and need to cool before I frost them."

"Bo, you're gonna burn your hand." Chelsea grabs a paper towel and hands it to Bo.

"It's not that hot." But he takes it anyway and covers the bottom as he peels back the wrapper. Then he takes a bite and nearly drops it. "Okay, maybe a little hot." He holds his mouth open.

"Spit it out then, goof. Don't burn your tongue." Chelsea scoffs.

"I'm good," he mumbles, then finishes chewing. "I'll let it cool for a second before I take another bite though."

Chelsea looks over at us and rolls her eyes.

"So, should we get a pizza or something? I'm getting hungry, and I can't wait to shower." He wraps an arm around Chelsea.

"I'm hungry too. I can call in an order while you shower first." I pull out my phone.

He nods. "That works. Get whatever you guys want." He drops his arm from Chelsea, but takes her by the hand. "You wanna come with me?"

"I literally can't believe you just asked me that in front of them." She covers her face with her free hand.

"Babe, I'm pretty sure they know we've seen each other naked."

She hits him on the stomach as they start walking.

"And I think they have us beat on the shock factor." Bo laughs and looks over at us. "Sorry, I couldn't help it."

"What can I say? I like to keep you all on your toes. Expect the unexpected and all that." I hold out my arms.

They laugh as they walk toward his room.

I turn back to Brooke, and her eyes are focused on her wedding band.

"What kind of pizza should we get?" I ask her to try to bring her gaze to me.

"Doesn't matter to me." She starts twisting her band.

"Brooke …" I set my phone down and take her hands in mine and set them on my chest. "Let's eat and visit with our friends for a while, and then we'll go into my room and talk."

She nods. "Okay. Sorry. I don't mean to be weird. Am I being weird?"

"You seem like someone trying to make sense of everything that's happened in the last twenty-four hours. And I get it. But we'll do it together, okay?"

I take her face in my hands and kiss her. When she melts into me, I deepen the kiss. I want her to be here with me.

"Hey, lovebirds. What are we doing for dinner?" Charlie walks in, interrupting us.

Brooke clears her throat. "We're gonna get a pizza."

"That works. Do you want me to order?" She lifts her phone in her hand.

"I got it. Just tell me what everyone wants." I grab my phone from the counter.

"Maybe just a cheese, veggie, and whatever you boys want. I assume my brother went to Noelle's since Chelsea is here?"

"Yeah, I guess. He told us he would see us later, but that was it." I tap on the app and place the pizza order.

"I figured." She takes a bottle of water out of the fridge, then turns to face us.

Brooke's hands are resting beside her now, but I'm still between her legs.

"So, how are you guys feeling about everything?" She studies us.

"I feel great." I smile widely. "A little sore still from the game and pretty tired, but I got to come home to this." I wrap my arms around Brooke's shoulders and tug her in tight.

Charlie has a smile on her face. "Good. And, B, how are you feeling?"

What's she doing? I'm sure they talked about it before I got home.

"I'm good," she says quietly.

"Awesome. Maybe you guys should go try to figure out where Brooke can put her things." She gestures toward my room. "I'll call y'all when the pizza gets here."

"Sounds like a great idea," I say, lifting Brooke off the counter, but I keep her in my arms, so she wraps around me again.

When we get to my room, I see her bags sitting neatly in front of my small dresser. Not sure how we're going to fit everything in here, but I'll toss out all my clothes just so she can have space.

"I wasn't really sure where to put my bags. I've never really been in your room before."

"Yeah, I guess you haven't. But this is fine for now. I just need to clear out the drawers. I don't have a ton of stuff. And only a few things in the closet." I set her down on my bed. "I can always run to Target and get some bins for under the bed, too, if we need them."

"Silas, is this … is this okay, really?"

I kneel down in front of her and push her legs apart so I can fit between them, then run my hands up her thighs. "Brooke, this is more than okay. Yeah, so we did this in a very unconventional way, but my feelings for you are real. Like I've already told you, I have zero regrets."

"But what if us trying to make this into something real is a mistake? You have a lot going on, and I feel like, I don't know, that timing is just not the best. I'm in school, I have my own goals." She takes a deep breath in. "I don't want to hold you back or anything. And I wouldn't want to be a distraction for you either."

"Cupcake, you might be a distraction, but not in the way you're thinking. Yes, I have a lot to prepare for, but as far as I'm concerned, having you by my side through it all will just make everything better." I lift a hand to her face and brush her cheek with my thumb. "Are you having doubts about this?"

"Honestly, I just don't know. Yes, I wanted to have fun and do some things out of my comfort zone, but maybe getting married was taking it too far." She laughs, but there's no humor in it. "I mean, I didn't even know you had feelings for me."

"Really? You didn't? I'd try to be near you whenever you were here. The night of Noelle's party wasn't the first time we'd fallen asleep on the couch together." I raise my brows. "The kiss at the basketball game? Well, that was just a golden opportunity, and I took it. And the first person I looked for after the game yesterday wasn't my family; it was you. I wanted to celebrate the win with you."

"You did?" She smiles sweetly.

"Hell yeah, I did. I think about you all the time. I'll do anything to show you how I feel about you."

"We haven't really been on an official date. Maybe we should just get an annulment or something, then date and try to do this the right way."

Fuck. That.

I shake my head. "Nah, I'm not gonna do that."

"What do you mean?"

"I'm not getting this marriage annulled."

"Silas, I'm not saying we would go our separate ways neces-sarily. I just mean that we could start fresh without the pressure of being married."

"I don't feel pressured. You do?" Shit.

"*Pressured* isn't the right word, I guess, but you have to agree, this is a major commitment. We're young too. I'm only nineteen. I'm just trying to wrap my head around it all, and I just don't know what to do."

"Do you have feelings for me?" I know she does, but I want her to say it.

"I told you I did." She sets her hands on my shoulders. "And I don't say things I don't mean. I might be cautious about it, maybe take time, but this? I didn't lie to you. I do have feelings for you. Probably for longer than I should admit."

"Okay, that's all good though. And you're not wrong. We did this backward, but it doesn't change the fact that I want to make this work, and I know we can."

"Football is going to be your priority for a while. It has to be, and I completely understand that. I really do. I just need to figure out how I fit into all of it." She searches my eyes for an answer.

"It does make sense. But I really want you to trust me."

In my gut, I know that us being together isn't a mistake. And I believe that we're meant to be. I can't explain it, but I feel it. I think she does, too, but she's scared. She needs to know she'll be a priority for me.

"So, let me date you. Woo you. Whatever you want to call it. Let's spend time getting to know each other better. I want to know everything about you."

"I want to know everything about you too." Her hands slide up my neck and into my hair.

I love it when she does this.

I need her to feel like she has the control here. I think that's the only way she's going to give this a chance and not run for the hills. And give up on me.

"I have an idea." I rub my hands up and down her thighs.

"What's your idea?"

"Give me until April."

"For what?"

"To prove to you that this isn't a mistake."

"Silas, just to be clear, I don't think you're a mistake. I just think maybe now that we're out of the Vegas bubble, we need to be more realistic. That doesn't mean I don't want to be with you."

"And all of those feelings and thoughts are completely valid. So, I'm going to let you decide if we stay married or not. But I'm asking you to give me until the draft to make you fall in love with me."

"Silas," she practically whispers.

"Come on, Cupcake. Give me a chance."

"What if you don't fall in love with me? What if you decide you don't want this?" She drops her hands from my neck.

"Baby, I'm already there. You own me." I bring her hands to my chest.

"Really?" A smile spreads across her face.

"Abso-fucking-lutely." I kiss her and run my hands up and under the Walker football sweatshirt she's wearing.

"Hmm … no bra?" I cup her breasts, running my thumbs over her nipples.

She shakes her head. "No. I showered when we got back, and I just didn't put one on."

I move down to the hem and grab it. "I'd better check, just to be sure."

"Silas." She giggles when I stick my head under the sweatshirt, but gasps when I suck one of her nipples into my mouth.

I pull her sweatshirt off and throw it over my shoulder.

"What about the pizza?"

"I'm gonna have dessert first tonight." I smirk.

"Oh my God." She laughs.

I kiss my way down her chest, and with one hand, I push her gently to lie down.

Then I take the waistband of her shorts and pull them, along with her underwear, down her legs. Her skin is so soft, and she smells so fucking good; I'm barely hanging onto my control.

I rip off my shirt and center myself between her legs.

On the first swipe of my tongue, she gasps and arches her back. "Silas," she breathes.

"Best dessert I've ever had." I swirl my tongue slowly around her clit and bring one of her legs to rest on my shoulder. "Do you like this, baby? Do you like it when I lick your pussy?"

"Yes," she moans.

She starts to move her hips, so I let her grind on my tongue, letting her take what she needs.

She grabs on to my head—without being told to this time—pushing my head into her, and holds it while I run my tongue from her opening up to her clit. Then I stop long enough to wet my finger and slide it between her ass cheeks.

"Relax." I move my finger slowly up and down, but don't insert it. We'll get to that another time.

"I've never done anything there."

"This is all we'll do tonight. How does it feel?" I press on her tight opening.

"I … I'm not sure. It's different, but not in a bad way."

"Focus on my tongue and how my mouth feels."

I look up and see that she's watching me. So, I let her see my tongue tasting, licking, and then I suck her clit into my mouth.

Her breathing is getting faster, and I can tell she's absolutely turned on. I don't think it'll take much more to set her off.

I increase my pace and flatten my tongue to intensify the friction. When I moan on her clit, her hips buck.

"Silas, I want you inside me." She puts her hands on either side of my head, pulling me up.

I kiss the inside of her thigh. "You want your husband's thick cock?"

"Yes," she rasps. "Hurry."

I strip off my sweatpants and crawl up her body and lift her under her arms to move her further back on the bed.

When I'm lying on top of her, I take her mouth in a searing kiss. I rub my dick up and down her slit, hitting her clit with my crown.

She opens her legs wider and reaches between us, takes my cock in her hand, and places it at her entrance. "Please," she begs.

I push into her slowly, making us both groan.

"Oh God, Silas. How does it feel so good? I didn't know it could be like this." She lifts her hips to meet mine, pushing me in deeper.

"I know, baby. It's the same for me. You are perfect. Your tight little pussy squeezing my cock." I wrap my hand around her neck, my thumb resting on her pulse point. I can feel her heartbeat thumping.

I shove into her hard, lifting my head just enough to see her face. Her mouth falls open, and she covers it with her hand.

I squeeze gently on her throat. "Let them hear you. Don't hold it in."

She shakes her head back and forth, arching her back and tipping her head back further.

Fuck, that's so hot.

"Goddamn, you are such a good girl, baby. You're greedy for my cock, taking it so well." I thrust my hips faster, deeper, making her body inch up the bed.

She removes her hand from her mouth and puts it on the headboard behind her.

"Please," she rasps.

"Please what?" I slow my pace and grind my hips so I put pressure on her clit.

"I ... I need to come." She takes my face in her hands. "Kiss me."

I tease her with my tongue, tracing her bottom lip before sucking it into my mouth. Then I release it with a pop.

She holds my head and slants her mouth on mine, her tongue diving deep. But as she gets closer to her orgasm, her breaths mingle with mine, and then I start to feel her pulsing around my dick.

"That's it. Come all over my cock." I thrust faster, my balls tightening, and the pressure rushes through me as Brooke and I come together.

I kiss her softly as we both catch our breath.

"How is it so good every time?" She winds her arms around my neck.

"Because you and I fit, Cupcake." I kiss her nose, then pull out of her and move to lie next to her. My fingers lightly trace the curve of her breasts, then down her stomach.

She inhales sharply. "I think you might be right."

"So, you feel a little better about us?"

She turns her body to face me. "I think we still have a lot to think about and discuss, but I accept." She smiles.

"Accept?"

"I think we date and see how it goes. And if we—not just me —feel like this isn't working by the time you get drafted, we'll go our separate ways." She places her hand on my arm, watching it move across my skin, then meets my gaze.

I look into her eyes and then at the soft, hopeful smile on her face. "I won't change my mind, just so you know. But I'll take it." I kiss her again because I need to seal this deal with a promise but without the words.

"Pizza's here!" Bo yells from outside my room.

"Guess we should go eat." She starts to sit up, but I stop her.

"Stay here. I'll be right back." I get up from the bed. "I mean it, stay put."

"Okay, I won't move." She giggles.

I get a pair of shorts from a drawer and pull them on. I take my T-shirt from off the floor and slip it over my head.

The bathroom is next to my room, so I run in and grab a towel from the cabinet, then run it through warm water. When I get back to my room, she's still lying there, as I asked.

I push her legs open, and when I see my come leaking out, it makes me want her all over again.

"What are you doing?" she asks.

I don't answer and instead place a kiss on the inside of her thigh before wiping the towel over her, cleaning her off.

"Thank you," she says, running her hand over my head.

"I'll always take care of you, Brooke."

I take her hands and pull her up. I lean down and grab her undies, shorts, and sweatshirt.

"Lift your arms."

I pull her sweatshirt over her. Then I sit on the edge of the bed and slide her panties up her legs, then her shorts. Her arms rest on my shoulders.

I kiss her stomach over her clothes and look up at her. "Let's go eat some pizza, wife."

She brushes her hand over my head again. "I'm starving now."

I pick her up as I stand. "Me too, baby. Me too."

I kiss her as I open the door and then walk her out of my room.

I'm gonna make this girl fall hard, and I'm never gonna let her go.

CHAPTER
FIFTEEN

BROOKE

WE'VE BEEN HOME NOW for almost two weeks and fallen into a pretty normal routine. Classes are back in full swing, and I've been busy adjusting to my new schedule for the semester. Silas, who is also back in class, is training for the combine.

The days are going by kind of fast, and I feel like we only see each other sometimes at night when we fall into bed. We've gone on occasional dates to dinner when we can fit them in, but it's been challenging to find time.

My last class of the day just ended. I'm heading out of the building, and I practically run into Eli as he comes out of one of the classrooms near the exit.

He stops walking and takes my elbow in his hand. "Brooke, hi." He has a tentative smile on his face.

"Hi, Eli," I sigh and roll my eyes, pulling my arm from his grasp.

"What have you been up to? How are you?"

"Honestly, I'm thriving."

"Oh, really?" He huffs. "You don't miss me at all?"

"Nope, not even a little. I actually forgot about you." I smile at him. "Now, if you'll excuse me, I need to go."

"Ha! I'm not sure if I believe you. Come on, Brooke. I'll walk with you back to your dorm so we can talk."

"I'd rather you didn't. And I'm not going to the dorm."

"Let me guess. You're going to the house."

"Yep, I am. I actually live there now." I walk down the stairs to the sidewalk.

"You're kidding me?"

"I'm not."

It's on the tip of my tongue to tell him about Silas when I see my husband walking toward us. He's smiling, but when he sees who I'm walking with, he scowls.

"Hey, Cupcake," he says, reaching for me and planting a kiss on my lips.

"Nice," Eli grumbles. "This is why you moved into the house then?"

"Oh, hello, Eli. I didn't even see you there." Silas gives him a sarcastic smile.

I place a hand on Silas's chest. "I just ran into him when I was walking out of the building."

"Did you tell him our good news?"

"Silas, not now." It's not because I want it to be a secret, but I really don't want to make a scene in the middle of the campus.

He ignores me, wrapping an arm around my shoulders. "Brooke and I got married recently." He kisses my temple.

Eli laughs. "Yeah, right."

"No, seriously." Silas holds up his hand, showing off his wedding band.

A part of me is giddy that he's claiming me in this way, but also, I'm slightly annoyed because he's putting on a show.

"Okay, we're going now." I turn and reach for his arm. I take his hand in mine, pulling him away.

"Whatever. You're not worth it. Go live in your testosterone-filled world."

Eli turns and starts to walk away, but Silas stops him.

"No, douchebag, you're not worth it. And I'm the luckiest bastard on the planet because she realized her worth and dumped your ass. Thank you for treating her so shitty. Now she sees how a man is supposed to treat his woman."

I mean, if that isn't a turn-on, I'm not sure what is.

Eli doesn't bother responding and walks away.

I look up at Silas as we start to walk. "Was that necessary?"

"Absolutely. Why? Are you embarrassed?" He squeezes my hand.

"No, I'm not. We just haven't said anything to anyone outside of our friends and family. I just…I don't know. I guess I haven't thought about handling it publicly. We should probably figure that out, don't you think?"

"Yeah, you're right, I'll talk to Scott about it too and see if he has any suggestions. Speaking of family, my parents are dying to meet you. I don't think they were nearly as shocked as your family was." He laughs.

"Okay, yeah. I'm not sure when that can happen though. It's kind of a bad time to go anywhere."

"Yeah, not a great time, but we can FaceTime them soon. Are you cool with that?"

He releases my hand and wraps his arm around my shoulder. It seems that he likes having me close to him. And I can't say that I mind.

"That works. Do you think they'll like me?"

I never met Eli's parents. And my family had an advantage knowing Silas, so this is a first for me.

"Cupcake, they are going to love you." He stops us and takes my chin between his fingers and tips my head up for a kiss.

"If you say so." I smile.

"I know so."

My cheeks flush with the way he says it so confidently. There's a gruffness to it, like in a possessive way.

He kisses me again when I smile, and then we turn and start walking again in the direction of the house.

"Wait, shouldn't you be at the gym?" I look up at him.

"I was, but I got done early. I wanted to pick you up from class because I have a surprise for you." He wiggles his eyebrows.

"Like a sexy surprise? Why are you wiggling your brows?" I giggle and poke him in the stomach with my finger.

"Oh, it absolutely will be sexy, but I wanted to do something special for you."

"Okay, now I'm curious. What is it?"

"Well, since everything has been kind of a whirlwind, we haven't really gotten to spend any time alone together, so I thought we could go on a little weekend getaway—call it a mini moon—just the two of us."

I could melt. *Mini moon.*

"Silas, that's really sweet, but are you sure you can take the time?"

"Yeah, this weekend is great time-wise for me, and where we're going, we'll be getting some exercise, so it's not like I'll be sitting on my ass, doing nothing."

"Okay, as long as you're sure."

"I wish we could go somewhere nicer and warmer." He laughs. "But this will have to do until we can take a proper trip. You down?"

"I don't expect anything like that. But, yes, this sounds like fun. Where are we going?"

"Have you ever been to Turner Falls?"

"Yeah, of course." I smile.

I love it there. The trails are incredible, and there are even caves to explore.

"So, I got us a cabin and thought we could do some hiking and just spend time together."

"Silas, that's actually perfect. Thank you for being so thoughtful."

"Well, like I said, a proper honeymoon is on the horizon, but it might just take a while." He kisses my head.

"Okay, but I really don't need something like that."

"Brooke, you deserve everything I can give you. And once I'm in the NFL, I'm gonna spoil you rotten." He laughs, then holds out his hands in a swiping motion, like he's tossing money.

"You're funny." I roll my eyes, but smile.

"What you said about announcing our marriage publicly—I would like to do that if you're okay with it. I mean, it doesn't have to be on *SportsCenter* or anything, but would you be okay with me posting it on social media? I'm pretty fucking psyched about being your husband, and I want everyone to know you're mine."

"I'm okay with it as long as you don't think it will hurt you in the draft."

"Nah, I'm not worried about that. Guys get married all the time in college. Shit, they even have babies. Look at Archie." He chuckles. "And maybe ours wasn't conventional, so we can keep the details to ourselves, but it's not a bad thing for these team owners to see that I'm in a committed relationship."

Committed. Wow. I still can't believe this is all real sometimes.

"Whatever you think is best, I'm okay with. We should probably let Beck know and maybe your agent so they're prepared."

"Why Beck?"

"Well, once they connect that he's my brother, he might get questioned about it, and I don't want him to be caught off guard."

"Good point. Okay, yeah. I'll let Scott know, and you can tell your brother."

"Great. Thanks." I smack him in the stomach.

"I don't think he wants to kill me anymore, so I feel like we're making progress there. But I still think you should handle that one. I'll hold your hand when you call him though."

"Gee, thanks."

"You're welcome, Cupcake."

We stop walking at the Stop sign to cross the street, and he turns to me.

"I can't wait to tell everyone you're my wife." He cups my face in his hands, and the kiss he lays on me makes me forget we're standing in a busy intersection in the middle of campus.

I pull back from the kiss. "You know, I can't wait either. I see the way girls look at you, and they need to know you're off-limits now."

"Oh, baby. I like that all too much. We need to get home—fast. Turns me on to hear you get all territorial." He grabs my hand as people around us start to cross. "I'll put it in my bio that I'm married too."

"Okay, then I will too."

He sighs, smiling and looking at me like a man ... in love. "You have no idea what you do to me."

"I think I might because I feel the same."

CHAPTER
SIXTEEN

SILAS

I WASN'T TOTALLY sure that hiking in the winter would be a good idea, but I think it's turning out to be a great fucking day.

Chelsea let us borrow her car for the weekend, and we left early this morning. We grabbed some food on the way here and then got checked into our cabin—which I have to say is pretty amazing—and dropped off our stuff.

It's a little chilly out, but hiking up some of these trails is keeping the blood flowing, and I can hardly feel it now. Brooke is a little more bundled than I am though. She's got on a cute little beanie and one of those puffer coats. I can't wait to take it all off her later.

"You know, I bet there is some kind of connection to your family. I mean, these are the Arbuckle Mountains. And your family is close enough that it could be a possibility."

"I'm not really sure. I mean, aren't these, like, one of the most ancient ranges in the United States?"

"I'm glad you asked." She smiles. "Yes, it is. Obviously, it's changed over time with land shifts and climate change. It's still changing today. Our weather patterns have shifted, creating drier air in Oklahoma, causing more drought conditions, making this area in particular more susceptible to flash floods. It's kinda sad when you think about it. Can you imagine what this must have looked like millions of years ago?" She looks up and around.

"I bet it was incredible. I think it still is. I can't wait to see the waterfalls. I didn't know there were caves behind them. We'll have to come back when it warms up and go explore them."

"Yeah, that would be fun. It's too cold and icy right now. The water might even be frozen. We went once when we were fairly young—maybe before Beck went into middle school. I loved it, but Beck didn't. He felt claustrophobic. The stalactites and stalagmites are really cool, from what I remember."

"I definitely want to see that. That's really cool. Do you want to go see the castle or just keep following the trails to the falls?"

There are castle remains here on the park grounds.

"Let's go to the falls first. I think we're almost there anyway." She pulls out the map we got when we came into the park. "Yeah, looks like we're maybe twenty minutes away."

"Lead the way."

She already is, and I'm enjoying watching the view from behind.

"So, Silas, tell me more about your life, growing up." She looks over her shoulder and smiles.

"Well, you know I'm the youngest in the family. I love my parents, but I won't lie and say I'm not a mama's boy because I love my mama something fierce. My siblings and I are close, but not like you and Beck are."

"Are you the only athlete in the family?"

"Two of my brothers played in high school, but they never went any further. They both stayed close to home so they could help on the farm."

"So why didn't you stay close to home? Although we're not too far from where you're from, right?"

I shake my head even though she can't see me. "Not too far.

It's maybe a three-and-a-half-hour drive from Walker. And I didn't stay close to home because my parents didn't want to hold me back from the offers I got to play at elite programs. I think, too, by the time I was on my way out, they had the farm taken care of between my brothers and didn't really need me anyway."

"That's good. You've definitely had a great college career. Did you always want to play at this level, or did it just kind of happen?"

"A little bit of both maybe. I was fast and strong, but I had some issues in school that no one seemed to recognize until I was in, like, middle school."

"Like behavioral or learning?"

"Cupcake, I'm an angel."

I laugh, and she turns her head, smiling.

"Right."

"Most of the time, I am. And I was a good kid too. Might be hard to believe, but I was kind of shy when I was little. I think it was because I struggled, and instead of getting made fun of, I became the funny guy."

"I can see that. So, what did you struggle with? Anything in particular or just in general?"

She stops and pulls out her map again, and we take a turn on the trail, where a sign also points to the falls. The path widens enough that I can walk beside her instead of behind, so I reach for her gloved hand. I love that she doesn't pull back. Like it's as natural for her as it is for me to touch her and hold her.

"Well, everything really because I'm dyslexic. And it wasn't until my coach figured it out that I had a breakthrough and realized that I was actually smart."

"That's pretty incredible, Silas. You're lucky you had a coach who was invested in your growth and was able to recognize that it was something that you could learn to manage. Do you have to use particular tools for studying?"

"I do. I wear my glasses, which help me see the letters clearly, but also help eye strain. I also have reading rulers, audiobooks and there are apps I can use, but I don't like to rely on those. I prefer to do it on my own, and between my glasses and ruler, I'm usually fine. Plus, I order books that have special fonts for people with dyslexia."

"I don't know that I've ever seen that. Can you show me when we get home?"

"Yeah, of course." I lift her hand and kiss it over her glove.

She gives me a soft smile, and she's so damn cute with the pink in her cheeks from the cold.

"And your major is something smart, right?" She laughs.

I chuckle. "Yeah, I guess it is. Biomedical engineering."

"What do you want to do with that?"

We're getting closer to the falls, and the trail is getting a little more traffic than what we've met so far. An older couple is moving slower, but I'm still impressed that they're out here at all. I pull Brooke over to the side to give them room to get by.

"Thank you, son," the man says.

"You're so sweet. Thank you." The woman reaches out her hand and touches Brooke's arm.

"No problem. Did you enjoy the falls?" she asks them.

"Oh, yes. We've been coming here since we were kids. Even before we got married. Seeing it in the winter is special, so we try to make it here at least once before the ice melts. Is this your first time here?"

"I came when I was younger, but this is my husband's first time here." Brooke says it so easily.

"Oh, that's nice. You two don't look old enough to be married." The woman smiles.

I wrap my arm around Brooke's waist. "Had to get this one locked down before she got away." I kiss her head.

"Good man. I had to do the same thing with this one." He points to the woman. "We've been married now for forty-five years."

"Oh wow, that's incredible. How did you make it work for all this time?" Brooke leans into me.

"A lot of patience and communication," the woman says with a snicker. "And get earplugs when he gets to the age where he starts to snore."

"I don't snore. She's full of bologna." He wraps an arm around her, and she laughs. "My piece of advice would be for you, young man. Know when to admit you're wrong, say you're sorry, and above all, listen to what she's telling you not only with words, but her actions."

"I love that." Brooke looks up at me.

"Those are some wise words there. I'll keep them front and center up here." I tap my head.

"We'll let you two get on with your day. Good luck to you." The woman smiles and nods as they walk by.

"Thank you. Be careful on the trail. Watch for the icy patches," Brooke calls after them, then looks at me. "How cute are they?"

I turn her to face me. "You're cute. And I'm so happy to be here with you. Thank you for coming with me."

"Silas, I should be the one thanking you. Every step we've made since Vegas, you've just made it so easy. And you're really fun to be around and hang out with, so I'm feeling pretty lucky." She lifts her shoulder and tucks her chin.

"I won't argue with you there. You have a great husband, but honestly, I think we're just good together."

She has a stray hair so I tuck it back under her hat.

A shy smile spreads across her face. "I do too." She places her hand on my cheek. "So, back to your major. Tell me why you picked biomedical engineering."

I turn and tuck her arm around mine. "Well, it's simple really. My dad had a heart attack, and he struggled with getting the right pacemaker. Like, his body just kept rejecting it. Not only was it painful for my dad, but the cost was insane. They had to leverage the farm, and it's just now slowly recovering."

"Okay, but where do you come in?"

"So, I want to help develop a machine that is more natural in materials, but also cost-effective," I explain.

"But how are you going to do all of that with your NFL career? You won't have a ton of time as long as you're playing."

She's not wrong, but I'm going to try to find ways to continue researching.

"I'm not really sure. I may look into companies to invest in until I can give my full attention to it, once my football career is over."

"I like that. I think it's important to have an after-football plan. You never know what can happen. You could have a long career or a short one."

"Well, let's hope, for the sake of our financial future, it's a long one."

We both laugh.

"Whatever happens and wherever life takes you, I know you'll be incredible. You want to know a secret?" She looks up at me with a goofy smile.

"One thousand percent yes. I want to know all of your secrets."

"I thought you might be smarter than you let on. I've watched you for the last few years. And I saw that mask come on when you felt like you needed to … perform maybe?"

"So, I didn't fool you, is what you're telling me?"

We get to a staircase that looks a little slick, so I take the steps in front of her so she doesn't fall, but I don't let go of her hand as I descend.

"Maybe it's that I could see more because I was looking." She squeezes my hand.

I don't look back over my shoulder at her, but I tip my head down and smile.

When we reach the falls, we find a place to sit. The stone is cold enough that I can feel it through the jeans I'm wearing, so I lift her and put her in my lap.

"I don't want that sweet ass of yours getting cold." I kiss her neck behind her ear.

"So thoughtful of you." She turns her head and kisses me quickly.

There are people roaming around the edges of the falls, taking pictures, and a few stopping for a snack or drink break. But I'm perfectly content, sitting here with my wife in my arms.

"Isn't this beautiful?"

She's looking out over the water cascading down the rocks. Some streams of water are frozen, making it almost look like something from a movie.

And it is beautiful, but when I look back at her face, nothing compares.

"Yeah, it's breathtaking." I pull her in tighter and breathe in her and this moment.

SEVENTEEN

BROOKE

THIS PLACE that Silas found for us this weekend is surreal. It's called the Birdhouse because it's nestled in the woods, and tucked into the trees a few miles away from the falls. The small cabin is on stilts, giving us a full view of the Arbuckle Mountains. I've never seen anything like it.

There's a king-size bed, a walk-in shower made of river rock, a huge garden tub, a tiny kitchen, and a dining table. A small electric fireplace sits under the windows, and a couch faces that stunning view. And it smells like pine and fresh air. Then outside, there is a round table on the deck, but it's too chilly to sit out there now that the sun is setting.

The warmth of the cabin is soothing after a long day in the cold. My legs ache from the miles we walked together, side by side. My belly is sore from laughing too hard on steep switchbacks that I almost slid down. My face is achy from smiling after every time he reached for me without looking whenever a trail got too narrow or steep.

Now we're working together to make a quick dinner. I'm making the steaks we bought, and Silas cut up some vegetables and potatoes for roasting. As I'm finishing up, he sets the table and opens a bottle of red wine.

The soft lighting, the fading sun, the view … it's really perfect.

"You want some water or something else with your wine?" Silas wraps his arms around my waist from behind.

"Water is good. But thank you for the wine. I don't have to drink, you know? It's not often that I do. And I know you can't right now, with training, so I'm okay without it." I rest my head on his shoulder.

"It won't bother me. I don't feel like I'm missing out or anything. I'm not a big drinker." He places kisses up and down my neck.

"Yeah, I guess that's true. With the exception of a few times, I haven't really seen you drink much." I tilt my head, enjoying the feeling of his lips on my skin.

"Makes me feel kinda crappy the next day, so it's just easier for me if I don't." He kisses my neck, then goes to the cabinet to get two glasses and fills them with water.

Silas walks back over to me at the stove, and he lays a hand on my hip. "Scoot over for a sec. Let me check on the food."

I slide over enough for him to open the oven door. "It smells so good in here." I peek in.

"Yeah, it does. We're gonna have us a fine meal tonight, wife." He pulls out the pan and sets it on the unused burners.

"Yes, we are, husband." I move around him so I can turn the steaks.

He takes two plates and scoops some veggies and potatoes onto each plate, then holds them out for me to set the steaks on. Then he leads me over to the table and sets our plates down, then pushes in my chair once I'm seated.

We eat and talk about our day. After the falls, we went to see the castle, and it was fun. Apparently, a professor from Walker built it in the early 1900s, and then it was abandoned and later became part of the park.

I'm enjoying doing things like this with Silas, because he's just as fascinated as I am to learn and see new things. And he doesn't tease me or make me feel like he knows more than I do.

"How's the wine? Is it any good?" he asks as I take a sip.

"It's good. I mean, I'm not a wine connoisseur or anything, but it tastes nice." I smile over my glass. "I probably won't have any more though. But we can take it home for Charlie and the girls."

He nods, but looks like he has something on his mind. "You don't drink much, and neither does your brother."

I shake my head. "No, he doesn't drink often."

Something in my expression must shift because he pauses. Really looks at me. "Is there a particular reason why?"

My chest tightens—not enough for me to panic, but enough to warn me I'm close to something I usually keep sealed shut.

I don't talk about my mom.

Not with friends. Not with family. Not with anyone except my therapist.

That's how I've learned to stay functional. To keep myself steady when everything else feels like it might tip. Avoidance isn't weakness; it's how I survived. Someone had to stay calm and steady.

That someone became me.

But Silas is different.

From the moment I met him—even when we were just friends—there was something about him that quieted the noise in my head. Being around him felt easy. Calm. Like I didn't have to brace myself for whatever came next.

And over the past few weeks, that feeling has only deepened.

He's become my safe space. The person my body relaxes around before my brain can catch up. Someone I know I can talk to without being rushed or fixed or dismissed. He's proven that over and over again—not with promises, but with the way he shows up. With patience. With consistency. With listening.

Somewhere along the way, my feelings caught on to what my nervous system already knew.

I trust him.

If we're going to make a real go at this—at *us*—then he needs to understand what he's stepping into. Because the truth is, my anxiety isn't something I'll ever completely outgrow. I just manage it better than most people realize.

I clear my throat, glancing at him. "Do you know anything about my family? Like, maybe overheard things?"

He shakes his head. "Not really. I remember hearing some murmuring about one of the games, but I wasn't here yet, and I just didn't think it was a good idea to ask."

That only confirms it.

I inhale slowly, grounding myself the way I've practiced a hundred times. This isn't spiraling. This is choosing.

"Beck definitely wouldn't have talked to anyone on the team about it other than Casey and Coach, but, yeah, my mom showed up to one of his games unexpectedly." I suck in a deep breath. "It just so happens that Beck and I were born in Pennsylvania, where the game was. She had been in jail and was out on parole. She can't leave the state to try to see us, and she's not legally allowed within a certain distance from us."

"Can I ask what happened to cause her arrest, or do you not want to talk about it?" He places his hands on the table.

"It's not something I usually talk about, but you should probably know."

"We can talk about it later. I don't want to upset you. I want us to have good memories from this weekend." He reaches for my hand across the table.

I take a sip of my wine with my other hand, then take a deep breath. "I don't remember a lot about her. Just images and faint memories. Most of what I do know comes from things I've heard in court or my dad and brother talking."

"Did she hurt you guys?" He rubs his thumb along the back of my hand.

I nod. "Yes, she did. She was an alcoholic. And apparently, she didn't start drinking heavily until after I was born. My dad has never said anything to insinuate this, but I've kind of always felt like I was the reason she did the things she did to us. She hurt Beck more than me really, but he would protect me, and unfortunately, he was the recipient of most of her abuse."

The words settle between us—heavy, vulnerable, real.

And for once, I don't feel alone, carrying them.

"I'm so sorry, Brooke. You don't have to say anything else about it." He sits up enough to scoot his chair next to me.

"No, it's okay. The things that happened to my brother are horrific, and honestly, I will spare you most of the details. But I do remember the day she was arrested."

I look at Silas's face. "I had been playing and trying to be quiet, but something I did must have set her off because, one minute, I was playing with my toys, and the next minute, she was yanking my hair and pulling me over to the stove. Beck was in the other room, working on homework or something, and came running in to see me being dragged across the floor. He fought with her until she let go of me, but then she was able to hold him long enough to put his hand in hot oil in a pan on the stove. I remember the smell of something burning, and I tugged on my mom's legs to let him go."

"Jesus Christ, Brooke." He places his hand on my arm.

"I think I must have blocked some of it out because most of it I heard in court, but my dad came in when she was hurting Beck, and that's pretty much the story of how she got arrested. She should have been in jail a lot sooner, but my dad traveled a lot for work back then and didn't realize everything that was going on.

"After the trial, we moved to Oklahoma for a fresh start. It had been in the news, and since we were so young, my dad wanted us to get away from all of it. Lucky for us, we moved across the street from the Kings, and I think they helped us more than they probably know. Carol and Tim became like family, and the rest in that part of the story is history." I smile, but it's forced.

"I hate that this happened to you guys. But can I say something?" he asks cautiously.

I nod.

"Why do you feel like it's your fault that she hurt you and your brother?"

I shrug one shoulder. "I don't think she wanted another baby, from what I've pieced together. And because my dad was gone so much, I think it was too much for her to manage on her own. My dad has never defended her to us, but he was aware of her mental illness when they got married. He just thought she was on her medication, but she wasn't."

"None of that is your fault though. You can't carry the weight of that, Brooke. Have you considered going to therapy?"

"I've been in therapy since I was young, off and on. But after she showed up at Beck's game a few years ago, I've been seeing someone regularly. I'm sorry. I probably should have told you all of this sooner. Does this change your mind about staying married to me?"

He takes my chin in his hand and kisses me softly. "Never in a million years would this change anything for me."

The kindness and gentleness of his voice overwhelms me, and I can't stop the tears that start to fall.

"Fuck, I'm sorry, baby." He wraps me in his arms.

I hold on to him, too, as I cry, but I don't stop talking. It's like he opened up the floodgates. "I think once I was old enough to understand what had happened, and probably before that, I tried to do everything right, be the perfect daughter. I didn't want to upset my dad or my brother, so I agreed with everything they said or did. And I really didn't want to be a burden or worry them because if Beck hadn't had to protect me, none of the abuse would have happened in the first place." I sniffle and wipe my drippy nose. "Logically, I know that's not real, but it's been a struggle to work through.

"And you should probably know that I have anxiety attacks from time to time when I feel overwhelmed or stressed. Anytime I feel like I'm not in control of my emotions, basically."

I lift one shoulder in a small, helpless shrug.

He doesn't interrupt. Doesn't rush in with reassurance or platitudes.

Instead, he shifts just enough to hold me more securely.

"What can I do to help you when you're struggling? Do you have any exercises that I should know so I can be there to support you?"

Who is this guy? I swear I hit the lottery with him.

"Well, I have different techniques that work—like the *five, four, three, two, one* method—and I also use physical grounding when it gets really bad. They're sensory exercises that are designed to bring back my focus and help me relax. And they really do work."

Silas sits back in his chair, but holds on to my hand. "Brooke, I need you to be honest with me."

I nod. "Okay."

"Has us getting married caused you to have any anxiety attacks? I don't want to be the cause of any distress for you. It would kill me." His eyes search mine, looking for the answer.

"I won't lie to you." I tip my head back. "The morning after, when I first woke up, I was a little disoriented, but then I started doing my exercises, and it calmed me down." I look back at him. "But the minute you opened your eyes and looked at me, all the panic faded away. Well, almost all." I smile. "Enough for me to have a conversation and get out of my head anyway."

"What about the night I kissed you at the game?"

I snicker. "Funny you mention that because my therapist and I had a conversation about that in my session before winter break."

"And what did you say?"

"The kiss wasn't something I had planned or had any control over. And I probably would have had an attack, but because it was you, I didn't. She thinks the familiarity of our friendship at the time is the reason I didn't have one."

"Well, that makes me feel a little better. But I am sorry. If I had known, I would have controlled myself better." He lifts my hand and kisses it.

"No, I actually think it helped prevent one. Because the attention on us in that moment was starting to overwhelm me, and the embarrassment of Eli's actions were making it worse. So, I think you were my sensory object. You took the panic away by kissing me." I lean forward and kiss him.

"I'm happy to do that anytime. You just say the word." He kisses me. "Or, hell, just give me a look. Maybe we should have like a Bat-Signal or something."

"A Bat-Signal?" I smile and shake my head.

"Or we just continue to grow our relationship, and I'll be able to feel it before it happens." He smiles slowly, almost shyly.

The need to be closer to him starts to burn through me. So, I get up and climb onto his lap, straddling him and wrapping my arms around his neck.

Husband.

A word that should feel strange in my mouth, but somehow doesn't.

"I want that too. I want to know everything about you. Your secrets. Your worries. And I want to be part of your celebrations too. But the one thing I want to make sure we don't lose is our friendship."

"We won't because we'll work for it. All of it." He keeps one hand around my waist and brings the other to my neck, thumb stroking over my pulse point. "You know what I think we need?"

I trace my finger over one of the tattoos on his neck. "What do we need?"

"We need a bath." He nuzzles my chest.

"Is that your way of telling me I stink from today?" I huff, playfully pushing him back.

"Not at all. I love the way you smell. It's just something we can't do at the house, and we have this big ol' tub here, so we should take advantage of it." He kisses my jaw. "And I want to get my wife naked and wet."

Heat rushes through me at his words. "Okay," I practically pant. "Let's take a bath."

He stands with me in his arms and walks us over to the tub. He sets me down so he can turn on the water and push down the stopper, and then he takes one of the bottles of bubble bath and pours some into the running water.

The tub is deep and is surrounded by windows. As the water fills, steam curls up, fogging the glass.

When he turns to face me, my hands go to his chest, and I start to unbutton his shirt. He stands still, letting me undress him slowly. Once it's done, I push it off his shoulders, and he pulls the sleeves, removing it completely.

Then he reaches for me and takes the hem of my sweater and lifts it off of me, tossing it to the side, on top of his shirt. He grabs my bare waist and runs his hands up my rib cage, then to the back to unclasp my bra. I shrug my shoulders forward, letting the straps fall down my arms to the floor.

I curl my hand into the waistband of his jeans and tug him closer. I pop the button and slowly pull down the zipper. With a newfound boldness, I reach into his boxers and wrap my hand around his erection.

"Fuck, baby," he hisses.

I stroke up and down a few times, then slip my hands under the band of his boxers to his ass and push them down with his jeans, bending to take them all the way to the floor.

When he steps out of the legs, I trail kisses up his thighs, stopping to swirl my tongue around his swollen crown.

He grabs me under my arms, pulling me up. "Not yet. I want to take my time with you tonight." His thumbs brush the sides of my breasts as he holds me, making goose bumps appear on my skin.

I bring my hands to his chest and trace the planes of his muscles and over some of the larger tattoos. His body is a work of art, figuratively and literally. Some of the ink on his skin could be on a wall; it's so good.

His hands move to take hold of my breasts, and he squeezes gently and pushes them together. "God, you're perfect." His voice is thick and deep.

I remove my hands from his chest and unbutton my pants, and his hands fall as I shove them down with my underwear.

When I straighten, Silas's gaze makes my knees nearly buckle.

"You're staring," I tell him.

"I just can't get over the fact that you're my wife," he says quietly.

Something warm flutters in my belly.

Then I take his hand and step into the tub first. I sink down into the water, letting the heat wrap around my body. When he steps in behind me, I scoot up a little to give him room to sit, and I watch the water rise and spill over the side as he sits behind me.

His arms wind around my waist, pressing my back to his chest, and he pulls me back with him as he rests against the tub. My head drops back to his shoulder, like it's exactly where it's supposed to be.

"Silas," I practically whisper, "thank you for today."

"You're welcome, baby." He kisses my cheek. "It was fun, watching you pretend like you weren't out of breath." His chest moves behind me, like he's holding in a laugh.

"Well, it's because I was. There was no pretending. I was just trying to act as nonchalant as possible next to my athletic husband."

He tucks his face into my neck to hold in his laugh.

"It's okay; you can laugh." I turn my head to see his face.

He doesn't answer, just kisses me.

His hands find my hips under the bubbles, and I place my

hands on his forearms as he traces his fingers over my hip bones and across my stomach, like he's not in a hurry. He just wants to feel me.

I can feel his erection sitting between my butt cheeks, gently sliding back and forth. I can't deny that it's turning me on. I mean, all of it is really.

His hands move down to my thighs, and his hands dive between my legs, spreading them apart. I place one of my hands on top of his and guide it to my center. I've never felt this bold before, but Silas makes me feel like I can take what I need.

"You want me to play?" He presses kisses along my neck, sucking below my ear.

"Yes," I practically moan.

His palm covers my mound, and he slides one long finger through my center, pushing it into me. He pumps in and out slowly while he presses down on my clit with his palm.

I start to circle my hips, seeking more, and he answers by pushing his finger in to the knuckle, thrusting it short and deep. I turn my head to kiss him, sucking on his tongue when he opens for me.

It's everything, but also not enough.

I turn in his lap, my knees brushing his thighs, making the water spill. His hands grab my hips to steady me—instinctive, protective—as I settle over his cock.

My hands run up his chest, and then up around his head, holding the back of it. Like I'm afraid he'll move away from me.

I study his face and see a beautiful man who is comfortable in his own skin. Who looks at me with reverence and curiosity.

"This feels … real," I admit quietly.

He leans forward and kisses me. "Because it is."

"I keep waiting for the bubble to pop," I say. "Like I'm supposed to wake up and realize it was a dream."

I want to live forever in this dream.

He chuckles deep. "Let me know when that happens."

"I don't want to wake up if it is a dream," I whisper against his lips.

Our kiss starts slow and gentle, almost like he's trying to reassure me. And I answer without thinking. It's instinct. I'm supposed to move with this man. Because we fit.

He explores my body as we kiss, learning my body. And he takes notice when he does something that makes me squirm in his lap.

I start to rock my hips over his erection, and the pressure inside me builds. I pull back just enough for his crown to reach my opening, and I sink down slightly to tease us both.

Silas hisses when I go in deeper, circling my hips.

Then my hands run up his chest, and I use it as leverage to lift myself up just so I can drop back down on him, taking him to the hilt.

I feel so unbelievably full, and yet I want more. But I don't think it's about coming anymore. I think it's about the connection I'm feeling with him right now.

I lean in to kiss him again, and this time, he's not patient. He holds my face as we kiss, our tongues tangling as the heat builds. Then he moves his hands to my hips without breaking the kiss and lifts me up and down his shaft.

Our bodies slide together in the water, and it's almost sensation overload. I'm getting close to coming already, but I don't want this to stop.

I try to slow our pace, but I can't. We move faster, more urgently. Our kiss breaks as we pant into each other's mouth. Licking and tasting as we move together. Water spills over the side of the tub, and I couldn't care less. He makes me feel … free. I like this version of me that I am with him.

Silas moves one of his hands from my hip and circles my clit with his thumb. Not that I need much to set me off, but that does it. Within seconds, I come apart.

"Oh my God." I tilt my head back as I let the wave of heat rush through me. "You feel so good. I don't want it to stop."

"Fuck!" he cries out. "Goddamn. Your pussy was made for me. I swear it." He thrusts up once. Twice. And then he stills.

I rest my head on his forehead, trying to catch my breath.

"You okay, baby?" he says, stroking my back.

I nod against him, and I can feel his smile stretch across his face.

We stay still longer than necessary, softly touching and breathing each other in.

When the water starts to cool, he finally mumbles, "We should probably get out before my dick prunes."

I laugh. "Well, we don't want that."

"Definitely not. I plan to use it again later." He kisses my forehead as he lifts me off him.

He stands first, steps out of the water, and grabs a towel off the bar next to the tub. He holds his hand out to me, helping me to my feet. And I'm grateful for it because my legs feel more like jelly than they did when we got back from hiking today, and it takes me a second to balance.

I step out of the tub, and he wraps the towel around me securely, then pulls me into him and holds me tight.

My head rests on his naked chest, and I can hear the steady beat of his heart.

This closeness I'm feeling to him right now seems a lot like the beginning of something that just might last. And less like a spur-of-the-moment decision taken too far.

EIGHTEEN

SILAS

I'M three days into the combine, and I'm tired. The initial adrenaline rush of being invited and just being able to show off my skills to the NFL teams is wearing off. Not that I'm not still excited or grateful because I am.

But I miss Brooke. I wish she could be here with me, but she can't miss a week of classes, and I understand that. I don't expect for her to put her life on hold for me just because we're together.

We've been able to talk every night, and it's been good for us, I think. Talking to her, I'm learning all the little things that make her who she is. And I feel like we've gotten closer as a couple too.

"Good job today, man. Your vertical is insane. I don't know how you can get up that high."

Cale Sellers is a cornerback from one of our rival schools, and I've always gotten along with him. His room is next to mine at the hotel, so we've been eating meals together and going to and from the venue in the same car. He's hoping to get drafted to New York.

"Thanks. My legs are feeling it tonight." I squeeze my thighs.

"I feel that. The forty nearly took me out. I just wanted to hit under four thirty, but it wasn't in the cards. Callaway was on fire today too. Same with King. He's fast for a tall guy. You Walker boys are dominating the combine."

He holds out his fist when we reach our rooms. I tap his fist.

"For sure. They're both going high in the draft. I'll see you tomorrow, man."

"Yep. Later."

Bo and Casey are here with me, but I haven't seen them much other than meals. We traveled here together though, so I'm sure we'll catch up when we head back to Oklahoma.

When my door closes, I pull out my phone to text Brooke.

> Silas: Hey, I just got back. Are you around?

I watch my phone for a second to see if those dots appear. When they don't right away, I set it on the dresser and sit on the bed to take my shoes off. Just as I stand, my phone buzzes.

> Brooke: Hi! I'm home, but I'm trying to finish some homework. Can you give me, like, forty-five minutes?

> Silas: No problem. I'll take my shower while you finish up.

> Brooke: K. Talk to you in a bit.

I take a quick shower, then slide on a pair of boxers. I crunch on a protein bar and drink some electrolytes to replenish everything I burned today. Then I settle in on the bed with my computer, put on my glasses, and pull up my calendar to see what I need to submit for homework this week. It's a lot to juggle right now, but I'm determined to get my degree, and with just a few months away from graduation, I can't slack off. Graduating is too important for my long-term goals.

I take care of a few things that don't take long, then read

through some emails my agent sent me. Including some film of my performance today.

I check the time on the screen. My eyes are starting to get heavy, and I feel like all it would take for me to fall asleep is to lie down, but I don't want to miss my call with Brooke.

A few minutes later, my phone rings, and a picture of her from our visit to Turner Falls appears.

"Hey," I answer, smiling.

"Hi. How are you?" She smiles, looking like she's genuinely happy to see me.

"Pretty good. Long day today. My legs are sore."

"I'm sorry. It seems like no matter how often or hard y'all train, it still stains your body."

"Yeah, but that's all part of the job. I'll be fine by tomorrow."

"What did you do today? You had the 40-yard dash today, right?"

"We did and ran the gauntlet too."

"I think I remember Beck had to do that last year. It sounds like it's hard."

"Yeah, he did. And it is definitely hard. You have to run in a straight line, turning side to side to catch balls being thrown at you. It takes a lot of focus, and also anticipating where the ball is going to be."

"I can imagine," she says, yawning. "How did you do on the 40?"

"Really good. I had the second best time in the group."

"That's awesome, Silas. I'm so happy for you." I can hear the smile in her voice.

"Thanks, cupcake. It'll all pay off. I just wish I had a better idea of where I'm heading."

"Yeah, it's like a total crap shoot it seems. I wonder how many first round draft picks have really been like 'fuuuuck I don't want to go there'." She giggles.

"Right? Although the amount of money they get as the number one pick probably makes up for the disappointment."

"True. Where do you hope to go? I don't think we've even talked about it."

I hear her shift, and sounds like she's getting under the covers maybe.

I want to see her, so I hit Facetime and she answers right away.

"Hi," she says shyly. "Good lord. Shirtless and has his glasses on," she mumbles.

"Hi," I smile.

She's so damn pretty.

"I wanted to see your face. Is this okay?" I move my computer off my lap and set it on the bedside table next to me.

"Yeah, of course. I wanted to see your face too." She snuggles under the covers in my bed. Or I guess, our bed.

Neither of us says anything for a beat; we're just smiling at each other like fools.

"So, where do you want to go?"

"Oh, right. Your beauty distracted me." I wink at her.

"Stop! You'll make me blush." She covers her face up to her eyes.

"Uh-uh. I want to see your smile." I motion for her to drop the covers.

She does and rolls her eyes. "Fine. Happy?"

"Yes, I am. Thank you." I lie back on my pillow and turn on my side, propping my phone on the extra pillow. "Where do I want to go? Hmm. I honestly don't really have a preference. I just want to go somewhere, you know?"

She purses her lips and nods. "So, if the Browns called you up, you would be okay with that?"

"Well, actually, yes. Their defense is one of the best in the league. To get to play with and learn from some of those guys would be incredible."

"I guess you're right. Bad example. Okay, but you have to have some thoughts about it." She raises her brows.

"It would be nice to be close enough that it's easy for you and my parents to come see my games as often as possible." I shrug my shoulder.

"Me?" She points to her chest.

"Well, yeah, we are married." I chuckle.

She shakes her head slightly. "Right. I just didn't realize that I would be a factor?" She says it almost like a question.

"Why wouldn't you be? I know it won't be easy to make schedules work sometimes, but we'll figure it out." I watch her face, and she looks a little unsure. "That's what we're going for anyway, right?"

"Sorry, yes. I guess it just still feels a little surreal sometimes. I mean, we got married on a whim for fun, and now we're talking about big decisions for your future." She looks away from me.

I swallow the lump forming in my throat. "I get that. And you're right, but I guess for me, it's turning into something more. At least I hope it is. I like the idea of planning my future and seeing your face in that picture." I pause and wait for her to look at me again. "I don't want you to feel any pressure though. So, if you ever feel like you are getting overwhelmed, I want you to be honest with me, okay?"

She nods and smiles softly. "Yeah, I promise. And I like seeing your face in my future too."

"Good." I smile in return. "So, I'll be breaking all kinds of NFL records, and you'll be chasing storms. But we'll do it together somehow."

"Chasing storms?" She laughs. "I mean, I guess, in a way, you're right. I just won't be on the front lines with the storm chasers. It'll be more behind a desk or at my home office that I plan to have."

"That's a possibility? You working at home?"

"Yeah, for sure. Especially if I go into the private sector or consulting. I've actually been thinking about your parents and what we talked about with the shifts in their crop production due to weather." She turns to her side, mirroring me. "It's something I would like to explore more as a long-term focus. And now it has more of a personal connection too."

"That would be amazing, and I support all of that. So, it's a lot of research then?"

"Mostly, yes. Some field work would need to be done, depending on what I'm doing, I suppose."

"Well, it sounds like something we can work with." I search her face, looking for agreement.

"I guess we'll see." She smiles and nods.

I don't want to push the topic any more tonight because we're both tired. And I'm trying really hard to let our relationship grow naturally. But at the end of the day, I do want us to make this work. I want her to fall in love with me in the same way that I'm falling in love with her.

I clear my throat to change the tone of the conversation. "So … Brooke."

"Yes, Silas?"

"Did you miss me today?"

She nods. "I did. Did you miss me?"

"You know it." I smirk. "Only a few more days until I can kiss those perfect lips of yours."

"I can't wait," she says softly with a smile. "So, um, Charlie gave me something today. It was a little embarrassing at first, but now I'm more curious than anything."

I raise an eyebrow, intrigued. "Oh, yeah? What did she give you?"

She inhales. "Hold on. I'll show you."

She scoots out from under the covers and leaves her phone on the bed; she moves out of view so I'm looking at the closet door. When she comes back into view, she's holding a black wand that looks sort of like …

Oh fuck.

Please tell me it's what I think it is.

"I can't believe I'm doing this." She covers her face with her free hand.

"Brooke … what's in your hand?" With the way she's turning it in her hand nervously, I can see it more clearly now. But I want to hear her say it.

She drops her hand from her face, but closes her eyes. "Charlie got me a vibrator. I kind of want to vomit at the next part, but she said this is her favorite one and helps her get through long times away from Beck."

I bark out a laugh. "Yeah, I'm sure that's not a visual you wanted."

"Not even a little, but after I ran into the bedroom with it, I got a little curious and started to read about how it works." Her face is turning red. It's fucking adorable.

"How does it work?" I bite back a smile because I don't want her to be embarrassed. I want her to feel like she can talk to me about sex and what she wants.

She holds it out, like she's giving some kind of presentation. "So, at first, I couldn't really figure out where like where it all went. But the curved part here that looks like a handle, it goes inside, you know …"

"Your pussy?" I smile.

She blushes, but continues, "Yes, that. Then the hole part is like a sucker. It actually suctions to the …"

"Clit?" I finish for her.

"Yes. But wait, there's more." She holds up a finger, seeming to relax a little now. "There's like a sonic wave that apparently hits a secret spot, like way up there, making the orgasm feel, like, ten times more intense."

"I'm fascinated, baby. I think you should try it out."

She smiles, then bites her bottom lip. "You think so?"

"Fuck yes. But I want to watch."

"Watch? Like here?"

"Uh-huh." I nod, smiling.

She sets the wand on the bed and covers her face with her hands. "I don't know if I can do that," she mumbles.

"I think you absolutely can." I shift on the bed, lying on my back because my dick is rock hard and pressing uncomfortably against the mattress. "I have an idea though. Can you switch to your iPad so we can be hands-free?" I pull my laptop back to the bed and set it where I had my phone so it's facing me.

"Silas," she whispers.

"Please, baby?" I give her a smile that I know she can't resist.

"Okay, but if I'm doing this, you are too." She reaches over to the nightstand next to the bed and grabs her iPad.

"You bet your ass I am. Although I don't even know if I'll need to use my hand at all. Just the thought of watching you come undone, it's making my cock leak already." I slip my hand inside my boxers and stroke my hard-on.

"I'll call you right back." She disconnects the call.

And for a minute, I'm not sure if she's going to call me back, but my phone rings again. This time, I answer it from my computer. "Hi."

"Hi." She's on her knees on the bed, facing the tablet that must be propped by something to keep it in place. She's wearing a tiny pair of sleep shorts and one of my Walker football shirts with my name and number on it.

"You wearing my shirt?"

She nods, smiling. "Yep. It smells like you, and it's comfortable."

"I like that you're wearing it, but I want it off."

"Are you getting naked too then?"

I push my boxers down and then fist my shaft. "Done."

She sucks in a deep breath, then starts to take off her shirt. No bra.

"Good girl. Now take your shorts off."

I see her swallow like she's nervous, but she lies down on the bed and removes her shorts. She's not wearing any underwear. Her legs part just enough that I can see how wet she is.

"Fuck me, baby." I bite my lip and groan.

This time, she smiles more confidently and runs her hand up her stomach and takes one of her breasts in her hand.

"Pick up your toy and turn it on."

"Before I put it in?"

She's going to make me come before she even starts.

"Yeah." I nod.

The hand on her breast falls, and she picks up the wand, holding it in both hands, then turns it on.

"Now use one hand and spread your pussy, then run it from your hole to your clit, getting it nice and wet."

She does as she's told, moving slowly through her center, up and down. I can see her chest start to rise and fall as she becomes more turned on.

"Okay, now I want you to slide it inside." I've never been more jealous of anything in my life.

I can see a slight tremble in her hand as she pushes the curved piece in, and she gasps.

"Oh my God."

"Can you feel the suction on your clit?"

She closes her eyes and nods, then rolls her head on her pillow.

"Tell me how it feels." I start jerking off, my dick like steel at this point.

"It's almost too much, Silas," she breathes.

"Talk to me, baby."

"It's like a mix of deep, pulsing waves and rumbly vibrations tumble through me, making me feel ... full."

"Drop the leg closest to the iPad and spread your legs a little further so I can see it."

Her leg falls to the bed, and she brings her knee up, spreading her pussy open, giving me the perfect view.

"Like this?" she pants. Both of her hands are on the wand.

"That's perfect. Fuck, baby. That's so sexy." My hand starts to move faster up and down my dick because I can already feel the pressure building in my balls.

"My whole body feels hot. I … I need to come." She removes one hand and takes a breast and runs her fingertip around her nipple, then pinches it between her fingers. Something I've noticed that makes her squirm when I do it to her.

"Ride it out, baby. Let it roll through you." My dick is slick with pre-cum as I pump.

"Silas," she moans.

"Are you close?" I'm starting to lose control.

She moves her head back and forth on the pillow and arches her back.

What I would give to touch her right now.

"Oh … oh … my … God. Silas!" she cries out.

"Fuck." I watch her as she comes and thrust my hips up into my hand as I come all over my stomach.

She opens her eyes and looks at me with a soft smile. "That was …" She shakes her head.

"That was something we'll be doing again. Remind me to thank Charlie when I get home."

"No!" She giggles. "I would die." Her body stills. "Note to self: don't laugh when you have a vibrator buried deep inside you."

I won't tell her that the whole house probably heard her. The walls are thin.

"Did you come?" she asks as I watch her pull out the vibrator.

I run a finger through my cum and show it to her. "Yep. Sure did." I grin wickedly. "And if you were here right now, I'd spread it across those puffy lips."

She bites her lip.

Goddamn. She's gonna ruin me.

After we've both cleaned up, we climb under the covers. I turn to my side to face her, and she does the same.

"Stay on the phone with me until I fall asleep?"

"Of course," I say, smiling.

I love that she doesn't want to hang up either.

She yawns. "Night, husband." She blows me a kiss.

"Sweet dreams, wife."

And I watch her as she falls asleep until I can't keep my eyes open any longer.

CHAPTER
NINETEEN

BROOKE

SILAS IS COMING HOME TODAY, and I'm really excited to see him. I didn't anticipate missing him as much as I have. And I think he missed me just as much.

The night we had phone sex will probably live rent-free in my head forever. But I'm also dying for the real thing. Maybe we can do a little preshow with the vibrator then …

My dirty thoughts are interrupted when Charlie walks into the kitchen.

"Whatcha doing?" She looks over my shoulder.

"Silas comes home today, so I thought I would make him some cupcakes to welcome him back."

"That's sweet. I bet he's ready to be back. Your brother slept for, like, two days when he got back. And you know he never sleeps like that."

I nod. "Yeah, he's pretty tired. I can see it in his eyes at night when we FaceTime."

"So, how's it going with you two? I see you're wearing his sweatshirt, and it seems you have confiscated most of his T-shirts." She smirks.

"It's going well. And, yes, I've stolen a lot of his clothes. I can't help it. They're soft and comfortable. And they smell like him. Besides, he steals my ability to walk, so I steal his hoodies. I feel like that's a fair trade."

Charlie gasps. "Brooke Linson! You naughty girl!"

When I look at her, her mouth is hanging open, but she's clearly amused.

"Is it weird if I say I'm proud of you?"

"Nah. I'm kind of proud of myself, to be honest." I start to frost the cupcakes.

"You've definitely been full of surprises the last few months. I mean, Silas's feelings for you were pretty obvious, and I thought maybe you were at the very least attracted to him. But getting married, becoming this little vixen … I didn't see that coming."

"Me neither. I don't even know if I can even understand it myself yet."

"Have you talked to your dad any more about it? Or Beck?"

I shake my head. "Not to Beck." I sigh. "I did talk to my dad the other day. He'd had annulment papers drawn up for us. I told him I wasn't ready to do anything yet, but it was like he didn't hear me. The thing is, I'm happy right now. And Silas and I are getting closer."

"Your dad just wants to protect you, is all. I think it's hard for them to let us go. My parents love Beck, and I know they're happy for us, but sometimes, I see my dad looking at me like I'm still a little girl." She wraps an arm around me. "Add in everything y'all went through, and I think it made him even more protective. You know?"

"I know. I just don't want to feel like it's already decided for me. I've always put my feelings on the back burner to keep the peace and not to worry anyone."

"Well, you're finding your voice now, it seems." She lets go of my shoulders and starts to take out the dishes in the dishwasher.

"I guess so. I promised Silas I would give us a chance, and

I'm glad I did. I mean, I knew he was a good guy before, but there's a lot more to him that no one else knows or sees."

"Beck said he's, like, super smart. I think he won the NCAA Elite Scholar-Athlete Award last year."

"He did?"

She nods. "Yeah, I think so. He never makes a big deal of it though. Like, he didn't say anything to us in the house."

"He is pretty modest, which is funny, considering he's a completely different person on the field."

"So true, but I feel like they're all like that. Kinda teddy bear at home and beast at their games." She laughs.

"In the bedroom too," I say under my breath, but she hears me and starts cracking up.

"Brooke!" she gasps, holding a bowl in her hand.

I can't help but laugh with her.

"I won't ask details, but I have to know. Is he pierced?"

"I don't think so. I've never seen him wear any jewelry."

"Noooo … I mean, his dick."

"Charlie. Oh my God." I feel my face flush.

"I heard he was pierced and that he's big too."

"You really want to know this about my husband? You have to look at him every day." I pick up my mint-green Stanley and take a sip of my protein water.

"And? He's not a blood relation to me, and I hear all kinds of stuff about these guys. If I were shy about it, I would never be able to look any of them in the eye."

"I guess you're right." I finish frosting the cupcakes. "No piercing, but I can confirm, he is tattooed almost entirely. And the rumors are true."

"I knew it. He just looks like the type to be packing."

"Okay, I'm not talking about it anymore. But I will say, I'm a really lucky bitch."

"Good for you. I love that for you." She walks back to me and takes my hands. "Brooke, I really am happy for you. I know your dad and brother are worried about how this is all going to play out, but if you were going to elope with anyone, you picked a good man."

"Thanks, Charlie. I still can't believe it sometimes. Like, I wake up next to him, and I'm like, *Is this real?*"

"Then you snap out of it when he bangs your brains out?" She cackles.

I shrug and smile. "Pretty much." I release her hands so I can put the cover over the cupcakes. "Or when I come down from my orgasm."

"Who's having orgasms?" my husband's deep voice grumbles as he walks into the kitchen.

I didn't even hear the door open.

"Broo—" Charlie starts, but I put a hand over her mouth.

Silas wraps his arms around me from behind and nuzzles my neck. "Cupcake, are you being naughty?"

I drop my hand from Charlie's mouth and spin in his arms to face him. "Me? Naughty?"

He hums, then takes my mouth in a deep kiss, right there in the middle of the kitchen.

We have been able to talk while he was away but it hits me at this moment how much I truly missed Silas. Not just the feel of him in my arms, and the taste of his tongue against my own. It's the feeling that I get when he's near. It's like I finally feel like I'm home.

"Hey, guys." Bo walks in.

"Hey, Bo," I hear Charlie say but I'm still lost in Silas' kiss. It's like a trance that I can dive deeper into with every flick of his tongue and curl of his lips.

Bo chuckles. "So, should we leave, or are we going to talk about food? I'm starving."

Silas and I break apart, and I look over at Bo. "How did it go this week for you?"

"Really well. I feel like I did what I needed to do to showcase what I can offer a team." He opens the fridge and pulls out a bottle of water.

"That's amazing, Bo. Just a few more weeks!" Charlie leans against the island. "So, what do we want to do for dinner? Brooke made some cupcakes, but they're for Silas." She winks at me.

"Baby, you made cupcakes just for me?" He kisses me quickly on the lips.

I nod. "I did, but everyone can have some."

"Hey, I thought they were mine." He peers over my shoulder.

"They are, but you won't eat all twelve." I put my hand on his chest. "You're still in training."

"Okay, I guess I'll share with everyone." He places a kiss on my forehead.

"What do we want for dinner?" Bo pulls out his phone. "Let me see if Chelsea's on her way. Casey went to pick up Noelle."

"I figured." Charlie pulls out her phone. "You looking for a cheat meal or a good meal? I can run out and get something if you want anything specific. I don't mind."

"You don't need to include us," Silas picks me up in his arms, and my water bottle. "I'm just gonna go lay my wife down and have my favorite meal. We'll see you all later."

"Silas!" I cover my face with my hands. It's one thing for me to be brazen or "naughty" when I'm talking with my future sister-in-law, but I'll never get over Silas's bravado when he's around his friends. He's unabashedly proud to share our love with the world.

Our love…

Is that where we're headed?

He laughs and walks us toward the bedroom, and when we get to the edge of the bed, he lowers me to the mattress, then hovers over me, looking me in the eyes.

"You know, I was raised to finish my meals, so I don't care if your legs are shaking; we're not stopping until I say so." He kisses one side of my mouth, then the other.

"Okay," I whisper.

We don't see anyone the rest of the night.

CHAPTER
TWENTY

SILAS

THE FIRST WEEK after the combine was pretty great. Brooke and I spent as much time together as we could when we weren't in class. It was awesome. But this week has been a different story.

She hasn't said it, but I feel like she's fallen in love with me—or at least pretty damn close to it. It's safe to say that I'm in love with her.

Head over ass.

But I want my declaration to her to come naturally. I want it to feel right for both of us. I don't even care if she says it back. I just want the timing to be right. And she did agree to give me until the draft, and we're just two weeks shy now.

My class schedule hasn't let up, and even after the draft, I'll have close to a month before I graduate. So, between school and meetings with my coaches here at Walker and my agent, that hasn't left much time for Brooke and me to spend together this week. And it sucks.

Her dad came down to see her today and took her out to lunch. She invited me to join them in an effort to show her dad that we really did care about each other, but I just couldn't make it work since they were going while I was in class. Then I had an appointment right after class and went to a car dealership after that.

I bought a truck to make it easier for me and Brooke to get around. And with everyone's schedules and personal lives, it's just not as easy to catch rides.

It's nothing fancy, but it's nice, and it will be good for us for now.

I thought she would be home by now, but she's not here. In fact, no one is in the house, which always feels kind of odd when it's so quiet in here. Not that we're loud and rowdy, but someone is usually hanging around.

When I walk into the bedroom, there's a moving box sitting on the bed—more stuff of Brooke's from her dorm. Inside, there's an Alexa, some books, a stuffed animal, and a cowboy hat, that I've seen her wear a few times. It looks like it's getting a little smooshed byy the books, and I don't want it to bend the brim, so I lift it out of the box and smack it a few times against my thigh to see if I can loosen the crease from the book.

I glance back into the box to see if anything else needs to be taken out and see a manila envelope with the words *Arbuckle Annulment* written in the center.

What the fuck?

My hands are shaking as I reach for the envelope—this stupid envelope that I can't believe exists at all.

I set the hat on the bed like I need both hands free for whatever this is about to do to me. Then I pick it up.

The paper is heavier than it should be.

I slide the contents out and try to read, but the words blur together, the letters swimming like they're actively trying to avoid me. I blink hard, forcing my focus, catching only fragments at first.

Mental capacity.

Duress.

My stomach drops.

Sure, we'd been drinking. But neither of us was drunk. Not even close. We knew exactly what we were doing. Hell—*she* knew exactly what she was doing. The marriage was her idea. She suggested it. Pushed it forward. Asked me if I was serious before we ever stood there and said the words out loud.

And I was. God, I was so on board it scared me.

What hurts—the thing that actually sinks its teeth into my chest—isn't the paperwork. It's not the legal language or the implications or the threat that this could all disappear with a judge's signature.

It's that she didn't tell me she was drawing up the papers.

I had no idea she was seriously considering this. No warning. No conversation. No chance to stand in front of her and tell her I'm not something she needs to protect herself *from*.

I lower myself onto the edge of the bed, the papers crinkling in my grip.

I thought she was giving me a chance.

We talked. We agreed to take it slow. To see where this went. I thought—*I really thought*—that her feelings were growing. That the way she relaxed around me meant something. That the smiles, the late nights, the quiet mornings weren't just politeness or fear or obligation.

I thought we were choosing each other.

And now I'm holding proof that maybe she's been preparing an exit the entire time.

My hands tighten around the pages, knuckles white.

If she's scared, I can handle that.

If she needs reassurance, I'll give it to her.

If she wants space, time, patience…I'll bleed it if I have to.

And if she leaves me because she doesn't want me then I'll have to let her go because then she's not mine to keep.

But this?

This feels like she never trusted me enough to let me in.

And that might be the part that breaks me.

I need to read through this more carefully, so I pull out my glasses from my backpack.

Just as I slip them on and pick up the papers again, Brooke walks through the door.

"Hey," she says, sounding tired.

She hasn't looked at me yet, so I don't respond.

Her back is to me as she pulls off her sweatshirt and tosses it into the hamper by the closet. Then she kicks off her shoes and sets them inside the closet.

"Is that your new truck out front? I'm sorry I couldn't go with you to get it. Lunch with my dad took longer than I'd thought. Then I pretty much had to run back here to get my backpack. I barely made it to my afternoon class on time."

When she turns to face me, she sees the papers in my hand. "Silas."

She doesn't look guilty, but she does look wary. "You went through my box?"

"I did." I drop the papers on the bed. "Your hat was getting bent, so I pulled it out so it didn't get ruined. But then I saw the words *Arbuckle Annulment* on the outside of the envelope, and … I don't know … I wanted to see why my wife had annulment papers. And I gotta say, I'm surprised."

"Silas, it's not like that. I didn't do anything. My dad brought them today."

"Your dad?" I ask incredulously.

"Yes, my dad. He had mentioned it on the plane ride home from Vegas, and I kind of forgot about it, honestly."

"How could you forget that your dad wanted to help us dissolve our marriage?" My brows rise, and I hold out my hands.

"*Forgot* isn't the right word." She shakes her head.

"Have you told him how you feel about me? Does he know you agreed to give this until the draft before any decisions were made?"

"Me caring about you has never been in question. Why are

you acting like this? This"—she holds up the papers—"doesn't mean I want to sign them."

"Maybe not, but why did you take them? You could have had him take them back with him if it wasn't something you were considering."

"I'm not! Silas, I hope you know that none of this has anything to do with what he thinks of you. He's just worried. He's being a dad. Us getting married, you have to admit, was really out of character for me. I'm not that person. I'm not the girl who throws caution to the wind and gets married in Vegas. So, I get why he would be worried about it. Don't you?"

Logically, yes. But I'm trying to process all of this.

"So then, why did you marry me?" I take off my glasses and set them on the dresser.

"I don't know!" she yells.

We stare at each other silently, and I watch her chest rise and fall.

"Silas, I've spent my entire life doing everything so fucking carefully so I stayed in the shadows. The guilt that I carry over the abuse Beck suffered because of me is suffocating. I've gotten really good at bottling my emotions and putting on a happy face so that neither of them worries about me because they've been protecting me from the ugly parts of our lives since I was little. So, neither of them saw how all of our trauma was eating *me* up inside. They have no idea about my panic attacks. They don't know that the thought of disappointing either of them is crippling to me." She crumples to the bed. Her head in her hands.

"I wanted a night that I could just be someone else. Hell, my own therapist and my brother both told me to let loose in Vegas, and for a minute, as I watched that newlywed couple walk off the Ferris wheel before we did, I thought, *I want that*. I want that kind of bliss, even if it's for one night." She looks up at me with tears in her eyes. "I'm sorry you got swept up in it. I would never want to hurt you."

"Do you care about me, or was I just a body? Could it have

been someone else you said *I do* with?" My heart stutters at the thought.

She shakes her head and stands. "No, I wouldn't have wanted to do this with anyone else. And, yes, of course I care about you. I did then, and I do even more now." She tries to take my hand, but I pull away. "Silas," she chokes on a sob.

"Brooke, when you said, 'Let's get married,' I didn't expect for us to be where we are now. I knew I had feelings for you. I knew I wanted to have you in my life as more than just my friend. And maybe it was on the fly for me, too, but selfishly, I saw it as an opportunity to see if you could feel the same about me as I did you. But if you're truly considering this, then I just …" I place both hands on the top of my head, pacing. "We're not playing house, Brooke. I want to be the first thing you touch in the morning and the last thing you taste at night. This is very real for me. And I thought it was for you too."

"It's real to me too. Can we just forget this for now? We both have a lot going on, and as I explained to my dad, it's not something I'm considering. Let's just focus on school and you getting ready for the draft."

"I think … I just need to think about all of this. It took me off guard because I hadn't even realized this was an actual conversation you had with your dad."

"It was on the plane on the way home. We haven't talked about it since then until today. This wasn't my doing." She cries.

I can't stand to see her like this, but I'm hurt. And maybe feel a little betrayed that she had talked to her dad about this and didn't mention it to me before now. And I might still not know if I hadn't seen those papers.

All of it—the ache in my chest, the way my lungs locked up the second I saw those papers—just proves how far gone I am.

I don't panic like that. I don't lose my breath over *paper*. And yet the idea of this ending, of her choosing to walk away, hit me so hard it felt physical. Like something vital was being pulled out of me without warning.

Which means I'm in deeper than I ever let myself believe.

I'm in love with her. Completely. In a way that doesn't ask permission or wait for good timing. In a way that's settled itself into my bones without me noticing.

So in love that if she decides this is over—if she signs those papers and ends it—something in me is going to break.

Not bruise. Not sting.

Break.

Fuck.

My hands drop from my head and I walk to her. "Brooke," I take her in my arms. "I need a little space right now." I release a heavy breath. "I'm not gonna lie, this sucks and it hurts. So, I'm going to go to the store, and run some errands to clear my head."

"Can I come with you?" She looks up at me. "Silas, please don't leave like this."

"Not right now. I'll be back later." I kiss the top of her head and let her go.

I replay our conversation in my head, and the thought of losing her starts to take over.

There's only one place I know to take this kind of fear. My mama.

She answers on the first ring. "Hi, honey."

"Hey," I say, voice rougher than I meant it to be.

She hears it anyway. She always does. "What's wrong? Are you hurt?"

I close my eyes. "No, Mama, I'm okay. Dad around too?"

"Sure. Hang on a second." There's a pause. Then the soft shuffle of movement.

"No, you need to press Speaker so we can both hear him," my dad tells my mom. "Silas? What's going on?" my dad asks, calm and steady, like the world hasn't just tilted.

"I need advice," I say.

When I told my parents Brooke and I got married in Vegas, they took it well. My parents aren't the type to involve themselves much into my business unless I ask.

My mom exhales. "Oh, that's never a good sign."

"Yeah." I laugh dryly. "I found annulment papers," I say.

Silence.

Then my dad clears his throat. "Did she ask for one?"

"No."

"Were they signed?"

"No." I release a heavy breath. "They were just … there."

My mom's voice softens. "Oh, Silas."

"I'm not mad," I say quickly. "I'm just—" I stop, jaw tightening. "I don't understand. Things had been going so well, and it just took me by surprise. She says her dad had them drawn up."

My dad speaks carefully. "How long have you been married now? What, like a month?"

I huff out a breath. "Technically, almost two months."

"And how long have you known each other?" he asks.

"A year and a half now."

"And how fast did everything happen between you?"

I don't answer right away.

"Well, considering we eloped, fast," I admit. I haven't told them about the kiss at the basketball game, but even then, it would still be fast.

My mom cuts in gently, "That doesn't mean it was wrong."

"I know," I say. "And I don't feel like it is. I want to stay *in* this marriage. And lately, it feels like she does, too, but now I can't help but wonder if she was already planning an exit or if it really was her dad."

My dad lets that sit.

"Silas, when people are scared, they prepare for the worst, even when they hope for the best. I'm sure seeing his daughter get married like that shook him up a bit. He's probably worried about her."

I run a hand through my hair. "So, you think this is fear."

"I think it's insurance," my mom says. "A way for her to feel like she has control. I'm sure it has less to do with you and more about his hopes and dreams for her."

That … actually makes sense. Too much sense.

"I don't want her to feel like she has a backup plan if things get bad," I say quietly.

"Then, if that happens, don't argue about the papers," my dad replies. "Argue for the marriage."

I look down at my ring, twisting it once. "I just don't want her to leave if things get hard. And this is making me think she might."

My mom's voice is firm now. "Then you show her why she should stay."

My dad adds, "And you do it without ultimatums. Without pressure. You make it safe for her to stay. Make it her idea to stay."

I swallow. "I really love her."

"We know," my mom says. "We can hear it."

"Son, you know we're here for you through all of it, but you also need to think about everything you have going on. You're a good man, and I know you're keeping her in mind as you make some of these decisions, but you also can't lose sight of what the goal is here. Create a future for yourself. You've worked hard for this. Your marriage should enhance your dreams."

"Thanks. I love y'all. I'll see you soon."

"We love you too. Everything will work out—you'll see." My mom is so sweet. She always sees the world in a golden light.

"You're still planning to come home for the draft?" my dad asks.

"Yeah, that's the plan. Hopefully, we can work this out, and she'll be with me too."

I hang up a few minutes later and sit there in the quiet of my truck again.

Two months ago, things were different. I was just a guy who wanted a girl. But now, I'm a husband, hoping his wife wants to stay married to him.

BROOKE

BY THE TIME Silas got home last night, I was asleep. I'm not entirely sure he actually slept with me or not though because his side of the bed is still neat, but the clothes he was wearing yesterday are in the hamper.

As much as I would love to stay in bed and drive myself crazy, overanalyzing everything that happened yesterday, I can't. I need to get down to the weather center for one of my classes, and there's no way I'll make it by foot or bike at this point.

I run out of the room to see if Silas is still home, but he's not, and I don't see his truck out the window either.

I do see Bo's and Chelsea's cars here though. Maybe I can get a ride from one of them.

I knock on Bo's bedroom door, and Chelsea answers.

"Hey, good morning. You okay?" She twists her wild curls into a top knot and yawns.

"No. I'm running late, and Silas is already gone. I hate to ask, but do you think you can give me a ride down to the weather center building?" I hold my hands together like I'm praying.

"Why don't you just take my car? I don't have class until this afternoon. Will you be back by then?" She walks over to the small desk in the room and gets her keys out of her crossbody bag she always wears.

"Yes, I have one class and a thirty-minute lab, and then I should be back by, like, twelve fifteen. Does that work for you?"

Bo is lying in bed, shirtless, and I suddenly feel like I'm intruding.

"Morning, Brooke." He waves.

"Hey. Sorry to wake y'all."

"No worries, seriously." He smiles.

"Yeah, that works fine for me. Here you go." She hands me her keys.

"Thanks, Chelsea. I really appreciate it."

"Where's Silas this early?" Bo calls after me.

"I'm not sure. I think he has some meetings today between classes. I didn't see him before he left." I'm not about to tell anyone about what happened yesterday. No one was here, and I'm gonna leave it at that.

"Oh, right. I think he mentioned something about meeting with his agent today."

"Okay, I gotta go get dressed. Thank you so much, Chels. I owe you!"

I make quick work of getting ready, and by the time I jump into the car, I have fifteen minutes to make it five miles down the road, which seems doable, but everyone and their brother seems to be walking to class and holding up every light.

Shit.

Once I make it through the busiest part of campus, the noise fades and my thoughts drift—inevitably—back to Silas.

I know why I've been holding back. I've known all along.

Giving myself fully to him would mean letting go of the careful balance I've spent years perfecting. It would mean admitting that I don't always have everything under control. That I can want something this badly and still be terrified of it at the same time.

Loving him isn't the scary part.

Losing myself is.

I've built my life on being steady. On not needing too much. On not asking for more than I can handle. I watched what happened when the ground fell out from under my family, and somewhere along the way I decided that if I stayed guarded enough—measured enough—I could keep everything from collapsing again.

Silas doesn't fit into that plan.

He asks for honesty without pressure. He offers support without conditions. And every time I let myself lean into him, even just a little, it feels so easy it scares me. Like if I stop bracing, I might never want to start again.

So I've kept parts of myself tucked away. Not because I don't feel enough—but because I feel too much.

Because giving myself to him fully would mean trusting that this won't end the way my parent's marriage did. That choosing happiness doesn't automatically mean paying for it later.

I grip the steering wheel and close my eyes for a second. Breathe. I know this feeling. I won't let it take over.

Five. The dashboard lights. The small crack in the windshield. My reflection in the rearview mirror. A tree swaying outside. The clock on the radio.

Four. The seat beneath me. The cool air from the vent. The wheel under my palms. The ring on my finger.

My breathing slows.

Three. A car passing. The click of my turn signal…

I'm so lost in controlling my emotions that I almost don't notice the sky.

It's not a dramatic shift. There's no movie-moment crack of thunder or mysterious darkness. Just a subtle wrongness.

The air thickens. And the light in the sky turns flat and yellow, like someone pressed a dimmer light on the sun.

My chest tightens and I grip the steering wheel harder than

necessary, telling myself to breathe. In through my nose. Out through my mouth.

Wind starts to rattle the windows of Chelsea's Honda Civic like whispered warnings.

You're okay.

But my heart doesn't listen.

It starts racing—too fast, too loud—like it's trying to outrun my thoughts. My hands feel disconnected from my body. The ring on my finger feels heavy and hot.

Silas.

Husband.

Safe.

All the words tangle together, as fear starts to creep in with every sway of the car and the ones in front of me.

The first gust hits the car hard enough to make it drift.

"Okay," I whisper. "Okay, okay."

Big golf ball sized hail slams down without warning, pounding against the windshield. The wipers automatically flip on and squeal as they move, but they can't keep up with the hail. The trees on either side of the road bend unnaturally, leaves and debris spinning in tight circles across the road.

My breath comes shallow now. Faster.

Pull over, a rational voice says.

But panic doesn't care about rational.

My phone buzzes in the cupholder.

I glance down for a second and that's when the world tilts.

The wind screams. Sounding like a freight train going a hundred miles an hour.

The Civic jolts sideways as debris skitters across the pavement before me—branches, leaves, something darker I don't let myself identify. The steering wheel starts to vibrate in my hands.

Then the sky turns green.

I know that color. Growing up in Oklahoma makes you learn real quick what a green colored sky means.

"Oh god," I panic.

My breath feels like it's trapped somewhere behind my ribs. My vision narrows, edges blurring. I can't get enough air. I can't —breathe.

The funnel touches down a quarter mile away.

Small. Narrow. But close enough.

Too close.

I slam the brakes making the tires scream. The road is slick from the melting hail and the car starts to fishtail as wind slams me into a guard rail.

I don't scream.

I go silent.

The car spins again, once, twice, then stops hard against something solid. A tree. I think.

Then suddenly the trees stop moving and the hail disappears but the wind still roars in the distance.

My heart finally slows enough for breath to claw back into my lungs in jagged gasps. I rest my forehead against the steering wheel. My hands shaking uncontrollably.

I'm alive.

The realization crashes through me harder than the accident.

Alive.

Married.

Silas.

Something wet runs down my face and drips into my lap.

Then everything goes black.

TWENTY-TWO

SILAS

I DIDN'T WAKE Brooke when I got home last night, and I didn't say goodbye to her this morning. Partially because I knew I wouldn't have time to say everything I wanted to. The other part, well, I'm still a little hurt, I guess.

Now, I'm meeting with my agent for breakfast to go over what to expect the days leading up to the draft and then draft day itself.

"So, you have quite a few teams interested in you, Silas. Off the record, of course. No offers or official conversations have been had on your behalf."

"I wasn't worried about that, Scott. But I am worried about who is interested. As I told you last month at the combine, I got married, so where I land needs to be easily accessible to her." Because I'm going to keep planning my future as if she'll be by my side. Fuck those papers.

"Ah, yes. Linson's little sister. How did that happen again?" He holds up a hand. "Actually, let's table that for a different day. We can put a spin on that whole thing once we know who we're dealing with. Some owners are a little more old-fashioned. They might not want to know that you recklessly eloped in Vegas." He huffs a laugh.

"That might be how it happened, but that's not how it is now."

"Okay, so then you tell me. What teams would you be interested in talking with?"

"Well, honestly, any that can get me here within a few hours, tops. So, Dallas, Houston, Kansas City, New Orleans. Maybe Denver, but that wouldn't be a top choice."

"Is she not planning to go with you?" He stops tapping notes in his phone.

"She's only in her first year, and I don't expect her to stop going to school for me."

"Why wouldn't she just transfer somewhere wherever you go?"

"Because she's a climatology major, and she's at the best school for that."

My phone starts to ring in my pocket, then stops.

"Okay, I'll see what I can do."

It starts to ring again, and I pull it out to see Beck's name.

Not sure if I want to deal with anything he might have to say right now, I ignore the call.

Within seconds, it's ringing again.

"Scott, I'd better take this. Beck has called me three times in a row."

He waves me off as I stand and move to the exit of the restaurant.

"Hey, Beck. What's up?" I try to keep my voice neutral, ready for whatever he has to say.

"Silas, Brooke's been in an accident."

My heart stops. "Where is she?" I fumble with my keys and walk to my truck.

"They took her to Walker General. My dad is on his way, but it'll take him at least two hours to get there. Get to her as fast as you can." Beck sounds anything but calm, like he normally does.

I get into my car, start the engine, and pull out of the parking lot. "Already on my way. But wait, how was she in a car accident? Was she by herself?"

"She was driving a Honda Civic, so I'm guessing she was in Chelsea's car. They said a small tornado hit that side of town about forty-five minutes ago. Did you not see it?"

I shake my head even though he can't see me. "I was in the gym this morning, and then I met Scott for breakfast after. Fuck, I just left him in the restaurant."

"I'll let him know what's going on. Just get to my sister. And call me with updates as soon as you can." He disconnects before I can reply.

I smack my hand on the wheel. "Fuck!"

The smell of disinfectant hits me as soon as I walk into the hospital.

I run up to the empty check-in desk—because of course it is—and look around for someone to help me.

"Hello?" I call out. I'm sure it's loud, but I don't give a fuck.

A little lady with white hair and a smile walks up, then sits down in the chair behind the desk. "Can I help you?"

"I'm looking for Brooke Linson. She was brought a while ago. Car accident." I tap on the counter while she slowly pulls up the computer screen.

"Oh, yes. There she is. Only family is allowed back at this time. They're still running tests on her."

"Okay, I understand, but I'm her husband."

"Well, that'll do it. You can go back, but I need your ID so I can issue a wristband."

"Great. Thanks."

She straps on one of those paper bands that suck to take off on my wrist.

"I'll buzz you through those doors. Then you'll take that hallway all the way down, then to the right. You should see her right away."

"Thank you." I take off through the heavy security door before she even stops talking.

I pace the hallway for a minute as I try to catch my breath, my heart still trying to kick its way out of my ribs.

I pull open the door, and there she is. She's sitting up when I walk in. Alive. Breathing. A nurse takes her vitals.

Her head has a gauze wrap around it, and she's covered in a blanket that's too thin for what she just went through.

The relief hits so hard that my knees almost give out.

"Hey," I say, keeping my voice steady because if I don't, I'll lose it.

She looks up, eyes glassy but clear. "Hey."

I stop a few feet away, hands clenched at my sides, like I don't trust myself not to crush her if I touch her too fast.

"You okay?" I ask, even though the answer is right in front of me.

She nods. "Yeah. I'm okay. Just a little bump and cut on my head. They have to keep me for concussion protocol though." Her voice is scratchy.

I exhale, slow and controlled, then step closer and take her hand in mine. I lean down and rest my forehead against hers. She's warm. Real.

"Fuck me, that was a scary call to get," I admit quietly.

She whispers, "I'm sorry."

"You have nothing to apologize for," I say immediately. "It was an accident."

We stay like that until the nurse slips out and the door clicks shut behind her.

That's when the silence hangs.

The heavy kind. So, I pull back and sit on the side of the bed.

"I started to have a panic attack," she says.

I nod. "Okay."

"Before the tornado. I was thinking about us."

A panic attack at the thought of being married to me is not a good sign.

"What about us?" I practically whisper, not knowing if I want to hear the truth.

Her breath stutters. There it is. The truth finally stepping into the room. "I didn't intend on filing the annulment papers. I wouldn't," she says quickly. "I swear."

"I know," I tell her. "Deep down, I didn't think you would."

"But ..." She lets out a shaky breath.

"But I left anyway," I finish gently.

She nods, eyes dropping to her hands. "I think my dad just needed to know I wasn't trapped. That I had a choice in my future."

That one hurts. I won't pretend it doesn't. But hurt isn't the same as anger.

"I never want you to feel trapped," I say.

"And I don't," she admits. "But we can't deny that life is moving fast here. There's a possibility that things could get hard for us."

I scoot closer to her. "I have no doubt they will, but just because things get hard doesn't mean we will fall apart," I say. "But I think we need to build a foundation on truth."

She looks up at that.

"Truth about what?" she whispers.

Now is the right time.

I take her hands in mine again. "Truth about how I feel about you." I lift her hand and kiss the back of it. "Brooke, I'm obsessively in love with you. And I really hope you love me too."

Her eyes fill with tears.

"Silas, I don't know what marriage is supposed to look like. I didn't have parents to model. Sure, Casey and Charlie's parents were around, but I think it must be different, seeing it than living it." She tilts her head and smiles softly. "But I do know that I love you."

Fuck yes.

"It doesn't matter what it's supposed to look like. We build our own life," I say without hesitation. "Together. With conversations like this—even when they suck." I kiss her gently.

When I pull back, she laughs weakly. "Yeah, this one really sucked."

"Yeah," I agree. "But you're still here. And so am I."

I lean in, resting my forehead against hers again, breathing her in, grateful she's okay.

She closes her eyes, settling against me.

"Hey, Cupcake?"

"Hmm?"

"I want to do this the right way. I don't want our marriage to be based on a spontaneous decision we made when we were young. I want it to be based on me loving you and you loving me. I want you to choose me, just like I choose you. Will you marry me again?"

Her eyes open, glassy, and the sweetest fucking smile spreads across her face.

"Yes. I will marry you. Because I love you."

"I love you so much; it hurts." I slide my hands, carefully, around her neck and lean in to kiss her.

We stay like that, kissing and just breathing each other in until Ryan rushes into the room an hour later.

"Brooke," he says, measured. "Are you okay?" He walks over to her and lays a hand on her arm and kisses her cheek.

"I'm feeling better. Mostly a little rattled by the whole thing now. But, hey, that could definitely be a paper topic for one of my classes." She smiles weakly, and her eyes start to flutter.

"You can't go to sleep yet, baby." I lightly squeeze her hand.

"But I'm tired. I just want to rest my eyes for a few minutes."

"No, Brooke. Silas is right. You have to stay awake for a while."

"Oh, Dad. Silas and I are getting married."

He looks back and forth between us. "Aren't you already married?"

"Yes, but we want to do it the right way this time. So, you can go ahead and shred those papers, like I told you to at lunch the other day."

Ryan starts to say something, but I interrupt.

"I understand why you did it. I really do. But, sir, we love each other. This isn't a joke to us. We want to make a life together, and I'll do whatever I can to make sure she's happy."

"What about school?"

"Well, I'm hoping to get drafted close enough that the commute is easy for us. Then once she graduates, she can decide if we stay here most of the year or wherever I'm playing. I just want her. The rest is just a bonus."

He pulls in a deep breath. "Okay then. You're both adults. All I can do is be here for you when you need me, I suppose."

"Thank you, sir."

I hold out my hand to him, but he pulls me in for a hug.

"Welcome to the family, Silas."

EPILOGUE
SEVEN MONTHS LATER

BROOKE

OKLAHOMA SUNSETS DON'T BELIEVE in subtlety.

They show up loud and unapologetic, stretching across the sky in streaks of gold and fire reds and purple, like they're daring you to pretend this moment isn't important.

Like they know this is our second wedding and it deserves a little drama.

The ceremony is set up in an open field, where an arbor is decorated in a mixture of white flowers and drapes, giving it an elegant but rustic feel.

It's perfect in the most Oklahoma way possible.

Simple. Honest. Unpretentious.

"You ready for this, baby girl?" My dad tucks my arm in his and kisses the top of my head.

"So ready." I look up at my dad's face, my smile wide.

My dad's eyes are a little glassy, and I can see his composure slipping. "You're so beautiful."

"Dad, don't make me cry. I actually made up my face for this." I laugh lightly.

He sniffs and pulls out a white hankie. "I'm so proud of the woman you're becoming. And I know I was hesitant about you and Silas, but I think you bring out the best in each other. You make each other better. And I'm not sure I could have picked a better man for my little girl. I wish you both a long, happy, and healthy marriage."

I take the hankie and dab my eyes because of course I'm crying now. "Thank you, Dad. I love you." I sniff. "I know we did this a little … unconventional, but he makes me so happy, and I hope I make him just as happy."

"Oh, sweetheart, that boy can't keep his hands or eyes off of you. He glows whenever you're around. I think it's safe to say he's a very happy and lucky man." He kisses my cheek this time and wipes a rogue tear.

I suck in a deep breath and tilt my head back to stave off more tears threatening to fall. "Okay," I exhale. "I'm ready. Take me to my husband."

Instead of answering, the music starts, and we make our way to the aisle around the guest chairs.

I can see Silas as I turn the corner. Waiting. Looking devastatingly handsome.

Jacket off. Sleeves rolled. Tie loose, like he made it halfway through tying it and decided that was good enough. His cowboy boots peek out from his pants. Buffed and shined.

This man faces roaring stadiums, last-second drives, and entire offensive lines hell-bent on breaking him in half. He's calm under pressure. Focused. Built for chaos.

But the second he sees me?

His jaw tightens. His shoulders tense. His hands curl into fists at his sides, like he needs to ground himself.

I've never loved anything or anyone more.

I start walking toward him, the prairie stretching wide around us, the wind tugging at my dress and hair, like it wants in on the moment. Folding chairs creak as people shift. Friends smile knowingly. Family leans forward.

Someone near the back mutters, "About damn time. I'm ready to party." Probably a Griffith.

Charlie is already waiting as my matron of honor, and Silas's oldest brother, Keith, stands next to him.

This might not be our first time promising forever. But it is the first time we're doing it without illusions.

This wedding? This one comes with thought, love, and more knowledge about each other and what we're getting into.

When I reach him, he takes my hands immediately, like he doesn't trust himself not to reach for me if I take another step. His palms are warm. Solid. Familiar. His thumb brushes my knuckle, a habit he does when he's checking if I'm okay.

Silas breaks his gaze from mine, just for a moment to look at the officiant, this one not dressed in a shiny gold suit, and nods. The officiant smiles and keeps things short. We've already said the legal words. Today is about the truth.

Silas is first to say his vows.

He clears his throat and exhales like he's trying to steady himself. And then he talks about football—because of course he does. "I've spent my whole life around football," he says. "Preparation. Discipline. Learning how to take a hit and get back up. The game taught me how to be tough."

He pauses, eyes dropping before lifting back to mine.

"But marriage taught me something harder."

The space between us feels electric.

"How to stay," he says. "When it would be easier to walk away. When things get messy. When I'm tired down to the bone."

He tightens his grip on my hand.

"I play a position where you don't get to look away," he continues. "My job is simple on paper—pick my person and don't let them go. Study them. Anticipate their moves. Stay with them, step for step, no matter how long the play lasts."

His voice roughens.

"Loving you has taught me that real strength is protecting

what matters. Showing up even when I'm exhausted. Choosing each other even after we've seen how hard things can get."

His thumb presses into my hand.

"I choose you," he says, voice low and certain. "Every down. Every drive. Every season."

My throat tightens, because leave it to him to turn football into a love language.

These vows aren't about proving anything.

They're about choosing each other—again.

When it's my turn, I don't pretend to be graceful or poetic. That's never been my lane. So I tell the truth instead."I study the weather for a living. I know how powerful it is. How even small shifts can change everything. I also know that nothing meaningful comes without risk."

I take a breath, grounding myself.

"Loving you is scary—because I know exactly how much you could hurt me. I didn't give you my heart blindly. I gave it to you completely, knowing the damage was possible."

My hand tightens in his. "Recommitting isn't romantic. It's brave. It's choosing each other after we've seen the storms, not before."

I swallow. "You taught me that trust isn't blind faith. It's built slowly—with consistency, forgiveness, and a lot of honesty. It's earned every day."

His smile nearly blinds me. Looking at me with pride.

"I choose you," I say. "Every down. Every day. Even when it's hard. Even when the wind knocks us sideways." I laugh lightly.

He doesn't wait for permission to kiss me. But it isn't rushed or showy. It's deep and grounding and like he's sealing a promise he has every intention of keeping.

Cheers explode immediately—loud and echoing across the prairie. And as the sun sinks and the sky turns gold and fire and purple, the string lights flicker on across the grounds.

He pulls away, slightly. Just enough to catch our breath.

"Remember that wish we made in the Bellagio fountain?" He says against my lips.

"Yeah."

"I wished for this. Seeing you walk down the aisle to me. I wished for it all to be real."

My smile spreads wide. "That was mine. I wanted this to be real."

"Looks like our wishes came true." He kisses my nose.

Could this man be more perfect?

We walk together toward the wedding pavilion, where our reception will be, hand in hand, married again. But this time, we're stronger, steadier, absolutely sure.

No stadium lights tonight.

No scoreboard.

No pressure.

No promises we haven't already tested.

Just two people who learned the long game is better when you're on the same team.

SILAS

The reception is in full swing, but I need a few minutes alone with my wife.

We just finished taking a few pictures on some nearby swings with our friends. There were three large swings that can hold two to three people on each seat. All the girls—Brooke, Charlie, Noelle, Chelsea, Emma, Arbor, and Lily—sat on the seats. Us guys—me, Beck, Casey, Bo, Archie, Ace, and Aston—stood behind them. It should turn out to be a pretty cool picture.

There's also an outdoor stone fireplace that has been decorated with the same flowers we used for the wedding, and candles in glass vases are scattered on the mantel and the stone around the fire. It's private and romantic and the perfect opportunity to dance with my wife. The music from the pavilion flows —ironically, they're playing "Can't Help Falling in Love" by Elvis Presley—loud enough that we can hear it.

I take her in my arms because I can't *not* touch her. "Can I have this dance, Mrs. Arbuckle?"

Her arms wind around my neck. "I'd be honored, Mr. Arbuckle."

I pull her in close, placing soft kisses along her neck. "How much longer do we have to stay?"

She giggles. "You want to leave already?"

"Well, I mean, yeah. The food was good, and everyone seems to be having fun, but I cannot wait to get this dress off of you."

When I saw Brooke walking down the aisle toward me, I nearly dropped to the ground. She's wearing a lace wedding dress, with sheer long sleeves and an open-back bodice, that flows to the ground. Brooke opted to keep her hair down and flowing. And I've never seen her look more beautiful. Clothed anyway.

"Okay, we can leave soon. I have to admit, I'm ready too. I want to take advantage of the time I have with you this weekend before you go back to Dallas." She leans up to kiss me.

I was drafted twenty-fourth in the first round by Dallas. It was one of my choices so I could be close to Brooke while she's still in school, and so far, it's working out well. Though this summer was a whirlwind, finding a place in Dallas and getting a condo here, where she could live while she was in school. Then we had to find a weekend that I had a bye because we really didn't want to wait to renew our vows. I have to leave on Monday, so as much time as I can spend with her alone, the better.

"How about we go start to make our rounds to say good-bye?" I twirl her as the song comes to an end, then dip her in a kiss.

"Ready when you are." Her eyes sparkle in the lights.

An hour later, we've made it to a small, private cabin, similar to the one we rented in Turner Falls on our mini moon.

The door barely clicks shut before she's in my arms and looking at me like she can't wait to see me come undone.

I don't hesitate. I back her up against the door, slow and deliberate, and feel her smile against my mouth when I kiss her.

This kiss isn't polite.

It's hungry. Familiar. Earned.

She moans when I take the kiss deeper, and it goes straight to my cock. I've never wanted her more than I do right now.

I slide my hands down her back and tug her as close as I can get her, and her body curves into mine.

When we pause to catch our breath, she starts to unbutton my shirt, then moves to my pants, making quick work of the button and zipper. The second her hand slides into my boxers, my eyes nearly roll to the back of my head. I've been waiting all day for this. It's been the longest foreplay of my life. Agonizing. And I'm not sure how long I'm going to last the first time.

I walk backward toward the bed, her hand still on my dick. Then I feel my way down her body, looking for the zipper. I'm tempted to rip it off just so I can get her naked faster, but she might kill me if I did.

I find it on the side and drag it down, then take the material at her shoulders and push it slowly down her arms, and the dress falls completely just as it passes her breasts. I take her thong in my hand and tear it and watch it fall to the floor.

We turn together, and she gets on top of the bed, watching

me as I undress. The hunger in her eyes tells me she wants to wreck me.

Her gaze tracks every movement.

Once I'm naked, I crawl on top of the bed, hands sliding up her legs. And when I reach her thighs, I take my time kissing and sucking, making her breaths shallow. Her hands find my head then, and like the good girl she is, she pushes my head right into her pussy.

"Silas," she moans when my tongue starts to work her clit.

I slide a couple of fingers inside her. With my other hand, I reach up and take ahold of one of her breasts, then pinch her nipple. "Come, baby. Come all over my tongue."

I can feel her pussy starting to contract around my fingers, so I pump them in and out faster. And when I suck hard on her clit, she cries out.

She lets go of my head and sits up to look at me. The look on her face is calm and sated. Because of me.

"Silas"—she strokes a hand over my head—"I really need you inside me."

I lick my lips, smiling, then kiss my way up her body. Stopping only to take a nipple into my mouth and suck. Once my cock is nestled in her pussy lips, I slide it up and down, working her up again. I stop moving when my tip reaches her open and push in just enough to drive her crazy.

I work into her, short and shallow pumps. Just as she's about to grab my ass and pull me in tighter, I push back and sit on my knees.

"Turn over, baby. Face down."

She gives me a shy smile. But I know she loves this position as much as I do.

"Get on your knees."

As she lifts her ass and places her body just the way I want it, I can't help but lean forward and bite her cheek.

"Mine." I lick over my bite to lessen the sting.

She looks over her shoulder at me. "Yours."

I run my hand up her spine, stopping at her neck, squeezing gently, my thumb resting on her pulse.

With my other hand, I run my fingers through her wetness and up to her asshole. She tilts her pelvis up when I do.

I take my cock and line it up. I push it deep enough that my head is tucked inside. Then I grab hold of her hip and slam into her. It's hard and possessive.

"Oh God, Silas."

"You feel so good, wife. I'm going to make you come so hard."

I pull back to the crown, then thrust back in again. Her hips match my rhythm now.

I release her hip and lean over her back, placing kisses along her shoulders and spine as I thrust.

"I'm getting close," she pants, looking over her shoulder at me.

"Me too, baby." I circle my hips and push deep.

"Oh my God, do that again."

So, I do.

When my thrusts become erratic, I sit back on my knees, and I take hold of her hair in my hand and tug, forcing her head to tilt back, but not enough to hurt.

"Silas!" she moans.

"That's it, wife. Come for me." I look down and watch as my cock moves in and out of her. My dick is slick from her arousal, glistening in the soft light. I spit on my thumb and press it into her ass, just past the tight ring of muscle.

The sensation makes her gasp and she pushes into me making my thumb slide in just a little more.

Seeing my wife come undone like this, drives me wild.

My balls start to tingle and pressure builds.

Just as I feel the first pulses of her pussy strangling me, I start to come. I can't hold it back any longer.

I pull out, and ropes of cum paint her back. "Fuck me, that's hot."

Our pace evens, then finally stops.

I let go of her hair, and it drops to the pillow under her. Her chest rises and falls as she tries to catch her breath.

"That was intense," she says, turning her head to see me as I get off the bed.

"Yeah, it was. And I swear, the longer we're married, the better it gets." I place a kiss on her lips. "Stay right here."

"I literally can't move right now." She giggles.

I smile, walking over to the bathroom to grab a washcloth. I wet it and move to the bed to clean her.

Once I'm done, I settle in next to her on the bed. We tangle together under the sheets, sweat cooling, hearts still racing. I tuck my arm under her pillow, and she moves to rest her head on my chest, leg thrown over mine, like she's daring me to go anywhere.

Not a fucking chance.

I kiss the top of her head and smile into the quiet, thinking about how we got here.

They say, *What happens in Vegas stays in Vegas.*

Except when you marry the girl you've always wanted.

And this?

This is the part I'll protect with everything I have.

My wife. My home. My forever.

Want to see what Silas and Brooke are up to now? Read their bonus chapter here.

What's Next
The Trade (Liam & Alie)

What to expect: Professional Football, Second Chance, Found
Family, No Love Triangle

Read on for a sneak peek inside Snow Blitz (The Trade prequel)
from the Gridiron Legacy series!

SNOW BLITZ
SNEAK PEEK

Liam

Why am I standing on a rooftop in the middle of winter, freezing my balls off? I did not sign up for this. I thought coming to some posh wedding meant we would at least be, you know, comfortable. I'd take the heat and humidity of New Orleans over this.

I came up to New York City for one of my college teammate's weddings. Brandon had been my roommate when I transferred to Michigan after I left Walker. He and his new wife live in New York since he plays for the Titans, so they got married at some fancy hotel in Midtown during a bye week.

Coming up here also gave me a good excuse to escape a little drama of my own. Last week, I'd broken it off with someone I had been seeing because I needed to stay focused on football right now. Too bad for Sabine, she'd thought our relationship was more serious than it was ever going to be.

Her texts have been coming in more frequently over the last few days, including two today, so, yeah, I'll probably have to change my number when I get back from New York. I have a feeling Sabine won't leave me alone otherwise.

Trying to warm myself up, I take a hefty gulp of my Macallan

18. Sure, there are heating lamps placed strategically around the rooftop with a glass wraparound to cut the wind, but it's still fucking cold. It was only supposed to be a short cocktail hour up here, and then we'd go to the main dining room for dinner, but I've been standing in this same spot, under one of the heaters, for close to an hour. If I had been better prepared and maybe worn a thicker coat, I wouldn't be acting like a pussy about the whole thing.

Glancing around, I take in the all-white wedding theme. Even we, the guests, were asked to wear white. It almost feels like we're in a white-out blizzard … inside a snow globe … that you can't get out of because it also started snowing about ten minutes ago.

Fuck, I'm trapped in this snow-globe world and starting to feel claustrophobic now.

A few of my old college teammates from Michigan are hanging around, but almost everyone brought a date, except me. They've tried to include me, and I can carry on a conversation with the best of them, but I'm just not feeling it tonight. I'll probably duck out after we eat.

They're great guys, but I miss my guys from Walker. We're on our own paths now, too, but we try to see each other now and then. Especially Archie Griffith. He's my best friend and the one I talk to the most.

My friends are either in the league now, too, or will be soon. And they're all falling in love. Not only are they falling in love, but they're getting married and—in Archie's case—having babies.

I pull out my phone because, now, I really miss them. *Damn, I'm feeling sappy.* I take a quick selfie and send it off to Archie, Beck, and Casey.

Liam: Wishing you guys were in NYC with me this weekend.

Beck: Aren't you at a wedding?

Liam: Well, yeah, but it's kinda boring.

Casey: Dude, I can't travel right now. We had a game today. You know this.

Archie: Sorry, buddy. I have a game tomorrow, and Emma is studying this weekend, so I'm on baby duty. Heading down to the ranch for a bit so Em can have a quiet house.

Liam: You guys suck. You should have come with me.

Casey: You love us.

Liam: Unfortunately. Assholes.

Archie: Have a good time. Maybe get laid or something. One of the bridesmaids?

Beck: Text us later. Charlie just got here and says hi.

Liam: Tell Little King I said hey.

Beck: Soon-to-be Linson.

Casey: Still a King right now.

Liam: Fine. I'll send you pictures of all the fun things I'm doing in New York. Without y'all.

Archie: Fun things to do... you mean pussy, right?

Liam: Any girl I meet in New York tonight will strictly be a hookup.

Archie: Don't do anything I wouldn't do. HA! Text me later, Pitzy.

I laugh, then drop my phone into my pocket. When I look up, I see the bundled-up bride standing next to a woman with long, dark brown hair in a long, bright red coat. I'm guessing she didn't get the all-white memo. Then I see my buddy Aaron Muldoon walk up to her. He places a hand on the small of her back, and when she turns her head to look up at him, I almost drop my whisky glass.

I've seen some beautiful women in my life, but she is unbelievably stunning, and I can't even see her whole face yet. But then they turn and walk away from the bride, and I get to see her head-on. She's got hair that looks like silk, with piercing blue eyes, a perfectly symmetrical nose, and her lips … *fuck me.* They're full and painted in bright red lipstick that matches her coat.

They're walking toward me now, and he leans down to say something to her that makes her laugh. I'm done for. By the time they reach me, I've managed to pick my jaw up off the floor and compose myself enough that I don't look like an idiot.

"Sup, man? How's it going? Good to see you." Aaron reaches his hand out and pulls me in for a bro hug.

"Muldoon, good to see you. How's New York treating you?" I ask him, but glance her way.

"Good, good. The season's been—" Aaron stops talking when he looks behind me. "Oh, shit, I gotta go say hi to someone. I'll be right back." Aaron looks at the woman as he walks away.

"Okay then. No problem. I'll just stand here by myself, freezing, but cool, cool." She tucks a piece of her hair behind her ear.

"Right?" I chuckle. "Whose idea was this? I mean, it does look incredible, but these heating lamps aren't doing a whole lot to cut the chill."

She straightens her arms and holds her hands out. "Picture this…New York City, it's snowing, love and Christmas magic are in the air, but I feel like I'm standing in a cryo chamber."

"Ha! Pretty close to the truth there. You ever been in one?" I tilt my head toward her.

She nods, smirking. "Oh, yeah. I'm a fan, but this is, like, really kinda crazy."

"It really is. I was just thinking about leaving after dinner. My hotel room is calling my name. I'll need a good thaw out after this. Until then, a stiff drink helps." I lift my glass to my lips and take another pull of my whisky.

"Whatever you have in that, I might need some to warm up." She tips her head toward my glass.

"Do you want some of this while I go get you a drink?" I hand it out to her.

"Hmm … risky, taking a drink from a stranger. But you look like a trustworthy guy, and Aaron seems to know you, so why not?" She takes my offered glass and sips. "Nice. Macallan. Eighteen?"

My mouth drops open, and then I shut it so I can form words. "You know your whisky?"

"Mmm. I do. My father is a big fan. I also love a good brandy." She hands it back to me. "So, are you here on the bride or groom's side? Guessing the groom since you know Aaron?"

"Groom. I know Brandon from Michigan. Think I was more of a courtesy invite than anything else. We were roommates, but not incredibly close."

She laughs a warm sound that blends with the music. "I came as Aaron's plus-one. His girlfriend missed her flight, so I said I'd keep him company. That said, he's more interested in working the room and catching up with people."

I smile. "Yeah, he's always been a social guy. Always the life of the party. Even when it's freezing."

She grabs my drink from my hand and lifts it slightly. "The whisky helps." She takes a sip, and I take it back from her, lifting it in my own cheers. "To questionable decisions and good whisky."

She laughs again, and there's a devilish twinkle in her eyes. I'm mesmerized by them until lights begin to brighten behind her in various shades of red, blue, and purple. I move to the side to see where they're coming from.

"It's the lights at Saks," she states, and I arch a brow. She further explains, "The holiday lights show at Saks Fifth Avenue. The sparkling wonderland of lights and music that graces the building's facade every ten minutes." There's a pause in her voice when she realizes I have no idea what she's talking about. "I forgot you're not from here."

I grin. "Midwestern boy. Kansas born and raised. How did you guess?"

"I hear the hint of twang. Have you ever been to New York City at Christmas?" She rubs her gloved hands together.

I shake my head. "I have not. And, unfortunately, I'm only here for the weekend and spending the better part of it in my own snowglobe of New York City instead of exploring it."

"Too bad because a guy like you could get into a lot of trouble in this city."

I'm just about to say something when a woman wearing a headset starts to speak. "Excuse me, everyone. Can I have your attention, please? Thank you so much for your patience tonight. There was a minor water issue that we're working to resolve. We should be able to go in shortly. In the meantime, we'll be bringing more appetizers out for you to enjoy. And don't forget to grab a drink at the bar." She waves her hand, then spins around and walks over to the bride and groom.

I glance over at this angel in red, and she meets my gaze.

"I have an idea," she says, grinning.

"Oh, yeah? What's your idea?" I move in a little closer to her.

"How invested are you in staying here?"

I mean, is this a trick question? "Uhh, not very."

"I …" She starts to say something, then stops.

"I …" I prompt her.

She laughs. "I was going to say, do you want to get out of here? Let me show you what a Manhattan Christmas is like."

Fuck. Yes. "Absolutely. But I don't even know your name."

She tilts her head to the side. "Let's go with … Vixen. And you can be … Blitzen."

"What? Why?" I chuckle.

"Because it's fun and Christmas is magical." She holds out her hand to me. "What do ya say, Blitzen? You wanna go make some Christmas magic with me?"

I place my hand in her small one. "Lead the way, Vixen."

ACKNOWLEDGMENTS

To my family, thank you for your support. You're my reason for everything. I love you all, eternally.

Compass Press, thank you for walking me through the author journey.

Jovanna Shirley, once again, thank you for your patience and expertise. My goal this year is to actually make a deadline. Please keep me around!

Jeannine Colette, what would we do without you? Seriously. I'm honored and privileged to have you on this journey with me.

Sarah Sentz, from cover to page, your feedback so incredibly valuable. I can't wait to tackle this year with you! Let's GO! P.S., you can't escape us. Ever.

Tina, thank you for coming in clutch, again, and making this baby shine. Your eye for detail is impeccable.

Sam R, thank you for reading early. Your voicemails and screenshots and your overall love for the series means the world to me. Thank you for everything you do for me.

Rickie, I'm still not over the spray tan tears! Please keep sharing your reactions with me, and your feedback, and I live for your highlights! Makes me feel like maybe it wasn't so bad afterall. MWAH

To my ARC Team and all readers, thank you for reading more of my words! Your reviews, edits, and just knowing you're reading still blow my mind. Thank you, thank you!

Wordsmith Publicity, Autumn and Roxie, thank you for helping me reach readers and for your guidance and support!

Read more books by Ava Sutton.

www.amazon.com/author/avasutton

WALKER UNIVERSITY STALLIONS

Counter Play Beckham & Charlie

Zone Protection Archie & Emma

Strong Side Casey & Noelle

Silent Count Bo & Chelsea

Lockdown Corner - Silas & Brooke

TBD - Aston Griffith (May 2026)

TDB - Ace Griffith (July 2026)

GRIDIRON LEGACY

Snow Blitz - Liam & Alie

The Trade - Liam & Alie

ABOUT THE AUTHOR

Ava Sutton is a sports enthusiast and author of spicy college and professional sports romance.

When she's not writing, you can find her nose in a book, scrolling social media or planning dream vacations she someday hopes to take. She lives in Dallas, Texas with her two dogs. Connect with her on Facebook, Instagram, and TikTok.
@avasuttonbooks
www.avasuttonbooks.com

www.ingramcontent.com/pod-product-compliance
Lightning Source LLC
Chambersburg PA
CBHW030758200726

PP18592100001B/9